THE HUNTER IN THE ROOM

Printed in the United States of America
Cover design by: MiblArt

First Printing, 2020

ISBN-13: 978-1-966238-02-7

THE HUNTER IN THE ROOM

ARIANA TOSADO

CONTENTS

ONE

"Everyone," Momma called from the front, her honey-colored eyes sweeping over her conjoined class, "welcome to the Hunter's Room."

The Redway Boys gawked all around in awe at what Sarah, Breanne, and I call the "Crimson Museum". Our class walked farther in, toward the quartz pillars displaying the most prestigious gadgets used in hunting. As of October last semester, the Callistro Academy had outgrown its self-defense school cover. Now and for the rest of high school, we were all Hunters-in-training.

Except, training is supposed to start freshman year, but we were already a month into our sophomore year when the Hunter's Room reopened "on emergency". Momma had warned us last semester that it'd be difficult to keep up grades for the rest of the rushed year—*especially* for the month that lay ahead of us. And they always say that second semester is harder than first.

The tall boy next to me nodded toward the back of the room, where the Hall of Generations sat. To think Sarah, Breanne, and I had snuck into it at the beginning of last semester, and now we were walking it as free students. "That's gonna be weird," Jak said, "seeing my family tree without my name on it."

"If you become like your dad, you'll get to," I told him, glancing at my classmates guiding his through the main archway. The Callistro Academy crest of a sword through a rose boasted itself proudly atop—all the more ironic to see Redway Boys strolling underneath it.

Jak huffed a toneless laugh as we meandered toward the Hall. "So I'll never be up there, got it."

Besides his light-brown skin and softer features, which he had to have gotten from his mom, Jak was the spitting image of his father. The only time I'd seen hostility in those brown eyes was when I'd stared William Bleu square in the face the night of the annual carnival last September.

Jak pressed his lips together. "And I'm guessing she's not on the Atera tree."

"If she were," I whispered, "we would've never met last semester."

"So it's a blessing in more than one way." His smirk was back, and he stuck his hands into his navy-blue blazer's pockets (which Momma would've scolded him for if she weren't distracted with the cut that Ava Baleen had accidentally given herself with her student ID).

Why was he bringing up last semester when we'd tacitly

agreed to never talk about it again? Was he trying to get insider information about Tristan's daughter because it had been his mother's dying wish for him to protect the Atera descendant?

Was he making sure she was still safe because there was a threat he knew about and I didn't?

Alexa had disappeared in the beach house fire that early morning on my birthday—Jak had even confirmed it the day after. But Mr. Dawson had come back. I knew, I *knew* I had to ask the question. But how could I cement that reality mere months after I'd escaped it?

I'd have to rip off the Band-Aid.

"Call me crazy for wondering," I began as we walked into the grand entryway of the Hall, "seriously, but you never said anything about Alexa before you left Capperson last year."

Jak laughed, ambling toward the golden entry arch to lean against it. "Do you *miss* getting kidnapped?"

"You know what I mean." I lowered my voice, staying beside him to monitor the wandering students and potentially listening ears. "They have a real reason to arrest me and my mom, we're accomplices."

Something shifted in him, as if I'd told him another part of the truth. Almost as if I'd told him that I was a magician and he only partially believed me.

"You are?" he asked, cocking his brows. "Because apparently you were lying about knowing where Tristan's descendant was hiding. It was just a defense mechanism to stop my dad from giving you an effective dose of truth serum."

So that was why he was bringing it up now: he wanted answers like I did. But "descendant"? That word hadn't been used between us for a while...

I said nothing, hoping to gather as much from him as I could with just observation. But with Jakson Bleu, you can never see what he's thinking or feeling unless he lets you. I thought he would've torn down those walls with me by then—but then I remembered that Jak also had secrets that were best left kept.

Not to mention the trust spell he was still under. Something that I didn't expect I'd have to figure out how to undo, considering that I didn't know I'd be seeing the boy again.

"But then," Jak said, casting his pensive gaze down the Hall, "you *were* telling the truth when you said you knew something."

"I thought—"

"How come you never told me she took you again?" His hurt eyes locked with mine. "After she took you and me at the carnival?"

I fiddled with the locket around my neck—the one he'd given me for my birthday. "I didn't really wanna relive it," I muttered, blindly staring at the plaid tie around his neck. "Any of those times."

His head pulled back. "Were there more?"

What was there to say? Was he going to turn against me now? Would he assume that I'd lied to him?

Wait. Who'd said that I *had* lied?

"Okay, look," he told me next. "I just need to know, was what you told me that night true? Everything about—"

"Who said I lied?"

"Alexa," he replied without skipping a beat. "A couple days after your birthday."

Two days. It had taken her two days to come back from the

dead. Alexa Delphine *had* come back from the dead.

My feet were ready to turn around and dart into the secret passageway hidden behind my family tree on the Magicians side. I'd been hoping against hope that Alexa and I would never meet again, but I think a deeper part of me had always known that her comeback was as inevitable as my destiny to become Adara.

"What did she say?" I asked, tension growing in the locket's chain the farther down I pulled.

"That you only knew where Tristan's descendant *was* hiding and they must've escaped sometime during the hunt in Capperson, so you weren't useful to them anymore."

I sighed in relief, but the tension didn't leave. "And you wanna know the truth."

"A little bit, Merlin," Jak said, his frown softening.

The cool silver of the locket warmed under my fingers. The words were bittersweet for a number of reasons. For one, this was the first time I was seeing Jak in four months; the potency of the trust spell was overwhelming, like being away from it for so long gave it a stronger pull. Second, he was practically *asking* me to prove my guilt! What if he could never forgive me for the truth?

"Everything I told you was true," I finally said, hugging myself. "I wasn't lying."

Which technically wasn't a lie.

But why would Alexa take the blame off me? Where was she now? Was I off the hook with William, too? Was I in even deeper water with the Redway Boys being here all January?

Alexa's alive.

She knows about us.

She knows about me.

"Hey, are you okay?" Jak said, reaching out his arm. "You look like you're gonna pass out."

"I'm—I think…" I pulled my hand to my forehead, as if that'd stop the room from swaying. Communication was my last priority as my hand moved over my heart. The pounding boomed in my chest. Thoughts and fear clouded my vision. What was going on? I didn't know and I didn't even know if I could afford to figure out.

And I didn't care enough to because Alexa was alive. That thought was always first.

Dad and Aunt Becca aren't safe. I can't lose them. I can't lose him, I just got him back, I—

Jak reached for my arm. "Come on—"

"No." I jerked away. My memory mindlessly walked me out of the Hall of Generations. "I'm sorry, I just—"

She knows everything! She has to be planning how to expose us!

"Emmy, are you okay?" I heard Sarah whisper, taking my shoulder. I turned around. Breanne stood right behind her. Both of them had left Adrien and Wyatt behind at a display pillar.

"Emma?" another voice chimed behind me, spinning me around. Teresa Darci was approaching with Ava Baleen, concern pinching together Teresa's slim face. "What's wrong, girl?"

Why do you think something's wrong with me, nothing's wrong with me!

"I'm okay, don't—" I began, waving them away, "don't worry, okay?"

If they find out something's wrong, they're gonna figure out the whole thing, I can't say anything—but I can't, but we have to—

Momma hurried over from the electromagnetic cardiograph

pillar. "What's wrong, honey?" she asked quietly, placing a firm hand on my back.

I just as quickly stepped away. "I'm fine," I said, forcing myself to be polite no matter how caged I felt. "Seriously, I'm fine, please."

But my hazed, anxious stare couldn't afford a glance at my friends, Jak, or my mother, or my nearby classmates glancing over. Burning mortification dove in waves in my chest. I kept my head low, pretending that my classmates didn't exist.

Why are you looking at me, stop it, stop it!

"Ladies," Momma announced sternly to the onlookers, narrow jaw firm, "I can handle this, please continue showing your guests around."

My classmates, just as scared of Momma as my friends and I were, scattered in a snap and began conversations whose English I didn't have the brain capacity to process (if they were even *in* English—we had Spanish, Italian, and Swedish under our belts by then).

"Emma," Momma said, careful not to touch me, "can you tell me what's wrong?"

I'm sorry. Alexa's not dead, our family's a walking open target.

I couldn't say that in front of anyone.

Every time I tried to voice the first word of a sentence that hadn't even formed in my head yet, an exhale was all that left, like I was made of air.

Momma faced Breanne. "Honey, can you take her to the nurse?"

"No," I stated, refusing more attention. "Don't, I'm sorry, I didn't want..." I shook my head and exhaled, resetting. And yet,

Alexa's name continued ringing in my head. "Forget it, I'm—I'm fine."

"Come on," Breanne said, "you need a break. Let's go see Julia."

"No, I don't want to!" I glanced around the room, begging for something to catch my attention and steal my mind. "I just wanna get back to class."

"Em," Momma said, straightening. "Go to the nurse. For me."

Ugh. I can never say no to my mother when she asks me to do something "for her".

Breanne linked her arm around mine and then walked me to the elevator. I looked behind me at Jak. His lips were pressed in a thin line, his hands stuck in the pockets of his blazer. Momma gently touched his arm and whispered something, and he took out his hands. When she continued past him, his eyes returned to mine. I moved them away, Breanne's inaudible words still rambling.

Alexa was alive. After Mr. Dawson had come home, my hopes had already dropped until Jak had said that she hadn't come back even the day after. And he'd never said anything about her since because we'd both decided to leave last September behind.

But Alexa, and she knows, and Dad's, and Aunt Becca—

"Emma?" Breanne's voice was feeble as we stood on the crimson carpet in the elevator. "Are you okay?"

How much time do we have before she turns us in, she has to have been planning something this whole time, that's why she's been silent since.

"Emma—"

"I'm fine," I snapped, finally starting to feel my lungs expand with air again. With one glimpse at Breanne's doe-like eyes and parted lips, regret burned in my chest. "I'm sorry, Bre, I didn't mean it like that."

"It's okay," she said softly. "But you don't seem like you are."

One of the things I love most about my roommates is how they can read me like a book. They know almost exactly what's going on in my head based on body language alone. (Momma's training definitely plays a role in that, though.) Sometimes I don't need to explain myself; other times, they're owed that anyway.

"I don't—" I said with a vocal shake I couldn't control. "I'm trying to be, I just—I don't know what's happening right now, I don't know."

She gently rubbed my shoulder with her signature soft smile. "It's okay. Julia can help."

The steel doors slid open, but my blank stare continued. I forced myself to keep my arm around my best friend's, needing something to lean against.

"What did Jak *say* to you?" she asked.

I stopped in my tracks. I couldn't tell her, I couldn't tell her anything.

"No, it's not him, it's—my own stupid mind."

"Don't say that. You're worried about something, that's not stupid."

I silently thanked her; I knew it wasn't, and she was saying that even without knowing the full story. The truth about my kidnapping on the early morning of my birthday had to slip out eventually—how else was I supposed to explain Alexa's sudden absence from my life? The (kind-of-true) story went that Alexa took me one last time to finally ask if I had magic and if I was Tristan Atera's daughter. I said no, and that was that.

To my friends, Alexa was officially a past issue. Which meant I was back to dealing with her alone, and I wasn't sure how to feel about that.

In the middle of the corridor, Breanne faced me. "Emmy?"

Thinking about the situation amplified the dazed sensation in my head, the locking in my chest. I tightened my lips to cage those words and settled on "I don't feel good."

"Okay," she said simply, gently tugging me along.

I didn't know if I was thankful or not that she dropped conversation after that. The last thing my mind could handle was keeping up my side of one, but no distraction meant facing my thoughts head on.

We didn't stop until we got to the nurse's office, where Julia walked us into the private lie-down room on the side. Breanne only felt safe to leave once Julia assured her that I'd be fine.

"First visit of the semester!" Julia's short auburn ponytail swished with her every step. "Welcome back."

The stress of first semester must have affected me more than I'd initially let on, with both Alexa and increasing workload. I'd had to come in every once in a while with either a headache or the occasional stomachache, but the other half of the time, I was escorting a classmate like Breanne had done with me today. Needless to say, I preferred being on Breanne's side of the situation.

But on the bright side, I was going to someone who really cared. Julia became our new school nurse when the Hunter's Room reopened thanks to the growing staff. Within that time, she and I had developed a friendship of sorts. So at least I could be vulnerable right now in front of a friend.

"Missed you, too." I exhaled, gripping the edges of the green vinyl mattress.

Creases formed in the corners of Julia's green eyes as she smiled. "Cool, because I doubt you're here so often because you like me."

I gave her a chuckle, slowly lying down on the crinkly paper. "Both."

I gazed up at the brightly lit suspended ceiling. Julia grabbed a thermometer from a drawer and then turned around to feel my forehead. The cold smell of sterilization was so strong that it alone could keep sickness at bay.

"You don't feel warm," Julia mused. "What were your other symptoms?"

I loosely held the thermometer, fiddling with my locket in my other hand. "I was talking to one of the Redway Boys and suddenly just... I was dizzy, I could see but I couldn't at the same time, I could barely feel my own body. It was hard to breathe right, like— my lungs were blocked. Like I was trapped in my body with this stifling feeling."

"How do you feel now?"

I stopped, sinking into the mattress. "Like I just recovered from throwing up but still have the fever. I'm still internally freaking out but I'm trying really hard not to."

Julia pressed her lips together, her hands on her hips. "What were you talking about before this happened?"

I took a deep breath to calm myself. "That... 'thing' I kind of told you about last semester. I don't think it ever ended."

I could trust Julia with a sugarcoated version of the story; she was a counselor in more ways than one, and she hadn't been involved whatsoever in the mess. All she knew was that I'd undergone a traumatic situation with some authority figures, and thankfully, she didn't care about how much or how little she knew about it.

She sat down in the black rolling stool beside the mattress. "You were talking about the traumatic events of last semester with someone, and then this happened?"

I nodded.

"Okay..." She nodded thoughtfully. "It sounds like you're dealing with a lot of unresolved anxiety about it. In which case, I think this was an anxiety attack. Have you ever had one before?"

"No..."

It made sense as to why; until now, I'd somehow convinced myself that there was no way Alexa was alive, and as time went on, it became easier to believe. I mean, nobody had come to snatch me from my bed in the past few months. And a life without Alexa? I had to enjoy that while I could!

"They can be a scary thing, especially your first," she said. "Do your best to avoid those thoughts, if that's what triggered this. Last semester is in the past, over and done with. Let that comfort you instead of letting it open the door to fear and panic."

"Yeah. I'll try," I said, slowly sitting up. But with Jak, his friends, and his *father* now living with us for a month, I felt completely powerless over my future regarding Alexa's involvement, let alone my anxiety about it. Then again, I'd never had that power to begin with.

"You're more than welcome to stay here until you feel better." Julia stood up from the stool and grabbed a small water bottle from the refrigerator in the room's corner. "So the boy you were talking to—is he cute?"

I narrowed my eyes. "That's subjective."

Except, with Jak, it's not. And Julia probably read that all over my face, snickering.

"Are you guys *perhaps*—?"

"Friends? Yeah."

"That's what I said about my first boyfriend before we got together," she said. "We lasted for two years."

"I have absolutely no time for dating right now. And my mom would kill me if I tried anything while they're here."

Julia gave a sweet laugh, condensation forming on her water bottle. "I almost pegged you as the type for secret relationships."

My head caught back in surprise. "Never! I'd never go against my mom like that."

"Well..." She strolled over to the counter and took a blossomed rose from the small vase sitting beside the sink. Facing me, she held it out with the water bottle.

"Hope you feel better."

My smile was wide and chest warm as I took the bottle and carefully accepted the thorned rose. "Thanks."

After celebrating New Year's in Rome, Sarah's aunt and uncle decided to host a late New Year's party in Capperson, too. And despite all the plus-ones Sarah had, I'd still managed to find myself down in the basement rec room alone. Well, until footsteps started thudding their way downstairs.

"Didn't think I'd find you here," Jak said. He ambled over to the other side of the pool table I stood at. "I never took you for the antisocial type."

"The music's too loud up there," I said, wrapping my black dress coat tighter around myself. The heater didn't function well down here. "What about you?"

"The music's too loud." His eyes bounced up to me from the

green felt. "And someone was missing."

I half smiled. "Did they send you?"

"No. I think I'm the only one who noticed."

Well, that's *comforting...*

His deep brown eyes stayed loyal to the red carpet under us, the shadows of the dim lighting adding a lot more weight than his question deserved: "Wanna tell me what you're thinking about right now?"

I fiddled with the locket around my neck. I almost didn't want the answer, but the question was a worse burden. "Same old. I just wanna know we're safe."

He traced his fingers against the wooden border of the pool table. "You and your mom, totally. But she's..."—he shrugged with an air of helplessness—"she's a magician."

As much as I hated it, that was enough said.

The glittery dress hugging my body was starting to itch, and a strained sigh left me. Questions had become a dangerous game, and asking them had become an irrational fear and all-too-necessary evil.

"Where's Alexa while your dad's at Callistro?"

"Leading the pack wherever for Tristan's descendant."

"In North Carolina?"

"Yeah."

What? Was Alexa leading her pack on a wild goose chase for my dad's descendant? Why was she doing my job for me? Why would she be leading them away from me, away from—?

Away from people who know her family's secret about being magicians.

We knew her secret and she knew ours. One wrong move

from either side and we were both going down. I didn't want to say it because, in a way, it was too good to be true—but it felt like the Ateras and Delphines were at a stalemate.

The door upstairs swung open, flooding the room with the holiday music blasting upstairs. Sarah and Breanne descended in their knee-high dresses, wedge heels clicking on the wooden steps.

"Oh, hello!" Sarah pushed a black bang from her elegant bun behind her ear. Her red dress flawlessly hugged her hourglass figure. "I hope we're not interrupting anything. Having fun, Jak?"

"Tons," he said, strolling from the pool table to them. "Thanks for the invite, seriously."

"I thought we came to celebrate *together*," Breanne said, glancing between us as she hugged herself. Her long-sleeved sweater dress was the fanciest thing that Sarah could get her into, but the mint green complemented her blond hair well. "What are you guys doing down here?"

"Growing up with my parents taught me to enjoy alone time." Jak's eyes landed on me, but it didn't feel like he was speaking to me. "'To be in company, even with the best, is soon wearisome and dissipating.'"

Breanne's jaw dropped with mine. I mean, it's not every day that a really cute boy quotes Henry David Thoreau.

"True, I guess," she said. "Do they never give you a break from... the Hunter agenda?"

William Bleu obviously used a pseudonym for his headmaster cover, but I had no doubt that he was working on the hunt for my family from his room at Callistro. That meant that any time Jak wasn't at the school was a time that he wasn't around his parents—or their peer pressure. But those moments were a bit rare, considering we needed Headmaster Dawson's approval to leave campus.

"I don't think any of us will be getting a break from it any time soon," Jak joked, running a hand through his dark-brown hair.

Sarah shrugged. "Better to be part of it than in the middle of it. I'm gonna go tell the guys you're okay."

She turned and trotted back upstairs at the same time my phone dinged in my dress coat pocket. I dug it out and had to remind myself not to smile when I saw the contact name:

N: Wanna get something to eat Monday after school

E: Sure, what time?

N: Meet ya at the fountain at 3

Interacting with Nolan had become just as easy as interacting with Jak over the last few months. If I'm being completely honest, it had become just as valuable, too; I could be a normal teenage girl around him. With Jak, I'd always be his parents' target, and he'd always know why.

Breanne walked to the wall adjacent to the pool table and picked up one of the cues hanging on it. "Want to play?"

I laughed. "Not against you."

"You can't win unless you keep playing." She smiled like a child, priming the end with blue chalk. "What about you, Jak?"

"She's just flattering you," he teased, picking up a cue. "I'll go easy, don't worry."

Another ding, and I looked down.

M: What time should I pick you up?

E: In an hour, I kinda feel... vulnerable here

M: I think you need to see Auntie afterward. Sound good?

E: Yes please

Another ding. Breanne looked up from the pool table.

"You're popular tonight," she said, setting the cue ball in place. I looked down at the new message on my screen. It belonged to...

An unknown number?

#: It's a nice evening for a party.
Know to always be wary.

"Guys?" I blurted. "Do you know who this is?"

Jak and Breanne came out from around the pool table to me and looked over my shoulder.

"That's not our area code," she said. Her voice went all too soft, even for Breanne Shaw, as she whispered, "How do they know that you're *here*?"

"Not Topa's area code, either," Jak mused, scrutinizing the message like it would change the harder he furrowed his brow.

"It can't be..." I began.

"It's not," he assured me, matching our eyes. "You're not

their target anymore."

"Maybe not *theirs*." Breanne shifted her doe-eyed stare to us. "But if someone's doing this, are we allowed to rule the possibility out overall?"

THREE

"So what's it like going to school with your boyfriend?" Aunt Becca sang from the recliner, sipping her tea. (Dad had challenged her to choose a healthier alternative to coffee for at least the first month of the new year. Apparently, with siblings, you either accept a challenge and win, or face a lifetime of shame.)

"You're not allowed to use that word," I said, setting my mug down onto the coffee table next to Dad's.

"Neither are you," he told me, leaning back into the couch with his arm around Momma. He'd been in my life for a few months now, but every word he spoke still sounded like a dream. His voice alone was a poignant memory of the steps we'd taken to even have this moment at all. Four months was nowhere near enough time to get used to it.

Tonight's anonymous text had left me on edge all the more, to say the least—and the last thing I wanted was to ruin family time right now. In full honesty, I didn't want my parents involved at all. They'd spent the last two decades running and fighting things like this, and I wasn't going to pull them back in after they'd *just* gotten each other back. If I was going to tell anyone, it was going to be Mr. Dawson—who could help with his magic *and* insight without being able to tell me what to do (technically).

"You should see them together, honey." Momma rested her hand on Dad's chest, cuddling into him. "Their relationship—"

"That word's not allowed, either."

When Momma shot him a frown of disapproval, he scoffed. "Sorry," he said, "you're just asking me to send my one and only daughter into the lion's den with no experience. Or a gun."

"If things go south, she can always toss him off a roof. Or into space," Aunt Becca said, icy-blue eyes peering up from her mug.

Dad narrowed his. "Are you saying you support this?"

She scoffed. "Seriously? I don't support the school she goes to, let alone her dating a boy from the *same type*."

"Okay!" Momma said, rubbing her temples. She chuckled. "Drop it. We need to get back."

"What? Can't you spend the night?" Auntie pleaded this even as she walked us to the front door.

"I have work that I'd like to get done before midnight, and Emma's friends are waiting for her," Momma replied, sliding on her coat. "Let's shoot for next weekend."

"Okay, you stay safe, kiddo," Auntie told me, grazing my

cheek with her thumb. Her brown roots were starting to leak through the platinum blond again. "Seriously. We lose you, we lose the entire Atera bloodline."

"Becca!" Mom and Dad snapped in unison. I mean, I don't judge Mr. and Mrs. Shaw for accidentally having Breanne's older brother at nineteen, but I'm not exactly interested in following those footsteps, either. And, you know, I'm still a *minor*.

"All I'm saying is, don't die!" Auntie said defensively, shrugging. "This family will never hear that enough. I'm not kidding, if we have to move again anytime soon, I'm giving up and turning myself in to Caldwell. I'm sick of living on constant lockdown, making a life-threatening relocation is the last thing I wanna add to it right now."

My chest tightened. All of that was fair; it must've been all the harder for Auntie to watch me and Momma freely leave the house every time because of it.

Momma took a deep breath and gazed at her like she always does whenever she admires "how much I've grown"—with the same melancholy. I'm grateful for how sisterly their bond is, especially considering how Auntie's fears were anything but irrational.

Momma nodded, amber eyes softening. "I know. I'm sorry. But you're safe here for now. Make the most of it."

Dad gave her a peck on the lips. "You, too."

Despite the fact that I'd been kidnapped in the middle of the night here twice, I still stand by how the manor is inexplicably comforting at night. It's either sleep deprivation from all the homework or the weirdest case of Stockholm syndrome I've ever seen, but it's true. When Momma and I walked through the elegant front doors that night, she was already taking off her pumps and sinking her feet into the crimson rug of the Grand Foyer. I would've done the same, but the clasps on my (Sarah's) three-inch heels didn't allow for an easy slide-off.

"I'm gonna head down and catch up on work," Momma said, sighing tiredly. "Don't stay up too late. And no boys."

"I know," I sang. "Good night, I love you."

She kissed the top of my head. "I love you, too, honey."

I waited for her to disappear behind the elevator doors past the Main Staircase before I approached the first stair. Exhaustion drenched every step up on the carpet runner, like my feet never wanted me to get out of these heels or this itchy dress, reach the top floor, and surrender to my bed.

"When I fall in love..."

I paused halfway up the stairs, my body matching the stillness of the near silence around me.

Did I actually just hear that?

"...it will be forever..."

A man's hum. But that wasn't Mr. Dawson—it was deeper, a little rougher. Who was humming in the Grand Foyer at this hour?

The humming paused. I could feel the muted steps of whoever now stood behind me at the bottom of the Main Staircase. The very weight of his presence socked me in the stomach, and I tightened my breath.

"Good evening, Miss Marie."

Oh, yes. I *did* know this voice. I knew it all too well, and it took every muscle in my body to force myself to turn around.

"Hello, Headmaster Bleu," I replied, tempted to soar past formalities.

"That's a beautiful dress." He rested his arm on the banister, square jaw as hard and unfeeling as the rest of him. And after feeling okay in said dress all night, that one comment cranked up my self-awareness dial. "How was your night?"

I called on my courage that had almost found the perfect hiding place. "Good. Thanks."

My fingers discreetly rubbed the wood of the banister as I chewed on the inside of my cheek.

A smile crept onto William's lips. "Did you find a picture for that yet?"

I glanced down at my locket. To my disappointment, my other hand was fiddling with it. William was reading me. I'd *given* him something to read.

What was I supposed to say? How was this locket any of his business?

"Are you okay?"

I bit back my response, because I highly doubted that he actually cared. "I'm gonna head up to my room, my friends are waiting for me."

"You don't trust me, do you?"

I cursed the fact that mortals can't hear telepathy, because I had a thought or a dozen to send him in that moment.

"Look," he said, round brown eyes suspiciously gentle, "you were right, you weren't who we thought you were. You're not a target anymore."

"Fine, but I'll *never* forgive you for what you did to me," I spat, my grip on the banister tightening at the bravery that had arrived at his call. "You tortured me, you pulled my life out from underneath me! And for what?"

"You were what we needed to move on. You were the missing piece to the puzzle."

He spoke too coolly, challenging the authority of my anger. I hated that—I hated the way his every word left a vibration in my head, like he was speaking in a code only he knew about and I just didn't know what sentence was real and what had a hidden message embedded in it.

Something was wrong about those sentences. About this whole conversation. But in front of him, I couldn't put my finger on it.

I looked behind me, tempted to continue up, but my words came to me in time. I rested my eyes on the tip of William's rugged nose. "Do me a favor: don't treat your suspects as targets. You can practice caution without assumptions."

His eyes stared up at me with a softness I only ever saw in his son's. My stomach twisted. "You're wise for your age," he said.

I turned around, his stare practically burning me with each step. I set my gaze ahead to stop myself from looking back.

"Emmalynn," William called as I neared the top. "I'm sorry."

C H A P T E R

FOUR

"This is amazing!" I chirped, Nolan's straight-A report card in my hands. I looked up at him sitting across from me, a tray of fries between us. "Didn't you say you were struggling this year?"

"I was!" He breathily laughed, about to run his fingers through his shaggy hair before remembering the beanie on his head. "I thought I was gonna fail two classes and barely manage to pass the rest. Seeing this was like someone bringing me a cake and saying, 'Your hard work was enough.'"

My lips were moments away from responding until my eyes snagged on what felt like a hangnail: "Greenwell". Nolan's last name was "Greenwell".

I know that name. Where have I heard that before?

No... I'd written that same name down in my first journal a few months ago, when Alexa had taken me to the Atera family beach house and told me about the Hunter who'd blackmailed Momma before I was born. But there was no way... Nolan couldn't... There was no way he was—

"What's wrong?"

My head snapped up to his curious green eyes. "Sorry, sorry, I... I was gonna say, your parents must be proud! Have you, um, told them yet?"

"The second I got home on Friday. That was the best feeling ever. Watching their reactions."

"I'm seriously so happy for you."

I slid his report card across the table and then took another sip of my soda. If I played this next part right, I could find out a bit about his parents and see if I at least had a lead. And if I did, I needed to get back to the school ASAP.

"Do you know what you wanna do after you graduate?" I asked. "Like follow in your parents' footsteps?"

He leaned back in the booth, his fair hand grabbing a fry. "Well, my mom's a paramedic, I think that'd be pretty cool. My dad... Okay, believe it or not, I don't know what he does. But he's randomly called away for a few days at a time every once in a while. He never talks about his job, though."

My heart started hammering, nerves burning alive as my mind jumped to Momma. That sounded way too close to the conditions of a Hunter career, and if I was right, Momma had been blackmailed all those years ago by Nolan's father. *Nolan's father.* He had to be Agent Greenwell!

Knowing that the Grand Hunter who'd chased me last year

was still alive, this felt all the more like confirmation: blatantly telling me that the hunt for my identity was never over and, if anything, had officially resumed.

I need to leave.

I grabbed my phone from my back pocket and glanced down at the black screen. "Shoot, I'm sorry, I have to go." I slid out of the booth and grabbed my half-empty soda cup. "I'll text you!"

Nolan smiled. "Can't wait."

I started my walk across the food court with strategy throbbing in my mind. It'd be wiser to hide Greenwell from Momma for now; I had to tell someone who not only would know what to do, but also had the power to do it:

—*I'm freaking out right now,*— I said to Mr. Dawson, the elevator straight ahead of me. —*I'm about to leave the mall, but I really* need *to talk to you.*—

—*Okay,*— he replied, —*get home safely. I'll see you in my office.*—

A wary Mr. Dawson closed his office door behind me, and I was ready for his every rebuttal—because I was also ready to lay my cards out onto the table if it meant getting help.

I turned around and faced him. "Promise me you won't say *anything* to my parents yet."

He arched a brow, his hand resting on the doorknob. "I never promise anything if there's a chance I can't keep it. Especially something as *unwise* as that." Straightening, he stuck his hands into the pockets of his blazer. "So?"

I quietly exhaled. I already knew that he was the right person to tell, and that would have to be enough courage to speak.

"Okay. Three things." I pulled out my phone and showed him the screen. "First, I got this text Saturday night during the New Year's party. I'm pretty sure they're implying that they know something, so I can't just delete it. But I need to know more about them before I can tell my parents. I don't wanna drag them into anything until I can figure out what to do—that's why I'm telling you."

He raised his head from the screen, pressing his lips together. "Okay. I can actually see your point there."

I quelled a proud smile and slid my phone back into my pocket. Following Mr. Dawson to his desk, I took a seat in front of him. "Good, because if they send me something else, it has to give me a clue, like if they're an ally or an enemy, or if they're just a wrong number. I just need time."

He held up a finger, leaning back in his desk chair. "All I said was that I saw your point. I didn't say I agreed with it. You do remember that your mom's one of the best in the business, right? Why aren't you getting her involved?"

I let the words in my head marinate for a bit. I wasn't sure if he'd fully understand, let alone agree, like he said. "My parents just got each other back. I don't want them to have to get up and fight when they're finally allowed to have their family again. And Aunt Becca isn't doing well, either. She said she's ready to flat out turn herself in if she has to move again because she can't stand living like this anymore."

Mr. Dawson rolled his eyes. "You know Becca's dramatic."

"Yeah, but—I also know that part of her actually does feel that way. Even if just the smallest bit."

He took a deep breath as his sharp jaw tightened. Now he seemed to understand. "Okay. Fine. Keep me updated on this and we're good. What else do you got?"

"Um... My fingers mindlessly wrapped around my locket as I searched for the words. "When I was out with Nolan just now, he told me how his mom's a paramedic, but his dad's always kept his job a secret. And I found out that their last name is 'Greenwell'. Which is the name of the Hunter who blackmailed Mom."

Mr. Dawson crossed his arms. I could practically see his mind filing through his thoughts and theories, and just as I was about to join him, he paused. My chest burned with a warning. I *knew* his next words, but my stomach still churned like butter when his sharp diamond-blue eyes leveled with mine.

"How do you know his name?"

It was now or never. And never wasn't an option. "Alexa. She survived the fire."

The muscles in his face dropped like a mask. He sighed, rubbing his face with both hands and resting his elbows on the desk. "Great," he muttered.

"Jak said she's leading the pack to another city for my dad's descendant."

When Mr. Dawson shook his head, I braced myself. "Okay," he said. "Based on what we learned about Alexa last year and how she wants your magic, she won't be able to come after the Ateras easily without exposing herself, let alone without a plan to isolate you both long enough to take your magic. If she hasn't come after you guys after all this time, at this point, all we can do is plan for what to do if worse comes to worst. Which means we *are* telling your parents that Alexa's alive."

I opened my mouth, but my brain refused to give me a rebuttal. I guess that was the other reason I'd picked Mr. Dawson to confess to: he could show me where I was right *and* wrong.

"And," he said next, "you need to tell your mom about Nolan's father potentially being the Hunter who blackmailed her so she doesn't risk being seen whenever she leaves the manor. If Nolan's dad *is* him, it's a miracle he's never caught her before."

I couldn't argue with that, either. I was just grateful that Mr. Dawson really did know what to do; he was able to help me get back some control, because nothing was ever in my control. I couldn't even do anything to stop or stall Alexa's plans right now because I didn't know where she was, or why she was there. What was I supposed to do?

I rested unfocused eyes on the desk, huffing. "I can't believe this is all happening while *William* is living here."

Mr. Dawson scoffed. "If I'd known he would be, I would've never agreed to Redway staying for the month. I've practically invited the devil into my home—I guarantee you he pulled some strings to stay here."

"Is it scary? Whenever you meet to discuss things?"

"Never let the enemy know you're afraid of them." He opened the lid of his laptop. "Then you let them know that they have an advantage and a chance. You give them their first and most important victory for the fight: confidence."

Maybe that was why I'd found Dad unscathed in the beach house basement after all those years; he'd been powerless, yet he'd fooled his enemies into believing he'd already won, like he'd been *letting* them have their fun while it lasted.

Ugh... My hand settled over my stomach. I swallowed, leaning against the right side of the chair. *What am I supposed to do if I can't do anything? How am I supposed to protect anyone if I'm not even allowed to use magic without getting caught and—?*

"You okay, Em?" Mr. Dawson asked, his chair squeaking as he leaned forward. "You're a bit flushed."

"Yeah," I said, swallowing again. "I'm gonna see Julia."

"Do you need me to take you?"

"No," I said, carefully standing. "I'm fine. Thanks, though."

At this point, visiting Julia felt more like visiting a friend at work—a friend who gave you free healthcare, which honestly wasn't a bad deal. When I walked through the door, she wasn't even surprised to see me again so soon, or maybe it was because of the red in my cheeks and how I'd come in holding my stomach. As usual, the office was empty, which made me wonder how Julia occupied every day when she wasn't taking care of one of us; kids are more often healthy than sick, and having only two hundred students further lowered the chances of "visitors".

"Stomach pains and hot flashes?" she asked as I sat down on the cot in the private room. After feeling my forehead, she walked to the cabinet behind her, grabbed a thermometer, and handed it to me. "You do feel a bit warm. You could've caught something over the weekend."

"I don't know." I lay down and stuck the thermometer into my mouth.

"Last week it was an anxiety attack, and now you're sick." Julia lightly shook her head, her auburn ponytail swaying behind her. "Maybe you should consider talking with the guidance counselor, or at least your mother."

I homed my focus on the roses in the spherical vase next to

the sink. They were a comforting beauty while the thermometer stabbed the back of my tongue. All I knew was that my eyes felt heavy enough for a nap and my hazy mind didn't want to keep me aware of reality for longer than a few seconds. Then again, that had become the norm ever since homework had *really* picked up last September.

Except, now I had an MIA Alexa and Nolan's dad being the agent who'd blackmailed my mom on top of it. It'd be no wonder if my stress levels had compromised me somehow.

Julia took the thermometer from my mouth a minute later, but not a hint of surprise touched her fair, soft face. "Hmm. Ninety-nine. Sounds like a stress-induced fever."

"What does that mean?" I said, propping myself up on my elbows.

"Well, you're probably not contagious—you've just put so much on yourself that your body is struggling to keep you healthy *and* functioning. You need to rest and relax, Emmalynn."

"Okay, I will," I said, sitting up and swinging my legs over the mattress, "as long as you don't tell my mom. She'll force me to stay in bed for the next three days, and I *can't* miss school right now."

Julia laughed, taking a seat in the rolling stool at the counter. "Wow, whenever I kept secrets from my mom, they were about a boyfriend or sneaking out to spend time with my friends who didn't go to Callistro. You're funny."

I tilted my head. Something didn't sound right in that story. "You weren't allowed to have friends who weren't Callistro Girls?"

She pressed her defined lips together, shaking her head. "Mom didn't approve of anyone who wasn't. She was *strongly* against magic and thought the only surefire way to make sure my friends were normal was if they went to a Hunter school. Well, I've never met any magicians, so she must've been right about something."

Based on the background she'd given me in the few months we'd known each other, I grew all the more curious. "I still can't believe you took this job over being a Hunter. Isn't hunting... more exciting?"

"I like being the support for the next generation." She smiled, shrugging. "Excitement's never been a priority for me. And I can't handle the battlefield firsthand. I've seen what happens out there. Some people are just... vicious."

Irony rang its bell, but I was the only one who could hear it: despite Julia being mortal, we had more in common than I would've ever assumed. The medical world actually used to fascinate me as a kid because it was scientific magic to me. All the more ironic, magic was normal to me while science was magical, which is even weirder because science has always been my worst subject in school.

Wait. What had Julia just said?

"'Vicious'?"

She took in a breath to speak, but nothing came out. A decision weighed down her green eyes, which seemed to forget that they were still on me as the seconds ticked by.

"Can I trust you?"

I blinked, suppressing my surprise. "Yeah. Of course."

"Good. Because I've never had anyone to tell this to, but I feel like I can trust you because—I can see myself in you. And if I'm right, then we're similar in this way."

This conversation felt familiar, almost too familiar. Why?

"Do you know what 'compassion' means, Emmalynn?"

Afraid that I'd incriminate myself, all I gave was a nod.

"I don't think I need to tell you how rare it is today. Borderline archaeological. It's so uncommon in the world—so what about for magicians?"

I chewed the inside of my cheek, fiddling with my locket. There was a wrong answer to that question, but that was the only thing I knew.

"Whatever your stance is on the issue," Julia said, "I physically can't look someone in the eye and kill them. It's not me. But that's really the only requirement to be a Hunter. And honestly, I'm just left sitting here asking how on this earth someone gets *paid* to do that. How?"

That was about the last thing I'd expected to come out of her mouth. I don't think even Momma would've been able to predict that there were other people just like me—or, more accurately, like her—at this school!

Wait. What was I supposed to say to that? Was I supposed to agree and tell Julia part of the truth about my stance, or keep playing my role as Emmalynn Marie, as a Hunter-in-training?

"Oh," I finally said. "I... Well... I get that. I'm actually having trouble getting over that, too."

"You could end up in my shoes." She shrugged. "You could be standing right here speaking to another Callistro Girl about the same thing in ten years."

I chuckled. "No, I have other plans. But I do wanna make a difference somehow, at least help people."

"Well, good, because nurses do that all the time." She

grinned at me, then leaned forward in her seat on the stool. "Seriously, though—can I trust you to keep that between us?"

I nodded again, as if she had a recording device on her and I couldn't let her snag any evidence of me admitting an alliance with magic.

"Thanks," she said. She gestured toward the door. "Okay, head up to your room. Take it easy, get some rest, and for your own sake, stay calm. Okay?" She placed a hand on my arm, gently rubbing it. "Relax for me."

I bit my tongue. That was easy for her to say. The biggest consequence of her actions as a teenager had been her mother's discipline—not her family's lives.

CHAPTER

I don't know where the Callistro Academy grabs their male staff from, but as of October, Headmaster Dawson was no longer the only man Callistro Girls whispered about in the halls. Teresa Darci theorized that Mr. Hartman, the new sophomore class math teacher, was originally an undercover magazine model assigned to lure in magicians with his handsomeness, but even Opal Dubois debunked the ridiculousness of that.

Otherwise, with a toned figure like that, I would've believed it at the drop of a hat.

Mr. Hartman walked to the front of his fluorescently lit classroom and then turned to face us. "I've been saying it since I got here, ladies, all you need is *confidence*," he said, both hands carrying the word as he emphasized it. "You know the material, you've done this before, you can do these questions. I try not to make the tests *too* difficult and only add problems you've seen before, so I need help understanding what the issue is."

I had a strong theory that the "issue" had nothing to do with his teaching—considering Breanne had seen no difference in her grades. After all, he was the first man with green eyes and black hair that I'd ever seen, and his defined cheekbones definitely supported Teresa's model theory.

Which reminded me, I'd missed out on his last couple of sentences just now.

"So I want to go over the most *common* mistakes made on last week's test. Let's clarify *any* misunderstandings." Mr. Hartman walked to the back of the classroom, to his tablet sitting on his desk. The projector displayed the screen on the front whiteboard as he pulled up the first version of the test and circled two questions on the first page.

"Friendly reminder: exponential functions are *not* the same thing as *logarithmic* functions. But I *am* glad to see that you're up to date on those."

I glanced around the room. Teresa Darci was flipping through her test; Caroline Walker was sitting dazed in her seat; Amelia Baker was glowering at her paper like she was daring the answers to change; and Breanne was staring back at me, waiting for me to answer the silent calls of her excited blue-hazel eyes.

She raised her brows as if to say, *Well?*

I held up my fingers: eight and then three.

With a child-like smile, she held up hers: ninety-four.

I playfully rolled my eyes. I could blame my lower-than-usual score on my current life situation and the fact that Grand Hunters were still trying to steal my magic, right?

I looked at Sarah in the back of the room. *Whoa.*

Sarah swallowed hard in her seat, hunched over her paper and rapidly tapping her desk with her index finger. One hand held her forehead, her elbow sitting on the desk.

Sarah *never* touches her face because it causes pimples. This test must've slammed her...

"Miss Shaw," Mr. Hartman called from the back, "will you please explain how you answered number five?"

I reluctantly returned my attention to Breanne. "Logarithms are exponents," she answered, looking back down at her paper. "Since the equation was in exponential form, I rewrote it as a logarithmic equation and solved from there."

"*Wonderful.* Thank you." Our teacher beamed proudly at her. "Exactly the route to go."

I thought back to Breanne's score. This unit was actually supposed to be one of the easier ones; I wondered what could have been running through her mind at the time of the test for her to have missed five whole questions.

I guess I'm not the only one unhealthily stressed out.

Let's just say, I'd loosely taken Julia's advice to rest and relax, which meant adding a nap after school, especially since it was Friday. After two days, dizziness was the only thing left of the fever, but my 1,000-word analysis on how Victorian-era Hunters cracked magician ciphers using copper and shoe polish wasn't going to wait for me to feel right again.

Which was rather unfortunate, considering only one Hunter was on my mind the entire time. It wasn't Paula Vinsky and how she'd used a dipped wire to decrypt an encoded scroll. Instead, my mind drifted further toward trying to crack Alexa's code with us—more accurately, with her own pack. At least Mr. Dawson had delivered the news about her being alive and the news about Nolan's dad to Momma for me (two hard conversations out of the way), but that just left me to figure out the logistics. Alexa still had Caralyn's documents revealing her alliance with magic, and I had to pray that Alexa was willing to keep that a secret. But she had let me go *twice* last year and almost a third time. We still didn't know why, and I wasn't sure we ever would. Why had she made the game almost too... easy? Did that have anything to do with where she was now? Would that affect how much time we had before she came after—?

"Emma!"

I snapped my head up, scolding myself as Sarah frowned at me from her bed. "How long have you been ignoring us?"

"I wasn't." I glanced between her and Breanne. I was pretty sure Breanne had been the one speaking before I'd tuned out, so I settled on her. "Sorry, homework. What were you saying?"

"It was *about* the homework," she replied with a softly furrowed brow.

Sarah tapped her textbook on her lap with the end of her pencil. "You okay?" she asked me.

With another glance between the two of them, I let myself revert to the girl I'd been last semester—the girl I'd always have to be in front of them. "This stuff... reminds me of September."

A moment of silence passed as if to pay respects. The girls knew how traumatic it had been, but they didn't know how *impactful* it had been, how indelible the memories were because they were anything but memories now.

"You're safe," Sarah assured me, leaning in my direction. "Alexa's not coming back, she and her pack went somewhere else to find Tristan's descendant."

That was what I'd originally thought; that was what I'd always wanted to believe, but it wasn't true. And knowing that it wasn't true was eating me from the inside out. I knew the truth but never *enough* of it.

"She's gone," I began, "but Jak's dad—"

"He isn't after you, either." Sarah closed the textbook, even though I knew she knew that she'd have to open it back up again to finish homework. "He's been here for a week and nobody's tried to kidnap you. You're safe, I promise."

Don't make that promise, I thought. As long as Alexa knew that I was Tristan Atera's daughter, there was no such thing as truly escaping her. She was parched for power, and only the Ateras could give it to her.

My mind paused. Power. *She thinks we're the only ones who can give her great power. Unless...*

Unless she knew of someone who was meant to become the most powerful sorcerer on the planet. Someone who was known in the magic world by a different name.

I forced my focus back into the real world long enough to assure my best friends that I was fine. I definitely would be now that I had a prospect of my mission for this semester: if I somehow managed to throw Alexa off the scent, it'd buy me more time to protect my family. Maybe I could even permanently deflect her if I played my cards right... Mr. Dawson likely only knew that I was Adara because he was such an integral part of my life. If the entire magic world didn't know her identity, Alexa could never figure it out unless I told her—and if she believed that "Adara" was her real name, that chase would last even longer.

In the middle of Breanne explaining the chemical reactions of shoe polish encryption to a bored Sarah, my phone buzzed under my pillow. Breanne had challenged us to do our homework with screens out of sight, and I almost wish that it had worked that night.

#: Nobody else can fulfill your fate.
Open your eyes before it's too late.

From the same number that had texted me at the party—so they weren't done with me, after all. What was this message supposed to mean? First a warning to be wary, and now they were telling me to open my eyes? To what?

"What's wrong?" Sarah asked, opening her textbook.

I realized too late that I was wearing my confusion. I ran to the first excuse in my head: "Wrong numbers keep texting me, it's just weird."

Breanne spun slightly in her chair, her thin brows furrowing. "Like the one that texted you Saturday night?"

"Oh, yeah, same exact thing," I told her, because for once, the last thing I needed was her mind on this case. "I finally asked who it was and it turned out to be some prank on a friend—also at a party."

The divot between her brows deepened. "Huh. Weird."

I pressed my lips together and shrugged, then looked back down.

The message was seen, but a response never came.

The rubbery, plastic smell of the gym hugged my nose as I opened the door Sunday afternoon. The heater was running to keep the manor cozy in the heart of winter, yet Mr. Dawson was setting down a bag of ice into a plastic cooler in the back of the gym.

"What's that?" I asked as I crossed the room.

He looked over his shoulder at me before tearing open the bag. "The subject of our lesson today." He stood and closed the lid of the cooler. "Let's start with strengthening your telekinesis."

I threw my head back and groaned. "Can't we do something *not* basic? I want a challenge, I wanna learn about different areas of magic."

He arched a strong brow at me. "Like what?"

I can't believe he's not arguing with me immediately on it.

I walked the length of the table next to me, gesturing with my hands. "Well, you've just been teaching me the same thing over and over again of messing with the laws and physics of nature. But I wanna start doing *serious* things like... messing with the internal chemical reactions of the human body or something."

Mr. Dawson took a step back, defensively holding up his hands. "We already established that you're not allowed to use me as target practice anymore."

I accidentally stop the flow of blood in his arms and sentence him to an overnight stay at the hospital *one* time and he never lets me forget it.

I rolled my eyes and leaned forward on the table. "I don't *exactly* mean that."

Wary curiosity bent his sharp features. "Then what are you talking about?"

"Things I can actually use against an enemy, like trust spells and hardcore forgetting spells—"

"*Why?*"

I kicked at an invisible pebble on the glazed floor and crossed my arms. "Alexa used that stupid trust spell against me last year. She used my feelings to try and get what she wanted. I never want to be a victim of that again. If I know how to do them..."—I let the words sit on my tongue for a bit, letting them fall with my sigh—"it'll be easier to reverse them."

"Oh." Mr. Dawson slowly nodded. "She never broke it. You can still feel it on Jak."

I think I was embarrassed to admit that I still wanted Jak to be part of my life; I let my silence answer.

"Emma, if you want to reverse something, you use a reversal spell. You know that."

I straightened. "That works with spells cast on people, too?"

"On anything that you want to reverse. It's just more difficult to cast on a person because you can't physically see what you're trying to undo."

"So, how do I do it?"

He turned back to the cooler and rolled it closer to me. "Practice your telekinesis first. Then I'll show you how."

Easy.

I set my focus on the plastic box in front of me. Whispering a telekinesis spell in my head, I lifted the cooler into the air.

I can do better than that.

My magic turned it upside down, letting gravity pull the lid open—and drop the open bag of ice onto the floor.

No!

I dropped the cooler onto the glazed floor as if to stop the already fallen cubes. A sharp bang resonated across the gym. I was almost tempted to run back to the doors to make sure that I actually had locked them, but Mr. Dawson was sighing and shaking his head—if he wasn't worried about unexpected guests, then I didn't have to be, either.

"I forgot you opened the bag," I murmured.

"Clearly."

I bent down, stood up the cooler, and then gathered all of the ice into one place. *Calfacio.*

"Emma!" Mr. Dawson exclaimed, stepping away from the large pool of water before it could touch his brown loafers. "What're you doing?"

Calfacio.

I stepped back from the puddle dissolving into steam. A cautious smile grew onto my face as I looked back up at Mr. Dawson and then stood.

He passed a hand over his face. "Well, there goes my lesson plan for the day."

"So..." I said. "Trust spell reversal now?"

C H A P T E R

SIX

None of us expected the surprise that Momma had prepared for us when we walked into her class Tuesday morning: for one thing, she's *always* in her chair while we find our seats, but today she stood at the front of the room. Second of all, her chestnut hair that she always kept down was now up in a bun (but I was pretty sure I was the only one who noticed the difference). The stolid mien on her narrow face shushed us the second our eyes met hers, and we settled into our black stools.

"We're doing something fairly different today, ladies and gentlemen," she began, pacing the front of the room with her hands behind her back. "You all have quite an advanced grasp of self-defense. But this semester, as you were warned, we're diving *much* deeper into your Hunter training.

"Hunters undergo brutal hours of training and simulations to fully prepare them for their career out in the field. Today, we're beginning our simulated hunts and missions—your first of many."

That was the cherry on top.

Callistro Girls and Redway Boys turned to one another with wide-eyed excitement. I caught glimpses of my best friends in the rows behind me: Sarah was silently squealing while a child-like grin lit up Breanne's face.

"If best-case scenario is that we end up as Grand Hunters," Jak began next to me, bouncing his knee, "and Grand Hunters hunt in packs, then that would mean we're hunting in groups—aren't we?"

"How funny would that be?" I said, humoring him.

"Settle down." Momma stopped at the front of the room. "There's a reason we spend an entire year practicing the concept of hunting. At the end of the year, for your spring final, we'll hold your most challenging hunt yet. It will demand *everything* you've learned in this class and count for half of your final grade. Get caught on that hunt, fail my class."

Okay, I might have been her daughter, but this was the very first time even I was hearing about this. The lowest final grade in the history of the Callistro Academy is a C+, and none of us wanted to break that record. (Not to call her out, but junior Penelope Lee earned that in 1964. She was absent for three weeks because she was assisting her father, a Hunter, on a real mission in the Caribbean. The mission earned her leniency in most of her classes, just not enough to maintain her average.)

Elizabeth Moody's brown hand shot up into the air. "Mrs.

Marie, isn't that... harsh?"

She had every right to exercise the question with diffidence; the entire class hushed like we were praying for the girl who'd just dared to question the sophomore class Hunter instructor.

Momma patiently locked her hands and rested them on her stomach. "Miss Moody," she began, "what happens when you're caught on a real hunt?"

She stayed silent; the question was rhetorical and only served to humble us.

"Your targets—your enemies—will *not* have clemency." Momma maintained equal eye contact with each of us. "Instead of earning an F as your final grade for the semester, you'll be killed the second your targets have the chance—the second you *give* them the chance by being caught. In here, it's pass or fail." She pointed at her door, her narrow features as cold as stone. "Out there, it's life or death."

The words resonated throughout my body. I knew the truth to them all too well. Even though nobody else knew from experience, my mother's as an ex-Master had doubled her class's respect for her within that one sentence.

"Severe punishment for small mistakes is real, ladies and gentlemen." She stepped onto the platform, walking to her desk. "You'll never get used to it, and we're not here to train you to get used to it. We're here to dull the shock as much as possible so that you can keep moving forward. If you think that that's not fair, that that's harsh, you're in the wrong class."

She looked back at Elizabeth, whose dark-brown irises seemed to quiver. "Did I answer your question, Miss Moody?"

"Yes, ma'am," her faint voice replied.

Not even Jak had enough courage to speak, crack a joke, or dare his own question. For a second, I was lost in the way his gaze admired my mother, her authority—something he could probably never respect his own parents for.

We all waited on Momma, and that was exactly what she wanted.

"So," she finally said, "because we had such a late start to training, your number of simulated hunts this semester has doubled. We can afford to take baby steps for now, but that in no way means that they'll be easy. Nothing is planned as soon as you begin. Anything and everything is fair game. Anything and everything could happen. That's how it will be out there.

"Your first hunt will be a diagnostic, and you'll be hunting as Grand Hunters inside the manor." Momma glimpsed her watch. "We have an hour and a half left of class, and we're using every second of it for your first mission."

She took out a small Tupperware container from one of her desk drawers, half full of slips of paper. "On average, the Grand Hunter-to-magician ratio is four to one. I have each of your names printed on a slip of paper here. Four of you will be magicians, and the rest will be Hunters."

Seventeen Hunters against *four* magicians? That wasn't fair—!

Oh. That's what she meant.

Momma opened the lid of the container, her eyes sweeping across the room one last time as she dug her hand inside. "For your first target," she announced, pulling out a slip, "Miss Cortez."

Jackie simply straightened her back, perfecting her posture, in response.

"Mr. Bleu."

No way. Really?

Jak's warm eyes met mine. No, I couldn't be seeing that right: he was suppressing a smile. A *smile*.

"Now I get to see how the other side lives," he whispered. Before I could blurt that his stepmom *was* someone from the other side, Momma called out another name.

"Miss Marie."

What?

The smile playing on Jak's lips dropped. Caution swarmed his gaze now. It was like he was asking me if I'd be okay with a role play so similar to last semester's reality, but this was just an assignment; my role in it was one that I'd been playing my entire life. This was just extra practice.

"And Mr. Schmitt."

Momma closed the lid and began our instructions before David could react. "Think of today's hunt as a game of hide-and-seek, but with a twist."

Yeah. A very *dark* twist.

"Hunters, catching your targets isn't your only mission today. Hidden cameras have been placed all around the school so I can track your progress. Your mission also includes finding these cameras and shutting them down to disable an outside source from looking in on your work.

"Magicians, utilize your training to stay hidden. Your classmates are learning how to be the offense in a Hunter's mission, but you are the defense. You'll be practicing the art of embodying the element of surprise. If you meet another magician, you may work together—I just can't promise that it'll be to your advantage.

It'll make your job more challenging, but the choice is yours."

Momma pulled out a black box from another drawer in her desk and popped open the lid. "You'll each be given a watch and earpieces so you can keep track of time and stay up to date with each other. When we have five minutes of class left, you'll meet me back here to briefly discuss how things went. Eventually, though, you will hunt until every last magician is caught, even if it takes you all day and night. Why?"

My classmates and I answered in unison: "Because that's how it will be out there."

In full honesty, it was kind of comforting that my classmates were just as unsettled by the notion as I was.

The Hunters stayed down in Momma's classroom while the four of us "magicians" were given a two-minute head start. We ran to the elevator together, and I couldn't help but wonder if our minds shared the same burden of adrenaline—like our lives were on the line.

We dispersed in the Grand Foyer, where I froze right there on the carpet. The majestic clock above the front doors didn't wait for me, ticking away. I had forty seconds left, and a hiding place still hadn't come to mind, not anywhere that my classmates wouldn't think to look first.

But watching the clock continue to move, I remembered that the last thing I *could* do was waste time thinking.

The staff knew about the hunt today, so I picked the library on the right side of the Foyer. Mrs. Reyes paid me no mind as I darted to the back of the room and stopped in front of the bookshelf in the right corner. *From Old English to Encryption* is actually a handle that opens the entire bookshelf like a door, revealing a secret space and a passageway that runs the width of the library. One of the narrow gaps between the books serves as a peephole. I was almost completely sure that it was a lesser-known passageway, but I'd have an escape route if my hiding space was exposed.

I grabbed the book and opened the passageway.

I prayed for every passing second to turn into another minute. I just needed to kill enough time to stay hidden until the end of class, but all too soon, quiet footsteps echoed across the library. I looked through the gap between two books: Ava Baleen, Hannah Lowe, and Redway Boy Carter McWayne.

"Emmalynn," whispered a familiar voice in my right ear. "*No cheating.*"

Translation: no magic. But Mother wanted me to treat this like a real hunt, and on a real hunt, I was going to use magic.

"There aren't a lot of places to hide here," Ava noted, large blue eyes glancing around like someone was about to jump out and attack her.

"True." Hannah stepped toward the large brick fireplace in the back, behind which the secret passageway ran. I could already hear her next sentence, which was my cue.

I turned to the wall on my right and searched for the handle. To minimize the grinding noise, I slowly slid open the wall and slipped through.

"But there are places that aren't completely *in* the library," Hannah said next, right on time.

Ava's and Carter's footsteps thudded behind her as they approached the bookshelf, but I was already at the other end of the passageway and opening the exit. I ran out and behind the curtains in front of the window beside me. Poking out my head enough just for a view of the armchairs in front of the fireplace, I had my next plan in mind.

I crept halfway across the room before whispering in my head, *Ite procul.* The left chair slid just enough to cause a groan against the wood. Ava, Hannah, and Carter darted their attentions over just as my telekinesis fluttered the curtains.

I was at the front of the room by the time the trio reached the passageway and dashed into where I'd left. Mrs. Reyes looked up from behind the counter just as I approached the doorway. She smirked at me, mouthing, "I won't tell."

With a grateful smile, I darted back into the Grand Foyer. One hiding spot was down, but I needed another one ASAP—this time somewhere another group of Hunters wouldn't already be looking.

Like... a place nobody knows about.

Momma *had* said that anything and everything was fair game. It wasn't my fault that I had an entire system of underground passageways to explore because nobody else knew about it.

The problem was, there was only one easy and non-risky entrance that wouldn't require me to go through the first-floor passageways and gamble being caught by the Hunters potentially in there searching. I just had to go through...

I muted my earpiece before knocking on Mr. Dawson's door. A few nerve-racking seconds of looking over my shoulder later, he opened up, and I weaseled inside.

Just as quickly, he shut the door behind me. When I turned to face him, he arched a brow.

"Dare I ask if this is an emergency?" he asked.

"Nope." I pushed the glass coffee table in the middle of the room back. "I'm here on an assignment."

Mr. Dawson passed a hand over his face. "The hunt. And you're gonna cheat."

"It's not cheating!" I grinned at him, folding up the navy-blue carpet. "Mom said anything's fair game. We're allowed to use the passageways, so I can use the ones nobody knows about."

"As long as you're not caught," he said, walking around me and toward his desk, "I'll pretend I never saw you."

"Thanks."

Aperta, I said to the floorboards in the center of the office. They slid into the ones behind them, revealing the staircase underneath.

A cold draft blew up and into my face as I took my first step down. "Don't forget to move the furniture back."

"Gee, thanks for the reminder," Mr. Dawson called. "I would've fallen through the gaping hole in my floor otherwise."

I snickered, stepping down the stairs until I my magic could safely close the floor. If not for the lanterns burning above me, I would've never had the courage to come down here so boldly.

The damp, frigid air nipped at my cheeks, and I pulled my blazer tighter around myself. Over the past few months, I'd learned that the only thing these passageways had were Caralyn's documents she'd put up behind my family tree. It was kind of disappointing, but it was fun to pretend that I *hadn't* explored every inch already and something else was waiting for me down here. I wondered how to pass the time while—

Ooh... Wait a minute. If I went straight down, I could walk *off campus* from here.

I looked at the watch Momma had given us before we left: I

had over an hour left. I could do so many things with that time! Town was practically calling my name!

I went down the cobblestone passageway before reaching the long staircase on the other end. I walked up, my legs burning by the time I could push up the fake tree stump. Daylight poured into the dim tunnel, and I squinted against it as I climbed out of the hole and stepped onto the snow-littered forest ground.

"When are we considered caught, Mrs. Marie?" Jackie Cortez whispered in my earpiece.

"When the hunt is over for you," Momma replied. "In other words, when you can't escape your Hunters. You'll know."

Well, no Hunter is coming out here. Unfortunately, it was way too cold to *stay* out here.

This isn't cheating. Right? Anything and everything's fair game.

Pulling my crimson blazer tighter around myself, I walked a little deeper into the forest. Maybe, just maybe, Caralyn had hidden something else here. A tree trunk with a camouflaged button in the shape of a hand, revealing secret weapons she'd owned; a secret opening in the ground that stored unheard-of gadgets; a secret code hidden in the shape of the bushes that was the door to a hideaway she'd built—

Snow crunched beside me in the distance. I froze. That was close by, way too close by.

I homed my focus on every detail my five senses could pick up: the bitter winter wind scraping my cheeks and grazing my legs, the aftertaste of the chocolate chip muffin I'd had just before class, the evergreen and redwood aromas. Now only a subtle wind whispered through the tree branches.

Jak had taught me last year how vital your peripheral vision is: that's where the most important things happen. And in mine on the left was a white-cloaked figure dashing behind a tree.

I whirled in their direction. I knew better than to call out to them, but my red uniform exposed me like a black bear in Antarctica. Maybe it didn't matter: the figure stayed behind the tree, patient. Like they were waiting for me to act.

I couldn't go back down into the passageways now! Not with a complete stranger in the forest, looming over the Callistro Academy for *Hunters*!

Quick. Keep everyone safe. What do I do?

I walked in the opposite direction, toward the path students took when leaving campus. I glanced behind me. Nothing had changed.

I had no plan, but I had to try anything that would eventually elicit a reaction; when I approached the tree stump, the figure slid farther behind the tree. That was it: I had to face them head on.

I charged toward their tree. Only then did they fearlessly step out, their back turned to me. My feet almost instinctually stopped, but the stranger wasn't heading in my direction anymore. They were walking away, back in the direction of town. Like this had been nothing more than a stroll through the Callistro Forest. I almost questioned if they'd even seen me, but I knew better.

Watch them until you're clear.

The second they disappeared past the school, I darted back down into the passageways. And, well, I stayed there for a long time.

CHAPTER

SEVEN

Okay, I took myself out of the underground passageways eventually because, in full honesty, being able to sit and do literally nothing while on a hunt did start to feel like cheating. I walked back to Mr. Dawson's office, and he telepathically verified that it was safe to come up.

I slipped out of his office and shut the door before turning around. Adrenaline bolted through me when I slammed into a figure just outside. I jumped back, catching myself before I could hit Mr. Dawson's door.

"Jak!" I hissed. "You scared me!"

He muted his earpiece with a grin, which reminded me that I had to unmute mine soon before Momma became suspicious. "Found you." He took my hand and then pulled me to the Main

Staircase in the middle of the Grand Foyer. Once we reached the top, he led us right, to the math wing.

Does the possibility of running into a Hunter not scare him?

"Do you wanna tell me," he began, walking to the very end of the hall, "why there's a full-length mirror here?"

I shrugged, crossing my arms. "Callistro Girls like to look their best."

"Okay," he said, pretending to believe me as he meandered back over. He stopped when we were mere inches apart, pushing a lock of brown hair behind my ear. "Can a mirror tell you how tempted I am to kiss you right now?"

Oh, he was wicked. No wonder he'd muted himself.

We hadn't kissed since that night last semester, when he'd told me about his mother. In full honesty, right now, I wanted to take him up on it; I remembered all too vividly the feeling of his lips on mine, and I wanted it again, to see if it was just as wonderful as I remembered.

"Why don't you?" I told him, tilting my head up against the inches he had over me.

A smile pulled apart his lips, one hand cupping my face. He leaned down, holding the kiss for a second longer than he needed to. It was like he already knew that I wouldn't mind.

He broke away, and I restrained myself from biting my lip, as if to cage the sensation of his lips on mine. Wow. I hadn't realized just how *much* I'd missed that.

"So what's it really for?" he asked.

I walked to the elegant mirror mounted on the wall and gripped the right side of the frame, opening it like a door. (Caralyn's riddle for this one was one of her best: "A world parallel to our own / That steps into the one not shown" was my favorite part.) I stepped inside the stone passageway with Jak right behind me.

"You sure you wanna risk the Hunters probably in here right now?" I whispered as Jak pushed closed the entrance.

"Just trust me, Merlin."

I followed him all the way to the passageway that led to Ms. Perketti's classroom. (It will forever be associated with the memory of Caroline Walker causing an electrical shock wave from a conduction experiment last November to super-charge Breanne's model rocket. Breanne *claims* that she'd built it without the intention of setting it off, but we all knew the truth after it flew out the window and exploded at three thousand feet up in the air.)

We stopped in the corner, Ms. Perketti's classroom just next to us. Another passageway ran down our left, or we could escape straight down if we had to. But the acoustics were too loud to conceal our steps if we had to run, and Ms. Perketti definitely wouldn't tolerate an interruption.

"We should keep moving before we're caught," I whispered. "We can't—"

Footsteps echoed in the passageway around the corner. And if we could hear them, they'd definitely hear us if we ran. We were trapped.

"I told you!" I mouthed to Jak, but all he did was smile, grab my hand, and turn to the cobblestone wall behind us. Wrapping his fingertips around the smoothest stone, he slid open the entrance to a secret, tiny space and pulled me inside with him.

When I say tiny, I mean *tiny*. I mean that it had been built for one and a half people, I had to turn my head to fit comfortably,

Jak's chest was pressed against mine, and his chin would've been digging into the side of my skull if he hadn't kept his head back.

Jak's chest was pressed against mine.

I could feel his heartbeat as clearly as my anxiety burning in my stomach. His heartbeat that was almost perfectly in sync with mine.

My shock lasted for only a couple of seconds. "How did you know—?"

He gently shushed me, our classmates' footsteps amplifying. I kept my head turned to the side and held my breath.

"Second floor's clear," Sarah's voice said. "Unless Ms. Perketti let someone hide in her classroom."

Teresa Darci scoffed. "No way. Hunt or no hunt, no one's brave enough to interrupt *her* class."

"Monsieur Goubeaux, on the other hand..." The smirk was all too audible in my best friend's voice. "He'll gladly let us check, I'm his favorite."

I stopped myself from laughing with Teresa; I'm not a foreign languages teacher, but if one of my students would only speak to me in a language I *didn't* know (thanks to Sarah's relatives on both sides of the family), they definitely wouldn't be my favorite.

I stayed quiet until the girls' steps eventually faded out with the grinding entrance far down the passageway. Then came Jak's breathy chuckle, that handsome, romantic grin in the corner of my eye. I kind of wanted to slap it off his face because it made me forget what I was thinking every time he flashed it at me, and I was pretty sure that that wasn't even his intention—that was just the natural effect. And that made me want to slap it off his face even more.

"They have hidden compartments like this in the secret passageways at Redway," he whispered. He'd definitely snuck in a stick of gum before class. "I've been able to explore a bit since we got here and find some. I just wanted to see if you trusted me enough to show me a secret for yourself."

Speechless and dumbfounded, I was almost afraid that my words would ruin the moment. There wasn't even a moment to ruin!

If you trusted *me enough.*

The butterflies in my stomach withered and dropped dead. The trust spell. I still had to reverse it, and now I *really* had to reverse it: what if it wasn't a secret passageway entrance next time? What if it was something that actually mattered?

"Scared, Merlin?"

I locked my jaw. "No," I said, stopping myself from turning my head to face him. "You're just... really close."

"That means either I let us out, or we stay here for the rest of the hunt."

My breath stopped in my throat—because he was completely right in that we really *could* just stay in here until the end of class. He was even keeping me warm despite how I was pressed against freezing stone on all sides. Not that I was genuinely considering it! But the fact that it was possible at all—

Jak chuckled again, like he could hear my every thought. "I'll stop, I promise."

I wanted to shove his head away to stop him from analyzing me. Jak never releases eye contact, and depending on the day, I'm either looking for the curse in it or, in the case of that day, the blessing.

"Would Headmaster Dawson let us hide in his office again?"

"I was coming out from a passageway that leads there," I said. "I wasn't hiding—um, can we leave now?"

He reached for the stone behind me, pulled on it, and opened the way we'd come from. "After you."

Minding the acoustics, I slowly released my breath as I stepped backwards and out of the space. I did not need this boy hearing how much he affected me, considering he probably already knew it.

"Mr. Bleu," Momma said in my ear. I silently thanked her for her timing as Jak and I unmuted our earpieces. "How have you managed to avoid your classmates so far?"

He rested his eyes with mine as he said, "I catch them before they catch me."

"Oh?" she asked.

"Yep." A soft smirk passed his lips. "In my peripheral."

Show-off. And as much as I hated to admit it, in the last few months, I'd used that advice a lot more often than I'd thought I would.

Jak and I managed to walk all throughout the second and then first floor of the manor (like Jak was going to leave me alone after we left the passageways). I showed him a few other passageway entries that he probably pretended to not know about. Half an hour before class ended, Breanne, Adrien, Wyatt, and Elizabeth caught David Schmitt in the elevator. Five minutes later, Jackie was caught in the secret passageway that led to the rec room. Meanwhile, Jak and I were camouflaged with the freshmen who went with Mr. Miller to get their language history books. (Jak did really well, considering that he's... well, not a girl, and his uniform is blue instead of red.) We left when the freshmen did, but we ducked into the English hall and into the passageway next to Mrs. Durrett's classroom after that.

That was when my mother told us, "Congratulations, Miss Marie and Mr. Bleu. You survived the hunt."

I looked down at my watch: we still had ten minutes of class left.

"Go ahead and meet us in the Hunter's Room."

Jak and I muted our earpieces. "What're you thinking?" he asked.

"That we should be going until we have five minutes left, like she told us," I said. "A Hunter will never *let* you win. You of all people should know that."

He scoffed, sticking his hands into his blazer pockets. "Of course I do," he teased back. "I was just worried I was gonna have to remind *you* of that."

My smirk gave way to a grin. I opened the door to the passageway, unmuting my earpiece. "Five more minutes, Mrs. Marie."

Her silence was all I needed to know how proud she was.

"They're probably all down there now if she wanted us to come," Jak said, running ahead of me. "Let's get a head start by going back up. As far as we can go?"

"You bet."

It was no longer a hunt, but a game. Not hide-and-seek like Momma had said, but tag, and we were trying to avoid the "it" group. It was all or nothing now, and we were going to give it our all.

Jak and I ran back into the Grand Foyer and then began our ascent up the Main Staircase. My stomach growled for the garlic

and herb spaghetti with glazed meatballs on the lunch menu today. I thought about how my friends and I would sit together at
lunch and talk about the hunt, about how Jak and I had worked
together so well. Maybe about what the other hunts for this semester would look like, about how Sarah and Breanne had managed
to catch their targets, what methods they'd used today, their plans
for—

Whoa!

My foot caught behind my ankle as I took another step up.
My body twisted, bending my ankle in a direction it's *not* supposed
to bend in.

I fell flat onto the stairs.

"Emma!" Jak rushed down and took my hands to pull me up.
"Are you okay?"

"I'm fine," I said, setting both feet onto the ground—and then
yelping in pain.

"Can you walk?"

"I'm fine, just slow, come on."

I took another step up, but my ankle just as quickly short-
circuited with a sharp jolt.

"You can't walk," Jak said.

You don't say.

"Do you need me to carry you—?"

"No," I said, sitting down on the step and rubbing my ankle.
"Just go without me, someone's gonna catch you here—"

The ding of the elevator cut me off. Somewhere behind the
Main Staircase, the doors slid open. Momma appeared on the left
side of the stairs with her class behind her.

"What happened?" she asked, walking up the steps.

"I just twisted my ankle," I said. "I'm fine."

She knelt down on the step below me, examining my ankle as the last few Hunters came from the library and others from the Dining Hall. (By the looks of Sloane Moore, Kimia Holland, and Jason Field each shoving a devilled egg into their mouths, it was kind of no wonder that Jak and I had managed to escape easily.)

"Em, can you move your foot?" Momma asked, looking up at me.

"Not without pain."

"Go ahead to the nurse's office." She stood and pulled me up. "It's probably not sprained, but make sure everything's okay. Can I trust you to escort her, Mr. Bleu?"

"Yes, ma'am," he said, taking my hand and helping me down the stairs.

Yes, everyone's eyes were on us. Yes, I wanted to get out of there as soon as possible. Yes, I wanted Jak to stop helping me walk even though he was the only thing letting me walk at all.

Breanne smally shrugged beside the Staircase with a hopeful smile. "You weren't caught. Congrats."

Except, I was pretty sure that a Grand Hunter wouldn't send me to the nurse if I tripped on a tree branch or something and twisted my ankle. In fact, I knew all too well that that was not how it would be out there.

EIGHT

"Oh, look who it is."

I should've expected the smirk from Julia when I walked in with Jak, but I still wanted to leave the room the second we did. Laughter is contagious, and with Jakson Bleu, smirks are no exception.

"What happened?" Julia asked him, standing from her desk.

"She twisted her ankle running up the stairs," he said. "I guess she was thinking about me."

I smacked his arm with the back of my hand.

"I told you not to let the boys distract you, sweetheart."

Doing the same to Julia wasn't an option.

A couple of minutes later, I was back in my usual spot on the vinyl mattress in the private room. My left foot hung over the edge with my right propped up with a pillow and an ice pack on my ankle. Julia had said to leave it there for a few minutes and we'd find out any collateral damage afterward.

Jak sat along the foot of the mattress with his back against the wall. I watched his mouth, knowing that he wouldn't allow silence between us for long.

"You're pretty good." He nodded at me. "How long did you say you've been at this?"

"Technically my entire life." I shrugged, lowering my voice. "If you count needing to keep the cover."

"Have you guys ever trained together?"

I smiled. "Are you trying to get me to admit where she's been?"

"*Never*," he teased, narrowing his eyes. It was the very first *purely* friendly laugh we'd ever shared. Some part of me was relieved. "No. I'm just wondering."

I licked my lips, selecting my choice of lie. "Um... we've trained a few times, I guess."

Seconds passed before his eyes went to my neck. "How often do you do that?"

I followed his stare; my fingers were fiddling with the locket.

"Oh. I don't even notice anymore." I dropped the charm and leaned back against the cold fridge behind me. "It's just habit now."

A soft smile bent his lips. "I'm glad."

"It gets dirty really fast."

"Yeah, but"—he leaned his head against the wall—"it means something to you."

Could this boy go *one* hour without butterflies?

"I'll go get your stuff," he said, standing up and walking out of the room.

I couldn't help but wonder if these moments would stop once I reversed the trust spell. Which I kept reminding myself I had to do, but the moment was never right. It was either that Jak would easily catch me using magic, or I needed the faith I had in him, artificial or not. At least, it felt like I needed it. I knew I wanted it. He'd been one of my biggest allies last September, and the truth spell Mr. Dawson had used on him had proven that he was genuine. If I didn't have that trust spell to keep my faith in Jak, would my cynicism stop me from having any...?

I didn't know better back then—but I *was* trying my best, and all I could ever do is learn.

Those kinds of thoughts made me hate being alone in that small, sterile room. All they did was remind me of every reason that my relationship with Jak was wrong. They reminded me of every reason that I could never pursue what I honestly wanted to. It was supposed to be dangerous just hanging out with him—Nolan, too. Even my friendship with Sarah and Breanne was on borrowed time.

I bit the inside of my cheek and took a deep breath. Right now, I couldn't afford those thoughts. Borrowed time, sure, but time nonetheless, and I couldn't get stuck.

"What did you do to scare him off?" Julia exclaimed as she walked in, as if Jak were a prize-winning animal and we were up next at the fair.

"He went to get my things," I said, taking the ice off my now numb ankle.

She scoffed, grabbing the icepack to put it back into the

freezer. "Why didn't they make any of him when I was your age? You have no idea how good you have it."

Sure, Jak was the quintessence of chivalry and Nolan was that of sweetness, but I was willing to trade cute, nice boys for getting to live back in Julia's day when technology wasn't as advanced and it was probably easier to hide magic.

"So," she began slowly, sitting down on her rolling stool, "how was the hunt?"

"Great," I said, surprising myself. "Actually, it was kinda easy."

"You might be better for this than I was ever meant to be." Her soft green eyes fell away from mine, her mind seeming to grab her gaze. I'd never asked about her story before. I was still too afraid to in case it'd be like someone asking me, *What happened the first week of last September?* "I'm sad I won't be able to treat your battle wounds."

I smiled cheekily at her. "I won't have any for you to treat."

She cocked a brow. "Tell me that when you successfully climb a flight of stairs."

"*Okay*," I said, earning a laugh, "it wasn't my fault, I just—"

I cut myself off at the realization. An internal shudder snaked through me at the thought of if that hunt *had* been real. I wouldn't have made it. Alexa would've caught me if I'd tried to run away.

"You what?" Julia asked gently, pushing a stray auburn bang behind her ear.

"I got sloppy," I forced myself to admit. "But I guess I learned for next time."

"Hey," Julia said. The softness in her voice pulled my eyes up. "Don't let this get you down, pretend it never happened. Give yourself a fresh slate so you don't have anything to base your current performance on except your training."

I shyly smiled as footsteps thudded from the main room. "Thanks. That helps."

Jak reappeared in the doorway, holding up my backpack. "Hungry yet?"

"First things first," Julia said, standing and gesturing to my ankle, "how does it feel when you stand?"

I swung my right leg over the edge of the mattress, slowly applying more and more pressure until it matched the amount that I needed to stand. "Okay. I can get by if I'm careful."

"Great!" Julia made a sweeping motion toward the door. "Then take it easy for the rest of the day and you should be fine, my dear."

"I'll make sure of it," Jak said, handing me my backpack so that I couldn't smack him again.

I took it. "Only if I let you."

"I approve, Jak." Julia nodded at him with her hands on her hips. "You keep doing what you're doing."

"*So?*" Sarah asked impatiently that night, eyes intent on Breanne as I walked into the bathroom. Both of them were sitting on Sarah's bed, per Sarah's demand after Wyatt had pulled Breanne aside after dinner. "Where were you two?"

I squeezed toothpaste onto my toothbrush and glanced in Breanne's direction. She was biting her lip with a child-like smile, furiously picking at the light hairs on her arms. It was like she was holding on to her next words for dear life and yet about to explode with them.

"He asked me out."

I paused with the toothbrush halfway to my mouth as Sarah unleashed a squeal.

"*Finally!*" she exclaimed, pear-green eyes alit as she threw her arms around Breanne. The bed bounced with her as she tossed her black hair over her shoulders and leaned in closely. "How did he do it? What happened *exactly*? Did you say yes?"

"Wait," I stated before Breanne could answer. "Does... he know?"

"No," she said, like she was perfectly all right with that. One look into her doe-like eyes assured me that for the first time ever, she was, and it thrilled me. "He just knows that something happened last year that ruined romance for me. But he's respected it and has *never* brought up dating until I accidentally did last week. When he wanted to talk tonight—"

"Wait, wait," Sarah said as I started brushing my teeth, maintaining her mile-a-minute speed. She sat crisscross-applesauce. "Tell us every detail and *exactly* what he said, verbatim."

Breanne giggled under her breath. "Um... it was along the lines of how he didn't know what happened but he didn't need to, I didn't deserve it. He said I'm the sweetest girl he knows and he's willing to wait however long..."

"However *long*?" Sarah exclaimed eagerly.

Breanne's cheeks swarmed red, her hands tightening into fists on her thighs. "I, um... kissed him—"

Right on time, Sarah squealed again and wrapped Breanne in her infamous death squeeze. I would've squealed with her if I hadn't been rinsing my mouth.

"What now?" she demanded, almost bouncing Breanne straight off the bed. "Are you dating? Are you gonna spend winter break together? Do you plan on doing long distance, or are—?"

"And you wonder why I hesitate to tell you anything," Breanne said, the shy girl in her crossing her arms, but her excitement couldn't leash her smile. "Emma's not freaking out."

I dried my mouth and laughed, taking out my face wash. "I just had a toothbrush in my mouth, I'm so happy for you!"

Sarah took in a breath to speak, but then her lips bent into a sly smirk. She caught a glimpse in my direction and then returned impish eyes to Breanne. "Fine. We can talk about Mrs. Bleu over there instead."

"Stop it!" I whined, setting down the bottle and waiting for Breanne's reaction that would tell me whether it'd be safe to resume. "Where, *where* did marriage come from?"

"Where's your denial?" Breanne pointed at me like a six-year-old who wanted you to pull her finger. "What desires do you hide and why?"

My eyes rolled to the back of my head. "Because Sarah's crazy and doesn't even know that we kissed again," I said, shutting the bathroom door on two gaping mouths.

I helplessly smiled to myself as they both scolded me through the door. It was a bit of a relief after narrowly avoiding the topic of Breanne's ex. Honestly, I hate even calling him that—he doesn't deserve to be part of her history.

We never talk about what happened for a number of reasons: 1) We'd seriously rather not talk about it. 2) Breanne doesn't need to relive it. 3) Every time it's mentioned, Sarah's filled with the destructive (and, well, murderous) impulse to do illegal things to the boy it involves. 4) If we didn't talk about it, we could keep moving forward. Or, at least, it was easier to believe that.

But we never considered what we'd do the day boys would make our hearts flutter again, or when Breanne "got back in the game". I mean, we knew that our guys were universes apart from last year's. But that night, Breanne making a move on Wyatt was still a progressive and miraculous sign. She wasn't just ready to move on; she *was* moving on. She was finally harvesting the fruits of her patience, caution, and strength.

I could learn a thing or three from her.

C H A P T E R

NINE

"**E**mma,**"** Breanne whispered from across our room, my name breaking through the hazy, tired fog of my awakening mind. Her voice traveled closer as she tiptoed to me. "Are you awake?"

"No," I groaned with my back to her, cuddling into my comforter. Last night, I'd had a weird, plotless dream about the mall, a group of teenage boys, and a faceless classmate, and I'd spent the entire dream trying to figure out what was going on. Now I just wanted to forget and sleep.

"Liar," Breanne whispered, plopping herself down onto my bed. "I'm bored, let's do something."

As much as I love the girl and her quirkiness that seems to fully blossom in the early morning, it was Saturday; I really wanted to enjoy the peace and stillness that I knew wouldn't last.

"Please *try* going back to sleep, Bre."

"I did."

"Then finish the annotations for Mrs. Durrett and the diagram for Ms. Perketti."

"I *did.*"

I propped myself up with my elbow and looked over my shoulder at her. "How long have you been up?"

"A little before 7."

I turned over and looked at the clock on the bedside table: 7:30.

"I don't know, wake up Sarah and we'll do something."

She chuckled as loudly as was safe. "You of *all* people know why I can't do that."

During a sleepover in fifth grade, Breanne and I had gotten up at the same time and could already smell Mrs. Shaw's chocolate chip waffles from downstairs. I was too impatient and tried shaking Sarah awake so we could go down, but she's a lot more cut out for the Hunter game than I thought: she defended herself and twisted my arm in her sleep. She profusely apologized for the rest of the morning, but it was fine because Mrs. Shaw gave me extra whipped cream.

I turned over in bed and took my phone off the nightstand. A message was already waiting for me.

J: Wanna take a walk around the school?

"Who's that?"

"Jak," I said as I typed a response. "He wants to walk around school."

Breanne's eyes lit up. "If he's awake, Wyatt probably is, too! I'm gonna ask if he wants to go to the library." She hopped off my bed and ran for the closet, picking her outfit for the day.

Well, that definitely worked in both of our favors.

Sarah stayed sound asleep even as Breanne and I got dressed and ready. I was almost willing to bet my magic (*almost*) that Sarah had spent half the night texting Adrien, meaning Breanne and I had at least a couple of hours to kill before she'd wake up and notice we were even gone.

Jak met me in front of my dorm after Breanne left, and he and I decided to head down to the first floor. Unfortunately for me, not even the early morning could ruffle his handsomeness. The tips of his hair almost seemed to curl up a bit more. He'd changed into jeans, a thin gray hoodie, and his leather jacket on top of it. And—I'm going to be completely honest—he smelled *really* good.

Perfume, I thought as we reached the staircase. *I forgot to put on perfume!*

"So," Jak began before I could turn back toward my dorm, taking the first few steps down, "what had you up so early?"

"Breanne," I replied. "She got an early start today and wanted to do something. You texting actually gave her the inspiration to see if Wyatt was awake."

"*Oh*," he chimed, nodding, "that's why she came out first. Then you're both welcome."

I nudged him, crossing my arms for added warmth. "Been a couple of weeks, how're you liking it here so far?"

He glanced at the tall ceilings, then the windows overlooking

Capperson, and then the crimson carpet runner underneath us. "Nice place you got here."

I was grateful for the currently unpopulated floors; I can't tell you why, but pretending that Jak and I were the only ones away right now felt fulfilling. And, well, if anyone *did* see us right now, the rumors would probably last until the end of the month.

"Remind me what it's like at Redway," I said as we reached the Second Staircase.

Jak had told me last year that his school was a renovated prison from 1902—which tempted a lot of jokes. I wondered about the Redway founder and what the story was behind the establishment, to pick a *prison* of all things to repurpose for a school.

Jak shrugged. "The teachers are pretty cool. The Hunter instructors..."

He didn't speak again until we reached the top of the Main Staircase. "Put it this way: no offense to your mom, but she's soft on us."

I cocked my head. "What do you mean?"

"I mean that it's easy to tell she's good. She's *really* good. On a scale of one to Alexa, where would you put her?"

My chest tightened at the name. I tried to hide the fact that it weighed more heavily on me than he thought it did. "I mean, I might be biased, but... if she were to have continued hunting? About Alexa's level. She was gonna be in a pack right before she quit."

"Exactly. Do you think she's soft on us right now?"

I thought about it for a few seconds as we descended, remembering all the stories Momma had ever told me about her Hunter adventures. One in particular, I'm scared of living out: when she was sent to Vegas undercover as a magician to lure a Hunter who was *actually* a magician out from his cover. There are a lot of reasons I'm probably never going to Vegas, but the possibility of me running into a Hunter with that same mission resides in my top three greatest fears. Especially when that Hunter could do the extra research to know what my favorite food is and then drug it— like Momma did.

"I guess so," I said, stepping onto the carpeting of the Grand Foyer. "Yeah."

"Then you're not biased." Jak seemed to stop automatically with me. "And if the Amy Marie we're shown in the classroom is sugarcoated, she belongs at a place like my school."

"So they're really tough?"

"They have to be. It's like your mom said, nobody's gonna have mercy on us if we're caught."

I laughed, meeting his eyes that seemed to smile when I did. "So you want her to be tougher on us?"

"Oh, no," he quickly said, "trust me, the break's been *really* nice."

I pressed my lips together in thought, mindlessly meandering toward the history wing on the right side of the Foyer. "Is your dad being Redway's headmaster how he and Alexa met?"

Jak tilted his head, crinkling his brows. "Where'd that come from?"

"I don't know," I said as we rounded the corner of the corridor, now aiming for the student lounge room. "I just got to thinking about my mom and the schools and... I think I've always been curious about how they met. Like, how two of the greatest Grand Hunters the country's ever seen ended up not only in the same pack, but married."

He nodded, digging his hands deeper into his jacket pockets. "I can't tell you."

"Oh. Then how long have they known each other?"

We reached the entrance of the lounge room. "My best guess is a few years," Jak replied. "Probably since I was, like, ten. I met her for the first time after I turned twelve, and it was so my dad could announce that they were getting married. Nothing was ever 'officially' announced to me except that."

I gasped. "They were dating for a *year* before you finally met her?"

Walking to the back wall, he leaned against one of the bookshelves. "They eloped four days later." His lips tightened with suppressed laughter, which managed to escape. "She was actually pretty nice to me, if you can believe it. She treated me almost like I was her own son."

"What about now?"

He stood up from the bookshelf and made his way toward the door, and I followed. "She'll crack a few jokes with me about a hunt, she'll ask what I'm feeling up to for dinner, and she'll tease me a bit. So she's still pretty nice."

I swallowed my own laughter ready to break out; I couldn't imagine Alexa Delphine doing those things (except maybe the first one) for many different reasons, including when she'd kidnapped Jak at the Capperson Fall Carnival last year and debriefed him about the girl she'd probably teased him about. None of those things screamed "motherly" to me.

"So, is how they met a touchy subject, just confidential, or...?"

"I can't tell you, Merlin," Jak said again as we walked back down the hall we'd come from, "because I don't know."

Huh. That was... unexpected.

At this point, any other topic was better than this one. "Okay. Then are you usually up this early on the weekends?" I asked, approaching the back of the English wing. "Because this is the only reason I was able to forgive Breanne for waking me up."

He stayed quiet the entire way back to the Grand Foyer, where he nodded his head in the direction of the English wing. I waited for an answer the whole time until we made it to Mrs. Durrett's door. Jak slid aside the daisy painting hanging on the wall next to it, and then pulled me into the secret passageway—keeping his hand around mine even as he slid the door closed.

Finally, he turned back to me. "Would you still rather be asleep?"

"I... didn't say that."

"I can escort you right now." He pulled me with him as he leaned against the entrance of the passageway. His hands slid to my waist, and I cursed how having to look up at him made my swallow all the more visible. I saw the idea to kiss me flash across his brown irises; the intuition was electric. Every movement was intentional, from the flicker of his eyes to the smirk twitching the corners of his lips—that was how I knew that that was his plan. To get me to think that he would kiss me then and there, to prepare me for it, before he released me and continued walking farther down the tunnel.

What a tease!

The shock didn't freeze me for too long, but I did have to jog to catch up. "How many times have you pulled that one?"

"Pulled what one?"

"Are you dodging—?"

"Zero." He shrugged nonchalantly, like I'd asked him what one minus one was. "I was trying something new. What would you rate it?"

I backhanded his arm. "That."

"You're a good liar."

Not according to Momma. Apparently I don't blink enough when I lie. Hopefully Jak wouldn't get to know me better before I had the chance to correct that.

He offered me a smile and then continued down with reverberating steps, turning left. I would've followed him to wherever he was heading next if he hadn't paused in the middle of the intersection. I stopped, waited a few seconds, and then went to step forward, but Jak's arm reached out in front of me.

"Did you hear that?"

"Hear...?" I whispered back, caution kindling in my chest.

Jak waited again. Silence. I was too scared to be impatient, because if Jakson Bleu is on high alert, it's because he doesn't know everything about his surroundings when he should—or, at least, he knows that something is *wrong* with his surroundings.

He took my hand and pulled me in the direction we'd come from, and I followed with ease. "Come on, let's go back."

"If you're messing with me—"

"I'm not," he said, turning around to firmly match our eyes. "I'm not, Merlin."

I knew that he meant it, because he was letting me see what he was thinking: he wanted out of those passageways.

We were back at the entrance when my curiosity meshed with my survival instinct. I turned my head just as Jak slid the entrance open. An all-black figure hugged the corner of the passageway. Fabric covered their entire head as they stared. Watching as Jak and I left the passageway.

I nearly jumped out with him. He didn't seem to notice.

We were being followed.

"I'm sorry," he said, shaking his head as we power walked through the English wing. "I thought... I thought I heard footsteps or—"

"I did, too."

That was a lie, but I knew that Jak wasn't crazy, and I needed him to know that I knew that. Goosebumps pricked my back. The hairs on my arms were standing up, tickling me as they slowly settled.

"Um..." I whispered, "maybe it was just—another student."

"That was the problem," Jak said, resting his hands in his pockets again. "I didn't need another student following us and hearing about..."

Us. Tristan's daughter. Jak's parents being active Grand Hunters and nowhere near retired.

I nodded, offering a small smile for comfort. "Yeah."

It seemed to work, because he returned it like a thank-you. "Library next?"

"If you want, but Breanne and Wyatt are there."

His smile stretched into his infamous smirk. "Let's see how long we can last without them knowing we're there."

"Wouldn't that be spying on them?"

"Only if you intend to eavesdrop."

There were a dozen ways I could fault that logic, but pretending otherwise gave me the necessary relief to follow a now carefree

Jak into the library. But nothing could shake the fact that he was only so blissfully ignorant because he hadn't seen the person who'd followed us in the passageways—someone who was anything but a student.

We entered the library and stayed on the right side of the room, sticking ourselves between the bookshelves. Breanne and Wyatt sat in the back, in front of the unlit fireplace. Jak and I tiptoed along the wall of books until reaching the one that opened like a door. Wyatt and Breanne were deep in a discussion about Henry David Thoreau's philosophical backing in *Walden* as Jak and I ducked. We pushed the bookshelf more and more open until we were able to just squeeze by. We closed the entrance with extra caution, trapping ourselves inside the secret room I'd hidden in during the hunt on Tuesday morning.

"I'm hesitantly impressed," Jak whispered, looking through the peephole.

I softly elbowed him.

"It was a compliment, Merlin. But now we need an escape plan."

I grinned. "You're not embarrassed of me, are you?"

"Oh." He smiled back. "Look who's flirting now."

I shook my head, opened the passageway that ran behind the fireplace, and guided us to the end. Opening the other entrance, we crept out as quiet as a couple of Hunters. There Breanne and Wyatt happily sat in front of the fireplace. A textbook was splayed open on the small table between them, their pencils scribbling notes in their composition books in their laps.

Jak and I shared a glance as we closed the exit and then skulked by.

"I always retain information a lot easier in the morning," Wyatt mused, running a hand through his shaggy black hair. "I don't know why, it just feels like my brain works best at this time."

"I'm that way, too!" Breanne beamed, shifting her position in the chair. Her long blond hair rested on the page of her book. "But... it helps to have a study partner."

I was pretty sure that that was the first time I'd ever heard Breanne Shaw flirt.

She really is moving past freshman year. Warmth that had nothing to do with the running heater radiated in my chest.

Jak smiled down at me, but I tiptoed past before he could say anything. Exiting the library and walking back into the empty foyer, it was back to my questions game with him. More accurately, trying to figure out what question *to* ask him.

I wondered if the next one that popped into my head was actually worth it. Well, it wouldn't result in any accidentally brought-up trauma, and that was enough for me: "What's your favorite color?"

"Am I boring you?"

I groaned. "*No—*"

"Purple. You?"

I nodded, even though the answer surprised me a bit. "Blue. Kind of like—"

"No need to explain, it already makes *plenty* of sense—"

"*Shut up*," I simpered as we approached the middle of the foyer, biting back a giggle. "I like a sky or baby blue. What about mornings? Are you usually a morning person?"

"Sure. I prefer waking up earlier than later, if that's what you mean."

"Me, too. I like it being this quiet and empty."

"Yeah?" Jak stopped again with his hands back in his pockets. "Is there something you can't normally do when people are around?"

I laughed. "Hang out with you without gossip, for one. You, on the other hand, don't care about what people see."

"Nope." He took a couple of steps toward me, stopping when he was close enough to lean in. "But that doesn't mean I prefer a crowd."

I was so sure that he would kiss me—I wanted him to take the sides of my face, to bring my lips up to his—until his chocolate-brown eyes darted to something over my shoulder. He instantly straightened, erasing the past few seconds.

I looked behind me, caught the man coming out of the head-master's office, and then stepped away from Jak. He clenched his jaw as William's stare found ours.

I expected Jak to reset in some way: clear his throat, do something with his arms like cross them, look down at the carpet. But all he did was exhale, his arms relaxed at his sides. His eyes never left William's as he approached.

"Hey," Jak said stolidly.

One word of communication was all it took for me to realize, the only other time I'd seen these two interact was when they'd had an all-out brawl the night William had interrogated me. Based on the tension practically crackling between their two frowns, the only difference now was the lack of fists.

"Good morning. And good morning to you, Miss Marie."

"Likewise."

William's eyes shifted to the boy next to me. William was just shorter than him. "You're up early. Having a good time?"

"It's an upgrade," Jak answered, subtly inching closer to stand in front of me.

William snickered. For a second, it felt like he was trying to have a real conversation as he flatly asked, "Really? What makes Redway so awful?"

"Would love to go to school without my dad and his wife breathing down my neck, for one."

I quelled my surprise and risked a glance at Jak. With his jaw clenched, he maintained defiant eyes on his father, who seemed to have expected that kind of answer.

"I'll gladly 'breathe down your neck' if it means you're doing well in school."

"If it means I'm doing what you want me to," Jak sneered, catching me further off guard. "Which is—"

He cut himself off, snapping his mouth shut. I dared to

glimpse William in a vain attempt to predict his reaction, but I couldn't even read if he knew how that sentence was supposed to end.

"What're your plans for the day, Headmaster Bleu?" I asked for the sake of civility. My rationality doubted things would escalate beyond this—at least not in a way that I'd be aware of—but I didn't want to risk anything.

"I just finished running through a couple of reports with Headmaster Dawson. After that, I need to call the school and check in on things over there."

I'm really glad Mr. Dawson can handle his own so well. I didn't know if I'd be able to handle a meeting with William about anything—the only one I *had* had with him had ended in disaster.

"Well, I won't keep you," he said, turning to the Main Staircase. "Have a good day."

I was hesitant to say anything as we watched him ascend, and Jak definitely wouldn't speak until we witnessed William disappear past the Second Staircase. Even then, though, I'd have to wait until Jak's next words; whatever they would be would tell me what was and wasn't safe to talk about.

"What do you think Sarah has planned for tonight?"

In other words, don't talk about what just happened.

The Redway Boys would only be with us during January, so Sarah had insisted on dedicating our Saturdays with the guys while we could. Finding something to do was a walk in the park (literally, in last Saturday's case) since Sarah always had something planned. It temporarily kept us away from our responsibilities behind the school's walls, though, so none of us had any complaints.

I chuckled. "Who knows? Are you excited?"

"Always. Funny how 'normal' is actually a break for us."

"Try this one," Sarah said to Adrien that evening, popping a yel-low petit four into his mouth as we left Dom's Bakery. "It's lemon, but it's *so* sweet!"

Last month, when Dom's had moved in, they town had opened a little back area behind a few of Capperson's stores. A wall of snow-dipped evergreens stood tall on our right, and there were a few benches aesthetically placed in the open area. Only a handful of people came back here, but it was clean, quiet, and private—the perfect place for an evening stroll. Dom's Bakery had a backdoor specifically for this purpose, and what better way to finish off a gourmet meal from Callistro (other than the tiramisu they were serving tonight, but this was more private)?

"Oh, yeah, it is," Adrien mused, nodding at the concrete in thought. He then returned a loving, blue-eyed gaze to Sarah; wrapped his arm around her; and met his lips with hers, taking her by surprise. "I still prefer that."

Jak's smiling eyes fell onto me as we passed them. "Wanna try that, Merlin?"

"The cake?"

Breanne laughed on my other side, looking over her shoul-der. "You're ruining my dessert!" she called to Sarah.

Sarah smirked in her direction, tossing her hair over her shoulder. "What're you talking about? Your dessert's standing next to you."

Suppressing laughter, I looked away from Breanne in fear of

witnessing retaliation—until I accidentally leaned too far into Jak, stumbling over my feet. Nobody needs to guess who caught me.

"They must've put something in the cake," he said.

I scrambled to my feet, muttering a thanks as Sarah dragged Adrien with her to catch up with us.

"Well, I guess we have to start heading back," she said with a sigh, linking her arm with his. "But today was fun."

"As always," Wyatt said, narrow dark-brown eyes smiling down at Breanne. He still kept his distance from her until she closed it, taking his hand.

Our jackets—and each other—sufficed for warmth against the winter night. A light breeze fluttered by, lending the bushes a gentle sway that lulled my walking pace into the same rhythm. The light from the lampposts lined in front of the trees mixed softly with the dim sky, and for a few moments, I let myself settle into it all. The back of my mind whispered that evenings like this would eventually become rare. According to Mr. Dawson, I only had so much time before Adara came into power. Leisurely strolls around her hometown didn't really seem like something the world's most powerful sorcerer would have time for.

Nobody had anything to say for the rest of the walk home. We were already tired from the evening out, and nothing sounded better than grabbing a cup of hot cocoa and warming up in front of the library fireplace before bed. Sometimes silence is the glue that bonds a group closer together, especially when you can relax in the fact that your friends are there at all.

But as all good things do, the bliss came to an end.

We'd just entered the forest when my phone buzzed in my coat pocket. I reluctantly pulled it out. From my notifications, the anonymous number stared back at me:

#: Who is your ally, and who is your foe?
Who, most importantly, could already know?

It was like the sender had heard my every thought. Like they were taunting me about it, telling me that even they knew that my friendships were on borrowed time.

Or like they were ready to ruin them.

That's it, I thought, my eyes landing on the school in the distance. *I can't wait anymore.*

ELEVEN

Come on!

Extracting IP addresses from a single text message and finding the exact location it's been sent from won't be taught until next year's off-the-field Hunter classes. But I figured, if Breanne was able to figure it out freshman year, I could during sophomore year!

I'd figured incorrectly.

Three days of sneaking and six error messages telling me that I needed to enter the valid "command prompt" later (whatever that was), I had to close the program Tuesday morning when I heard Breanne turn off the faucet in the bathroom. Not only would she see that I *wasn't* testing if I could track Jak's texts (the only time she's ever approved of stalking), but she'd also be able to see the search and data history of what addresses I'd located if I did continue. Besides, I didn't trust Sarah to walk out of the closet and *not* ask why I was trying to stalk a random number.

On top of all that, Mr. Dawson wouldn't approve of me looking further into this without my parents' knowledge, but my parents would shut down the entire operation before I'd even have a chance to explain. Where did I have to turn to now?

I reluctantly let go of my thoughts when third period and I entered the mini gym for Momma's lesson that day. If I stayed in my head for too long, I'd miss her instructions, and she wouldn't repeat them even for me.

Her steps and voice resonated as she paced the front of the gym. "Today I want to perfect our straights and combine them with our righthand uppercuts. This time, though, boys paired with boys and girls paired with girls."

Despite the disappointment on some of my classmates' faces, the rule didn't matter to me; socializing was in the very back of my mind right now. On top of having to keep the anonymous number at bay, Momma and I were finally going to visit Dad and Aunt Becca after school—which probably meant that we were going to discuss what to do about Alexa being MIA.

Seeing Sarah walk up to me, Jak made a special effort to wink at me before turning away and pairing up with Wyatt.

My best friend scoffed. "I only backed off because you saw him first," she teased, leading me to the right side of the mini gym. "And I'm still mad you didn't tell us about your first kiss the second it happened. It was literally your *first!*"

"I wasn't gonna wake you guys up in the middle of the night for *that*," I deadpanned. "We've moved on."

"We *did*," she said, placing her hands on her hips, "until you dropped that there was a second."

"Settle down, settle down," Momma announced as pairs scattered across the mat. "Focus. Face your partner. Set!"

"Let me get something straight," Sarah whispered, mirroring me as I brought my fist in front of my chin. "You've been on a date, you've kissed twice, but you're still not officially dating?"

I knew this question was coming sooner or later. Mostly because I'd asked that question a hundred times before reality barreled into me and made me remember that I couldn't afford those luxuries.

"I don't know," I replied. "But don't talk about it when he's in the same room!"

"He's on the other side, he's not gonna hear us from here."

"Aim for the right side of your partner's face," Momma called. "Ten straights for each arm and then shift to the other side. Begin."

I shoved any and all Jak thoughts aside. Besides Alexa, that anonymous number still had too much of my attention—and that, I felt like, I still had to handle on my own. Mom and Dad would *never* approve of me figuring out who they were, but before I could leave it alone, I needed to figure out if *they* were an ally or foe! And even then, how had they gotten my number? Their messages had leaned more toward a warning, meaning it couldn't have been Alexa. On the other-dimensional chance it was a random friend or family member, why would they freak me out like this? Was it just for fun?

Jak. This *had* to be Jak.

I looked in his direction on the other side of the gym as

Momma strolled around. Third period was obeying her with near silence.

No, it can't be him. He hadn't known anything when the number first texted me at the party. And I was pretty sure that he knew me well enough to know what pulling something like this would do to me—meaning he'd never do it.

"Some of you are dragging a bit," Momma sang as she passed a stumbling Ava Baleen. "You're fighting with force instead of speed. That can cost you the battle one day."

Momma enjoys going back to the basics every once in a while because she says that they help us perfect the foundation of the difficult moves (which I found to be true when practicing my pace choke last year). Despite being the basics, I still struggled with remembering to push my shoulder first. Sarah, on the other hand, was confident *and* practiced; that gave her the key all on its own for a perfect straight.

"Are you waiting for him to ask you out again?" she whispered. "So you can ask him about it?"

"No," I replied, honestly too tired to think of a cover story. I couldn't help but wonder, if not for me being a magician, where *would* Jak and I be by now?

"Then what is it?" Sarah asked. "If he likes you and you like him."

"It's not that—"

"Keep in mind where and when you're adding weight," Momma announced. "First your pelvis, then your shoulder, and *then* your fist."

Okay, stop and focus, I told myself. *You've done this before. You know you can do it.*

I was definitely overthinking things by now and letting the air overwhelm my energy. That definitely didn't ease anything as frustration began clouding my execution.

Sarah's movements slowed in front of me, and I almost paused. "Oh," she said. "Is it *Nolan?*"

Well, at least she was able to create a cover story for me.

"Not now," I finally said, fumbling another straight. I shook my head and briefly closed my eyes. I imagined my shoulder being pushed forward with all of my strength that seeped into my fist flying forward, willing it to be. Then another, then another—

Sarah yelped. I blinked out of concentration, watching as she brought her hands to the side of her right cheek.

My mouth hung open. *No. No, did I just–?*

"Miss Duncan?" Momma called, striding to us and gaining our classmates' attention. "What happened?"

"I'm fine," Sarah said, holding her cheek. "It—it's fine, I accidentally moved right."

"I'm so sorry," I blurted, knowing that she was lying. "I am so sorry, I shouldn't've—"

"It's fine!" Sarah breathily giggled, keeping her voice light. "You barely grazed me."

"Let me see," Momma said.

Sarah reluctantly gave way, as if out of fear. Either fear that it was worse than she thought, or fear on my behalf regarding the consequences.

The small crowd around us softly gasped. I forced my eyes to meet where Momma's hand hovered: blood. I'd scraped Sarah's once flawless cheek open.

"It's tiny, at least," Momma mused. "Miss Marie, can I trust you to take her to the nurse safely?"

Yes, it was a joke. No, I didn't take it as such, because even though teachers at the Callistro Academy address students by their titles and last names, I still wasn't used to it from Momma by that point, which only intensified the embarrassment boiling in my stomach.

"I'm so sorry."

"Accidents happen," Momma told me. "This is why we're training you, ladies and gentlemen. Control and precision are fundamentals when it comes to self-defense and combat. If you win a fight without them, it's a miracle. And in our world, it's an impossible miracle. Thank you for the lesson, Miss Marie."

I walked Sarah across and out of the mini gym, where we stepped into the carpeted halls of the school. Whether they were actually looking at me or not, everyone's eyes were heavy on my back, even as Momma commanded them back into position.

"Okay," Sarah said as we started down the hall. "Now you owe me, it's Nolan, isn't it?"

"Sarah, I am so sorry—"

"It's *fine*," she said, nudging me with her elbow. "It'll scab and fall off. I'm grateful you didn't get my nose, you should be proud of yourself! That was a powerful straight. Have you been secretly training after school without us?"

Training, yes. Self-defense training? No.

"I wish I had more to tell you," I eventually told her, rounding the corner of the hallway. "Nolan has something to do with it, but—I honestly don't know what I'm doing and I'm trying to figure it out, but it's not really my main focus right now."

Sarah's bright-green eyes softened on me as she crossed her

arms. "Then you can't let Jak kiss you again, my love. Not until you know where you're at."

Yeah. I know. For some reason, I couldn't bring myself to confess those words aloud. Maybe once I did, I'd have to let go of another part of my relationship with Jak that I wasn't ready to.

"Are you feeling okay?" I asked, fiddling with my locket as we turned into the hall where the nurse's office lay. "Still?"

"Yeah. It just burns."

I dragged my gaze down to the carpet runner as we walked. I couldn't suppress the fact that my magic *had* caused the graze on her cheek. My best friend couldn't know who I was, yet my magic had hurt her. I couldn't even apologize to her in the way that she deserved.

As if she knew what was going through my head, her face lit up like a firework. "Oh, wait until you see what I have planned for this weekend!" she chimed as we stepped through the doorway of Julia's office. "We have to go all out since—"

"Yikes, what happened here?" Julia stood from her desk, already scrutinizing Sarah. "Another Hunter causality?"

I shyly raised my hand. "My bad this time."

"*Really?*" she asked curiously, eyes widening. "You? Are you sure?"

"Yeah, she's stronger than the rest of us," Sarah said, strolling to one of the five vinyl mattresses on the right side of the room. She sat herself down on the middle one.

"Then... good job?" Julia shrugged at me with sheer confusion before heading to the back of the room and then grabbing a basic first-aid kit.

"I closed my eyes for a split second," I admitted. "I honestly didn't mean to, I was just trying to focus—"

"Stop it," Sarah stated, leaning back on the cot with her hands. "It's not a big deal, just go back to class and tell your mom I'm fine."

But it was a big deal to me because I couldn't give her the apology she deserved. So the only thing I could do for myself now was tell myself that she didn't want it.

"Okay." With a quick wave at Julia, I turned around and left. My fingers found my locket again as I started back down the hall, trying to keep my mind on anything else but Sarah—and how I was going back to class with everyone knowing what I'd, albeit accidentally, done.

I couldn't imagine how they would look at me if they knew that I wasn't one of them, if they knew that I was something the world was afraid of.

TWELVE

"How was school, kiddo?" Dad asked that afternoon, standing from the dining table and wrapping an arm around me.

A memory of Sarah in the nurse's office flashed in my mind, but I still told him, "Good."

"Well, you're not done yet," Mr. Dawson said as Aunt Becca met him at the kitchen island. Her dark roots almost matched the coffee she handed to him. "I was thinking we do lessons here today."

Oh, that's why he came with me and Mom today.

"Hey, actually, how about I teach this one?" Dad asked. "I have something in mind."

Dad's shown me a lot of cool tricks since he came home last

year, like how to make the dishes wash themselves, "juggling" (it's not really juggling if magic is doing all the work), and even a duplication spell for all of the socks whose mate I lost in the dryer (even if I still can't cast that one yet). But he'd never mentored me like Mr. Dawson had been doing.

I grinned, hugging him again. "I'd love that!"

"No offense taken," Mr. Dawson said. Auntie rolled her eyes as she came to sit at the dining table with Momma.

"I'll grab the cups," I said, moving toward the kitchen.

"Hey, hey, hey, what're you doing?" Momma asked from the head seat.

"This is what we always do," I said, confused.

She laughed, setting down her coffee. "We always practice with *Styrofoam* cups. Because *you* always end up destroying them."

"I'll be careful."

"No, Emma," she said flatly.

Dad nodded thoughtfully at me, his hands on his hips. "You sound pretty confident. Good."

We waited in suspense while he walked down the hall and into his bedroom. In his hands was his pair of seventy-five–pound dumbbells Momma had gotten him for Christmas last month. (He likes to work out since he can't go to the gym.)

He set them down onto the carpet, in the space between the living room and dining room, and waved me over. "Come on," he said, "this is your diagnostic test. Pick them up."

"I'm not training for the Olympics," I told him, as if he really didn't know.

"Pick them up with your telekinesis."

Telekinesis is like a muscle; the more you work it and practice it, the stronger it becomes and the heavier the objects you can lift. The most I'd been able to do by that point was ten textbooks—about fifty pounds—and it had taken me three tries. And I was only able to lift them, like, two inches off the table. But Dad wanted me to pick up 150 pounds!

I shook my head. "I can't do that."

"If you really wanna believe that." He shrugged, rubbing his square chin. "Just try it."

Silence buzzed behind us, but I didn't need to look back to know that Momma, Auntie, and Mr. Dawson were all on the edges of their seats at the dining table.

Ite procul.

A hard resistance pressed back on my mind, my magic, as if I were literally throwing the words at a wall.

I spoke them with more strain. *Ite procul.*

It'd been *months* since I'd needed to voice a telekinesis spell, but I'm always willing to trade pride for accomplishment when it comes to magic.

"*Ite procul.*"

That resistance remained, pressing just as hard against me.

"Remember to channel your *magic* onto the object," Mr. Dawson remarked from his seat next to Auntie. "These words alone have no power unless you give it to them."

"What he said." Dad nodded in his direction and then walked around to stand in front of me, the dumbbells between us. "Try picking one up with your hand first. Get a feel for what it's like to lift them."

I sighed and squatted down to a dumbbell. Wrapping my fingers around the handle alone warned me of the weight, but I tried to ignore it as I channeled my strength into my arm.

How does he do ten reps of these? I thought, bracing my entire body so I wouldn't throw something out.

The helplessness was familiar; it reminded me of all those times in Momma's class that I couldn't master a move quickly, when I kept messing up no matter how much I focused on the movement of my body throughout each step.

With my arm quivering and breath locked in my chest, I slowly lifted the dumbbell a couple of inches off the ground.

"Good," Dad said as I let it drop down onto the carpet with a hard, dull thud. "Okay. Now try to incorporate that into your telekinesis and let your magic help you lift."

I slightly shifted my position and weight. *Lift with your arm and legs, not your back,* I could hear Momma telling me.

It was like I *was* in class all over again.

Training's prepared me already, I thought to myself. If I could lift it with my hands, I could definitely lift it with my magic. Only my mind was stopping me.

With one hand still on the dumbbell, I grabbed the second with my other hand.

"Em—" Dad began, but I was already riding the flow of confidence and preparing myself.

Ite procul, I said, engaging each arm to my maximum capacity.

It was like... class today. With Sarah.

Ite procul!

I shut my eyes, allowed my magic to use its power, and lifted the dumbbells with a tremble.

There it was—the flowing magic I needed. I felt it activate inside as I tightly gripped the metal handles and opened my eyes, clinging to that power for dear life.

I couldn't talk or even look at anything else other than what my eyes were already fixed on; I was concentrated on my magic lifting for me, and I had to keep it that way.

I finally, slowly set them down after a couple of seconds, then looked at my father with pride. "That was fun."

"Yeah?" he said, beaming. "How'd you do that?"

I drew in a breath to speak, but one glimpse at Momma stole any previous excuse I had. I hesitantly turned to her. "Um... I remembered what happened in class today."

She paused and then processed my words. "Oh, yeah," she said, like I'd revived a forgotten memory. "What happened? You've never made a mistake like that before."

"What mistake?" Auntie asked curiously in the chair next to her, taking a sip of coffee.

No—don't lie. Sometimes the truth hurts and ends in punishment, but that doesn't mean that it isn't worth telling.

"I think—I think I accidentally made it more powerful. But I *never* meant to draw actual blood—"

"Back up," Mr. Dawson said, fully alert now as he held up a hand. Even Aunt Becca watched me more intently than I cared for. "You made someone *bleed?* You actually struck someone?"

"Sarah," Momma answered. "Well, it was a graze. She's fine."

"But you still drew blood?" Mr. Dawson asked me.

"Because of magic," I said. "I was frustrated with how my straights were coming out, I couldn't get the power I wanted because I couldn't get the execution right. I *briefly* closed my eyes and imagined what I wanted. I imagined my shoulder being pushed forward with the force I needed, and then it happened. It was magic. I felt it, it physically moved through me, like it was doing what I'd accidentally commanded it to do. That's—what I did just now."

Blank stares were exchanged all around the room like a round of champagne. Momma didn't dare a single word. After all, this wasn't her area of expertise. Admittedly, I was grateful for that.

Mr. Dawson, on the other hand, had to assume the best. "How come you never told me you knew a strengthening spell?"

"We..." Momma muttered, amber eyes stealing glances between me and Dad. "Because we never taught her that."

Mr. Dawson's sharp jaw slightly dropped. He couldn't even look at me now. Had I done something wrong? Why wouldn't he look at me, and why was Mom looking at me like *that*?

"Wait," Dad finally said, turning to me. "You just—knew it?"

"I didn't even know one existed."

"So you felt it," Mr. Dawson said, standing from the table. His eyes still avoided me. "You knew your goal, your mind *somehow* knew the feeling of a spell you didn't even know existed, and you cast it." Finally, he lifted his gaze to me, narrowing his eyes. "And you can't even pick up a pile of textbooks?"

"Thomas!" Momma snapped.

"No, no, we're onto something!" His mind seemed to be racing too quickly for his words to keep up. "I've—*nobody* has ever heard of this before, I'm not even sure it's possible. Unless Emma has a significant amount of a mage's blood, but even then, creating a new spell requires a lot more than just 'feeling it', and she didn't even create one."

Aunt Becca exhaled curtly. "So what does it *mean*? Why can

she suddenly cast things she's never been exposed or introduced to, that doesn't make sense—"

"I don't know!" Mr. Dawson snapped, startling us. Taking a deep breath, his shoulders dropped as he passed a hand over his face. That hand reached to ruffle his gelled-back, dark hair, but he just as quickly dropped it. "I'm sorry," he said. "I don't have the answers and I don't like that. All I know is that—this changes our entire situation."

His apologetic eyes fell onto me. There were keywords in that sentence that foreshadowed what he was about to say, which told me that I'd disapprove of it completely. Despite everything that had happened last September, despite all the evidence that told me to, I still didn't trust him completely if he felt that something was necessary. I braced myself.

"Your power is only growing, which makes you all the more valuable of a target. If the wrong person gets their hands on you—let alone Alexa—you might not make it to being Adara. You need to tell them what you told me."

I twisted the locket around my neck. He had told me months ago that druids can only see possible futures in their dreams. Any one decision, no matter how big or small, could alter someone's entire course. He had also told me that the only reason he knew that Adara was my destiny was that I'd taken multiple routes that brought me to that same ultimate destination anyway. That, though, was a result we'd have to fight for. Destiny is much like a plan: no plan is ever successful without big strides and hard work. And if you let it sit, waiting for it to complete itself, something or someone will come along and rip it apart.

"What is talking about?" Momma stated.

Not here. Not now. I'm not ready to ruin everything for them. I don't know who they are yet, I need more time—

"Please," I whispered to Mr. Dawson. But his eyes didn't change. My hope withered like a rose in winter.

"Em," Dad muttered. "What is it?"

"Some—someone…"—I gripped the locket tighter—"might know."

"What do you mean 'someone might know'?" Momma demanded, her body stiffening.

My eyes glued themselves to the carpet at her feet. "I've been getting—these texts. From someone who… who might know about me. They said something about my fate and—and asked who else could already know."

Silence really is deafening when your fears start strangling your senses. When I brought my head up to Momma, I found myself staring into the sharp eyes of a dragon.

"How long has this been going on?" she hissed.

I looked at Mr. Dawson, Aunt Becca, and Dad, none of whom offered any help and all of whom expected me to answer.

"Since the New Year's Party."

Momma's lips tightened as she stared down the beige carpet. Every one of my fears I was too scared to identify intensified with each second. My chest tightened, my mind clouding with the cruelest possibilities and what-ifs and mercies I was praying she would give me.

"Well?" Aunt Becca whispered the question like it was a dare, a game of Russian roulette. "What're we supposed to do?"

Dad sighed, his rugged jaw clenched. "I don't think there's much we *can* do until we know who this person is."

"Hang on," Momma snapped, her angry brows furrowing. "You told Thomas—you told *him* before you told me or your dad? Why, *what* possessed you to tell him, make him keep it from us, and then wait *weeks* before he made you tell us?"

"I don't—" I stammered. "I didn't want you guys to get... I just thought he and I could—"

"What did I tell you last year about keeping me updated?" Momma retorted, standing. My circulating fear almost made me take a step back. "Seriously, Emmalynn, what told you to wait THIS long? I could've spent the last couple of weeks tracing this person, we could've had them *captured*! This person could be on their way to exposing all of us right now because of you!"

"Amy," Dad stated, but it was too late. The rest of my breath had been stolen from my lungs, and Momma's shoulders just as quickly dropped with regret.

"I'm..." I whispered. Amidst my stinging eyes and nose, my words curdled in my throat. "I'm sorry, I didn't want—I didn't want you guys to—"

What have I done?

My breath hitched. "I'm—I'm sorry."

"Em," Momma murmured. "No, Emma, I didn't mean it like that, I'm sorry."

She might not have meant it that way, but it didn't change the truth. And the fact remained that whoever this person was, was out there, and Alexa was out there, and if I didn't gain control over my power soon, every irrational fear I'd had since childhood would turn out to be pretty rational, after all. For all we knew, Alexa and William were still on our tails and they were just harboring the element of surprise. For all we knew, they *were* the anonymous number. Or Alexa was withholding a plan to attack from William. We'd never be safe because of what we were, but because of me, we weren't prepared, either.

Momma might not have meant it that way, but this was my fault, this was all my fault. I'd tried to figure this out when the truth was, I couldn't. I wasn't able to.

I took too much time.

My stomach twisted into a knot. I stepped back.

I can't do this, I can't do it, it is my fault.

I shook my head, as if that would alleviate the pressure in my head. As if the overwhelming nausea would go away. As if that would change the truth.

I'm sorry, I'm so sorry.

As if that would stop the attack.

I thought I could handle it.

I hate this, I hate this, I hate this. Go away.

With another step back, I tripped over my own feet, falling to the carpet but numb to the sensation of contact. One hand held my head, trying to stop it from zooming in and out. The other was keeping me up. My parents had come running to my side. They were kneeling next to me, they were speaking, but their words couldn't penetrate my ears.

"No, stop," I cried, pushing them away. Their love and concern would suffocate me with guilt. I didn't want it. I didn't deserve it. They were in so much danger because of me. I didn't deserve it. I didn't want it.

Aunt Becca was asking something about me—if... I was okay? What was wrong?

I wanted to protect you.

Mr. Dawson's voice was the quietest among them all—I think he was still at the table—but it was still enough to vibrate my head.

Stop fussing over me! I shouted in my head. The words were trapped there. *Stop, please stop!*

I wanted them to know to leave, to let me deal with this alone. I didn't want to tell them. I wanted them to leave me alone in that house and let me deal with the consequences of our lives on all of their behalves.

"Please, honey," I caught Dad saying. "Please, talk to us."

I'm sorry.

I felt a light hand settle in the middle of my back, first feeling for my resistance to it, and then gently rubbing me when I gave none. That was Dad's touch. I knew it. I was giving in. There was no point in hiding this. A hot tear rolled down my cheek.

"Listen to us, all right?" he told me softly. "We're right here. We're here for you."

I'm sorry.

After a minute, I tried convincing myself that it was okay. That things were okay. I tried to breathe. Breathe. Breathing was good. Breathing would help. Breathing helped.

"Em," I heard Momma whisper. "I get angry when I get protective. When I can't immediately do anything. I lost your dad and I almost lost you last year. I can't let that happen again. I'm sorry."

I didn't know what to say to that, if she was even in the wrong—because I wasn't any less in it.

When my breathing became slower, quieter, Momma gently wrapped her arms around me and slightly swayed back and forth. I rested my hand supporting me on her arm, closing my eyes and finally sinking into her embrace. My mind raced, and my chest felt like a hole had been burned through it. But I prayed, desperate that Momma's hug would work. That prayer was answered when Dad joined in on my other side. They were both here. They were protecting me.

This was right, I reminded myself. This was good. This always helped.

THIRTEEN

I'd done all I could to avoid my parents getting sucked back into a Hunter fight, but it had backfired. Now there was nothing I could do about that except sit back and watch the adults work.

Momma got right to work trying to trace the number—which also backfired, because our anonymous texter had somehow managed to grab an industrial-level Faraday cage. Signal blocker. And unless we knew where this person was texting from, Momma couldn't use the stingray down in the Hunter's Room to bypass it.

Our next best option: waiting for another message and going from there.

That brought us to Saturday. And despite Sarah's warning the day I'd walked her to the nurse's office, I was still surprised to wake up to the smell of a hot curling iron and hair straightener. I already knew who was using what, just not which one Sarah would force me to use once she found out I was awake. I took my phone off the charger next to me to get in as much screen time as I could before one of them noticed—

"Emma's awake!" Breanne exclaimed.

Of all people, I least expected *her* to rat me out if it ever came down to it.

"Get up!" Sarah called from the bathroom, curling her second-to-last lock of ebony hair. "I have a full day planned!"

I moaned and sat up. It was 8 in the morning! Who got ready this early on a Saturday?

I paused. *It's Saturday.* I swiped through the notifications on my phone, none of which were text messages. That anonymous texter had sent me a message on one Friday night and two Saturdays. If the pattern continued, and considering the fact that I hadn't gotten anything last night, I wondered if today would end with text number four.

Perfect. What a great way to end the day.

Sarah walked out of the bathroom, snapping her fingers. "Come on, hurry!" she urged, gesturing rapid circles with her hand. "We need the whole day!"

Yep—perfect.

I hopped out of bed and trod to the closet on the opposite side of the room. "What do we need the whole day for?"

A smirk slowly stretched her mauve lips. She rested her hands on her hips. "We're knocking off bucket-list items today."

Breanne and I cautiously faced her.

"What does that mean?" she asked for me.

"Remember when I asked you guys this week for one thing you've always wanted to do? We're knocking them all off today!"

"Where did you find an ice-skating rink?" Breanne exclaimed from the bathroom, blue-hazel eyes wide.

"There's one just half an hour away that's open every fall and winter! I actually wanted to go there during winter break after next week, but I'm gonna be out of town." Sarah looked at me. "But on our way back from the rink, there's a bowling alley."

It sounded like an awesome day, but next time Sarah Duncan says that she has "big plans" for us, they're not allowed to be a surprise; I wasn't really sure that now was the best time to be experimenting with ice skating and bowling balls.

"What about what the guys wanted to do?" Breanne asked, unplugging her straightener.

"Wait and see," Sarah simpered, plopping down at the desk in the corner of the room.

Right—because after she'd said those exact words just before the infamous homemade caramel corn incident of eighth grade, that was comforting to hear.

I remembered from the past week how Sarah had said that she wanted to go all out for this Saturday in particular. Turns out, that meant indoor skydiving, learning how to play the mandolin, and making new ice cream flavors (note to self: do *not* mix relish and sauerkraut into butter pecan ice cream). Go figure, *her* bucket list item was to go on a triple date. Even though she and Adrien were the only official couple there, she still counted it.

The day ended with us sitting on the benches at the fountain in town square, gazing at the sunset as we sipped on hot chocolates from Dom's Bakery. It'd sounded like a crazy idea at first, but admittedly, Sarah had known exactly what she was doing today.

But when my phone buzzed in my pocket as my friends stood from the bench, that alarm blared in my head: today was over. It was back to the real world, and it was time for my next mission. Somehow, just somehow, my instincts knew what was waiting for me in my jacket pocket.

"Are you ready, Emmy?" Sarah asked me when I hadn't stood, lacing her arm around Adrien's.

As if she'd steal my phone straight off me, I stuck my hand into my pocket and grabbed it. "Yeah, um—gimme a sec."

I pulled it out, opened the text, and dared myself to read.

#: Heed my warning, for you must know now.
O Callistro Girl, you're close to being found.

Now? *Now* of all times, this was the message I got? The most threatening, let alone uncanniest, one yet, and Momma was back at the school!

"You guys go ahead."

I looked up at Jak gesturing in the general direction of the Callistro Forest. "We'll catch up," he said next.

"Stop it," I said, pointing an accusing finger at Sarah's impish grin already slithering to her face. Breanne was quick to obey, covering her mouth with her yellow sweater sleeve.

"I'm not thinking anything," Sarah chimed sweetly, eyelashes fluttering. Liar. "Get home safe."

I opened my mouth to tell them that I was actually coming, but my thoughts traveled faster: Jak knew just a sliver more about my world than my friends did, meaning he couldn't tell me who was sending the messages—but he *could* probably tell me who wasn't. It'd definitely take Momma longer than we'd anticipated to crack their identity. If I played my cards right, I could get just a bit more help. I was back to square one of having absolutely zero suspects, which meant that I needed to extend my list.

But why did *he* want to talk?

His eyes fell onto me once our friends were far enough down the street and out of earshot. "What's actually up, Merlin?"

Oh. He was just concerned; he'd read me. Of course.

I screenshot the text and sent it to Momma. Until I got a response, I'd need as much help as possible.

"Do you remember that number that texted me at the New Year's party?"

He briefly paused like he was already trying to predict how this conversation would go. "Yeah."

"They haven't stopped texting me."

His brows furrowed, and he put his hands into his pockets. "Did you figure out who they were? Do they know you?"

"I don't know. This is everything they've said so far. I get a text once a week."

I watched in anxious anticipation as I put my phone in front of him. His brown irises jittered as they ran through each line. I tried gathering the micro expressions, the contortions of confusion or intrigue, but they were minimal and ambiguous. As always, letting me know what he was really thinking was apparently too dangerous.

"This is..." he finally said, slightly shaking his head, "uncanny."

"That's what I thought just now."

"Do they know?" he whispered. "I mean—how could they know?"

"If I knew, I wouldn't be showing you this. We've been trying to figure out who they are, but they're using a signal blocker."

"If they're smart enough to do that, on top of what this is about, they're probably smart enough to take extra measures. VPN, burner phone, temporary SIM card..." He leaned back in his seat, sliding down a bit. I hadn't even realized just how *many* walls Momma might have to blast through to nail this person.

"Okay," Jak said, bouncing his knee. "So you need a bouncing board. I could get you thinking with a question, that could open a few doors."

Cold wind nipped at my cheeks and the tip of my nose. The snow lining the sidewalks radiated its icy temperature and crisp scent every time I inhaled. I almost wanted to press the back of my hand to Jak's nose to see if it was just as cold, but I stuffed my phone and hands back into my pockets.

I do think better with another mind. But if Jak was going to be asking me unanswered questions, I wanted them to be ones that he had a better chance at being able to answer.

Another text buzzed in my hand.

M: When you get back, I'm going to use an amplifier to try and interfere with the signal blocker, or at least look for any leaks.

Okay. Then I definitely need to get some ideas from Jak right now.

When I looked up, the sunset had stolen his gaze, reflecting his thoughts passing everywhere except to me. Finally, he gave me his eyes. "Does *she* know about this?"

"I'm trying to figure out how I should tell her."

"Who's at least a possibility?"

I scoffed, laughing. "Put it this way, I thought *you* were a possibility. It's anyone's best guess."

He hummed in satisfied thought, nodding once. "Okay. Then I think it's Breanne."

I burst out laughing before covering my mouth, ignoring the startled stares of evening shoppers and parents with their kids.

"*How* did you get Breanne?" I whispered.

Jak had the nerve to laugh. "First of all, you *know* she's smart enough to do this. It's practice, if nothing else. Second of all, do you really find the idea of her using you as a subject for another psychological experiment ridiculous?"

I still have nightmares of Elmo from Sesame Street chasing me around Disneyland thanks to the girl trying to test for the best way to achieve lucid dreaming. Now she's trying to figure out how to get me to *stop* having those nightmares because I won't let her do the same experiment on me to get rid of them.

"You're saying she could be using me to figure out... what? How to mentally torture someone until they admit their darkest secret? That sounds like an Alexa move."

Jak chuckled. "It does. No, you're close. Maybe she's testing out different psychological methods for Hunters behind the scenes. Like what my dad does. A William move."

"She'd *never* do something this cruel to me. Especially not after last semester. Not without my permission. And she was just as confused as we were about the first text at the party."

"First of all, you knowing would invalidate the results of the experiment. If this is her, she was playing her part."

His eyes were steady, too steady for what he was saying. He was really taking this like a science project, and I couldn't blame him for it. I mean, if I told him why the texts—more accurately, whoever was behind them—were potentially a life-or-death matter to my family, he'd probably turn me in himself.

"I'm just giving you ideas, Merlin. Bounce off."

Bounce off... The game was cruel enough to be a psychological experiment. And I only knew one person who was cruel enough to do that.

"I need you to tell me that it's not Alexa."

"It's not Alexa."

I rolled my eyes and slouched my shoulders in tired defeat. "I need you to mean it."

"I do."

I looked at him. Two streetlights along the sidewalk in front of us helped illuminate his light-brown skin and warmth of his dark-brown hair. Thankfully, his subtle smile told me that he really did mean it.

"Alexa isn't kind enough to give warnings," he said, knowing that I needed more. "She wouldn't warn you that her pack is back to hunting you. Especially not with her husband living under the same roof you are."

I exhaled, mentally exhausted. Okay. Not Alexa, not William, not him, probably not Breanne—I wasn't sure how much help that really was. Honestly, I contemplated telling Jak about the figure that had followed us in the passageways last Saturday. A small part of me was saying that that person had only been a product of my fear. Maybe Jak had misheard whatever he had that morning. After all, there'd been no details of the figure—only a black bodysuit, as far as I had been able to see.

"Then who is it?" I finally asked, accepting that my mind had nothing left to give me.

Jak continued bouncing his knee, eyes resting on the sunset like it would give him the answer. "Well—we'll keep trying to figure it out. But you won't have to do it by yourself."

CHAPTER

FOURTEEN

"Does anyone notice how this is the *first* function we're seeing that doesn't intersect with either real axis? What do we call those?"

Asymptotes. They're called "asymptotes".

Mr. Hartman feels the need to ask basic questions in class, but I couldn't really blame him after last semester's test scores (which were at least improving). I think it's nostalgic for everyone else because it reminds them of elementary school, but it just reminds me why I'm grateful that I had a teacher who let me tell her whenever she was going too slow—my mother.

I found Breanne a couple of rows away as Sloane Moore answered Mr. Hartman's question. Even with the lights turned off, I could see that Breanne was bored in her I-would-have-said-that way, mindlessly tapping her paper with the end of her pencil.

"That's *exactly* true," Mr. Hartman said, walking to the whiteboard at the front of the room. His gelled-back black hair almost blended in with the shadows that the turned-off lights created with the projector screen. "Give me your best educated guess: given the parent function, why would this graph never intersect with either the x- or y-axis *unless* translated?"

Breanne raised her hand.

"As always, Miss Shaw, I value your enthusiasm, but I'd like to hear someone else's thoughts, too."

"It's not that," Breanne said. She pointed at the clock above his head. "We have thirty seconds left."

Mr. Hartman followed her finger, glancing over his shoulder. "Oh, thank you. Yes, go ahead and start packing up. We'll pick up on Friday."

He returned to the table at the back of the room as we gathered our things. Our lesson flashed off the whiteboard, and Mr. Hartman strolled over to his desk beside it.

Breanne took her place next to me as I swung my backpack on. Sarah rushed up to us from behind me. "I need to talk to Mr. Hartman really quickly," she said, holding up our last homework assignment. "I don't get how I got almost half of these questions wrong. I even checked my answers!"

Breanne looked away, shifting her things in her arms despite her backpack hanging on her shoulders.

"You can wait here," Sarah said, as if to punish her, waiting for the last of our classmates to leave before walking up to Mr. Hartman's desk.

Breanne nudged me the second Sarah greeted him. "Forgot

to tell you yesterday, I won't be here during break next week, either. My grandparents arranged a family beach trip to Miami because they're sick of the cold—and so are my parents."

"Oh," I said, trying to shove forward some disappointment—because what I'd just heard was that I'd be spending my entire break with Dad and Aunt Becca uninterrupted. "It's fine. My mom and I will probably try to see some family, too."

"Well, do you want to head into the secret passageways today?" she asked, a sly smirk stretching her thin lips. "I'm still looking for buried treasure."

Oh, there was definitely buried treasure—or, at least, there *had* been, and it was capable of sparking anarchy. And it was still in Alexa Delphine's hands. I was still waking up every day thankful that I was the only Callistro Girl who knew.

"Sure," I said. "We can do our homework in one of the secret rooms."

"Yes!" Breanne's eyes lit up, and she hugged her binder. "And we can bring the guys with us."

"The six of us? In a small, private space?"

"The worst that'll happen is you'll be trapped with Sarah and Adrien ruthlessly flirting with each other. It's not like you're not used to it by now."

That was partially true, but only because I still wasn't used to *Jak* ruthlessly flirting with *me*. Being trapped with him while trying to write a sociology thesis on the development of American society from the Imperialism Era to the Roaring Twenties didn't sound, well, wise.

"Yeah," I said, shrugging, "but they get—*distracting*."

"Oh, no, I agree, but—" Breanne cut herself off, looking over at Sarah and tuning in to the conversation. She held up a dainty, fair finger and curiously furrowed her brows. "Hang on."

"I really would like to stay after class or during lunch for extra help," Sarah said in her sincerest voice. "I've just been really busy with... this semester."

"You helped Adrien with his homework last semester," Breanne commented, strolling over with me behind her. "I thought you guys even started doing homework together."

Mr. Hartman cocked his brows. "Is that so?" His green eyes stayed steady on Sarah as he asked, "Miss Shaw, do you have a boyfriend?"

Breanne was, to say the least, staggered, and I was no exception. "Um, well," she stammered, "nothing's... I don't know—but we, um—we're close."

"And she's my brightest student," our teacher told Sarah (which didn't really mean much—we were talking about a girl who'd assisted every first-place winner of the Capperson High School Science Fair in eighth grade and freshman year). "So, Miss Duncan, my only suggestion is that you pay just a *bit* more attention in class and less toward *other* things."

Sarah's hand sank, her grip on her homework loosening. "He's not the problem, I promise—"

"I didn't say he was. Only that boys *can* be a distraction if you allow them to be. Your mistakes here are *pretty* minor, but the more you make, the more points you lose on a serious test. Spend more time doing your assignments with friends instead. You *might* see a difference."

"Thank you," Sarah replied in a tone Breanne and I knew was her just being polite. She then walked across the classroom and through the doorway, and we followed suit.

It wasn't until we stepped down into the Grand Foyer from the Main Staircase that Breanne spoke up. "We were going to explore the secret passageways and maybe do some homework. Are you up for it?"

Sarah sighed, shoving her homework into her bookbag. "Sure. I guess the guys aren't coming with us."

I brought my backpack strap farther up my shoulder. "They can. We could make it a giant study session and make sure we all stay focused."

Sarah pressed her lips together, yet her lipstick didn't budge. "Only if we don't sit there for too long. The ground's really hard, and I'm already tired—"

"We could just do homework in our room," I assured her, then briefly turning to Breanne. "Let's go grab—"

I found her gazing off in the direction of Mr. Dawson's office. When I followed her eyes and caught William walking out, I understood.

He's humming it again, I realized, pairing his melody to the words of "When I Fall in Love". I cursed the fact that such a beautiful song was about to be permanently associated with William Bleu in my mind.

"I don't think I'll ever get used to that sight," Breanne said, eyes stuck on the headmaster of Redway Academy. "Knowing who he is and… what he did." She faced me then, probably because she didn't want William knowing that she'd been staring at him as he ambled to us.

"Good afternoon, ladies," he said, almost too politely, as he straightened his dark-blue blazer. "How was your day?"

"Fine," Sarah said for us, knowing all too well that Breanne was too intimidated to speak and I was still too angry. "And you?"

"Likewise, Miss Duncan, thank you." His smile didn't reach his rough eyes as they swept over Breanne. Then they landed on me. He never took them off as he said, "It was pretty successful, actually. Enjoy the rest of it, ladies."

He's up to something. He knows something.

As quickly as he'd come, he continued straight past us and toward the cavernous hall leading to the gym on the other side of the Foyer. His broad shoulders stayed squared with every step he took. And the farther he walked away, the more I wanted to follow. His eyes had been too intentional, either because he'd been sending me a message, or because he knew something I didn't and wanted me to know that.

My conversation with him on the Main Staircase a few weeks ago echoed in my head. He'd done the same thing that night, too, told me something that had been coded. Something had been wrong when he'd said that I was no longer a target... but why—?

I froze on the rug. That was it. He *did* know things I didn't, a lot of things. In fact, I was pretty sure that that was the whole reason I'd never once fully relaxed around him: he was powerless now, he couldn't hunt me anymore, but the problem was that *I* knew that.

I mindlessly followed Sarah and Breanne toward the Dining Hall on the opposite side of the Foyer, twirling the locket around my neck. We probably weren't going there for an after-school snack like we were trying to convince ourselves we were.

"You're gonna call me insane," I said, my decision already made, "but I need to talk to him."

"What?" Sarah sneered, stopping us as we reached the large doorway. "You're right, that's insane. There's nothing to talk about."

"You don't get it—"

"I love you, Emmy, I promise, I say this out of love, but this is why you're still hung up over all of that. You think there's more to it, and you keep indulging in that to where you're never able to let it rest."

You don't know. There's so much you don't know.

I glanced at William as he walked down the hall far across from us. "But..."

"If you want an apology out of him, I can guarantee you won't get one." Sarah's hands snapped to her hips. "What's done is done. As much as he deserves to suffer for what he did to you—"

When my eyes shifted back to the hall and confusion scrunched my brows together, my friends followed my gaze. William had disappeared. How had he done that?

"I know." I sighed, realizing that I had to humor Sarah if I was going to get any answers right now. "You're right, I know. There's just one thing I need to ask him. Just one, I promise. I need to know. Then this'll all be over." I slid my backpack off and handed it to her. "Go ahead, I'll meet you in a few minutes."

"Wait," Breanne said, reaching for me as I tried to walk away, "what're you going to—?"

I faced her, showing her every ounce of sincerity I had. "Please."

Just like I can read her eyes, she can read mine. Thankfully, after hesitating, she read everything she needed to, to set me free. I stepped away and walked back in the direction we'd come from.

Well, at least I hadn't lied.

Running across the Foyer and then into the hall, I waited until I saw the back of Sarah's and Breanne's heads at the after-school buffet in the Dining Hall. Then I'd be safe to slip into the secret passageway opened by a candle sconce with a fake candle.

I pulled open the entrance, slipped inside the small gap I'd made, and then faced the wall as I closed it. I felt the Grand Hunter's presence behind me without needing to turn around. I forced myself to gather enough courage to face him. He leaned against the right wall of the cobblestone passageway with his arms crossed and head down.

He knew I'd go after him. Anger bubbled in my stomach with the cold chill that ran down my back. The man knew how to read me. I guess he'd earned his position for a reason.

The air was infused with a damp quiet that rooted itself deep into the concrete ground. That was just as well; I wanted to get this conversation out of the way as soon as possible, even if that meant that I had to start it.

"How come you never made me forget that week?"

He took a breath in and then deeply exhaled, as if he didn't know. That was almost the answer I wanted.

"Why can I still remember everything? Jak said everyone else ruled innocent was forced to forget, but I didn't."

I remembered Jak's hesitance in telling me how the pack made their innocent suspects forget ever being hunted: using a magician to cast a forgetting spell. It was such a simple but cruel solution. Why hadn't I been put through it?

"There's more than one reason," William said, his big brown eyes locking with mine. I hated how much they looked like Jak's.

"Simply put, you were technically innocent, but you were different. For one thing, you *did* know something—we'd just gotten to you too late. Second of all, more than one of your loved ones knew that we were after you, meaning we'd have to erase the week from their memories, too, which is always risky because of how you can serve as a memory trigger to each other. But your mother and Headmaster Dawson both trained in the same field: they know how to keep a Hunter's secret. Why else do you think we took our interrogative measures so far with you? As cruel as it may sound, the more traumatizing an event is, the more likely you are to stay quiet about it."

I wanted to slap him for that alone. Especially because he was right.

"So..." I had to ask it. I had to ask it. I had to ask it. "So you meant it. A few weeks ago. I'm not still a target?"

William took himself away from the wall, standing up tall as he pulled forward the lapels of his blazer. I nearly ran out of the passageway on instinct. "We're no longer hunting you."

He walked toward me, head held high. For whatever reason, it felt wiser to stand still—and I was right, because he walked straight by me and placed his hand on the exit handle.

"Where's Alexa?"

The words had sprung from my darkest fears in the back of my mind, but I'd tried too hard to bury them. They weren't meant to be, and that was why they'd escaped.

Even William paused before answering, "Kingsport. Why? Do you miss her?"

Ha. You're not funny.

He slid open the passageway entrance, and I turned around

to face it as it closed in front of me. Standing there in the echoing silence, twisting my locket, I tried to think about anything else besides the conversation that had just happened. I wondered what Sarah and Breanne were doing right now, if they'd remembered to grab me something from the buffet in the Dining Hall and were now on their way up to our room. I thought about which route I was going to take to get there, which way would keep me as invisible as possible. I thought about the kinetic theory worksheet I had waiting for me in my physics binder, and I thought about how much safer my backpack was than I was right now.

That's what it felt like when a rag clamped over my mouth.

An arm slid around me, trapping my arms at my sides. Before my survival instincts could tell me to use my feet, I slipped out of consciousness and into the arms of whoever had followed me and William into the secret passageways.

FIFTEEN

J ust because you're not new to something doesn't mean it isn't any less terrifying the second—or, in my case, fourth—time around. Especially not when you have to pray that whoever had kidnapped you this time wouldn't find out the truth and send you straight to the White House.

Finally coming through the fog in my mind, I opened my eyes to a harshly dim, gray room. One low-light bulb hung from the center of the ceiling with a large stainless-steel door dead ahead. The iciness of the concrete below me rivaled the harsh brick against my back—the brick that scraped my bound-together hands every time I moved.

This isn't happening again, I thought. I was hallucinating, I was stuck in a dream, anything but reality!

My shaky breath hitched in my throat with almost every inhale. Terror throbbed in my chest. This was Alexa, wasn't it? This had to be, this was it, she was going to expose me, she'd finally—

No, no, stay calm. I need to get out. I can't just let this happen!

I looked around the small, empty room: no cameras. I could use magic—couldn't I?

Should I wait for the door to open? How would anyone know that I was awake if there were no cameras? Despite how sure I was about Alexa being my kidnapper, I couldn't safely *assume* anything. I needed to know my enemy before I gave them any intel with how I handled this situation, magic or no magic.

Then how was I supposed to escape? When was I supposed to use magic, if I even could—?

What felt like gloved fingers moved a lock of hair away from my face, only their touch telling me that they were even there. Invisible. This person was *invisible!*

I screamed, shuffling away and numb to the scraping of the brick against my hands. "No!" I shouted, darting my head around like I was following a fly. "Get away, don't touch me!"

Horror swelled in my throat, stifling my breath. I implored my fear to turn into bravery as I demanded, "Where are you?"

The fingers ran down my hair. I tried pushing myself away again, but my kidnapper's other hand gripped my shoulder to keep me in place. They could still see me, which meant I was every bit at their mercy. I didn't know who they were, their intentions with me, or even if they planned on keeping me alive after they finished whatever they wanted to do with me. The fear suffocating every instinct and thought in my mind kept me still as the invisible figure's fingers tugged at the ends of my hair. A snip whispered across the room, followed by a small brown lock of hair falling to the concrete.

W—what...? They wanted my hair?

Before I could see that lock's fate, before I could feel another touch, I slipped back into sleep.

Momma's woken up in strange places during a hunt a few times. To this day she's trying to figure out how she ended up in a cot at a Hunter base in Albuquerque when her last memory was sliding down a firepole into a tattoo parlor to catch magician Dahlia Raine.

So I was relieved, if anything, to wake up in the secret passageway I'd followed William into. The hardest part afterward was pretending in front of everyone I passed in the halls that I *hadn't* just been kidnapped by some creep who wanted my hair for some creepy, unknown reason. I guess that was just as well, because that was the reality I wanted to live in. And Momma always says that the most realistic lies are the ones we want the most to be true.

Why? Why is it always something?

My family was already running themselves in circles trying to figure out who the anonymous number was. Somehow, this person had outdone an ex-Master Hunter's work—which meant they had to have training of their own. Now an invisible kidnapper? How was I supposed to add *this* to my family's plate when they already had so much going on? If I told them about this, it'd force Dad and Aunt Becca straight out of the house! Auntie had already said she couldn't handle it, she at least needed more time to be safe where she was. Dad... To be honest, I was pretty sure that Dad was just better at hiding how he felt.

No, whoever had just kidnapped me, they wanted me, they wanted what *I* had. This was my fight, and I just had to keep them focused on me and away from my family. Stay on guard and figure out what they wanted.

To say I went through the next couple of days cautiously would be like calling Breanne "smart". At least with Alexa, I knew exactly what she wanted. Now, though, I was fighting on a battle-field saturated in so much fog that I couldn't see the ground. I didn't know either new enemy's pattern or motive; I had no right to go back to normal.

"Eat this," Jak told me in the Foyer on our way to Monsieur Goubeaux's class, grabbing my attention. He was handing me a blueberry muffin. "You barely ate at breakfast. Can't have you passing out in class."

I took the muffin as the four of us started the climb up the Main Staircase. "When did you become my mom?"

"When Mommy got busy teaching big-kid Hunter classes. I'm in charge of you now."

Sarah cackled as she and Breanne came up next to us. She tossed her hair over her shoulder as we reached the second floor. "You wish, pretty boy. She's ours."

I laughed, because I was the only one there able to throw them all down the stairs at the same time *and* give them amnesia without touching them.

Sarah rolled her eyes and then took a breath in, refreshing herself. "I'm gonna do Farsi today," she said as we rounded the corner of the hall. "It might be my last day to, Monsieur knows keywords now and he's learning everything outside of class. I'm on borrowed time."

"Just learn what everyone else is," Breanne said dully. "The languages *you* don't know."

"This is the last academic class I can have *fun* in," Sarah argued. "You banned everything else!"

Let's just say that "everything else" had involved a shock pen, invisible ink, a colorful pair of Christmas socks, and a traumatized Mr. Dale.

"Speaking of fun in class..."—Jak slid his hands into his blazer pockets, leaning forward for a better view of Breanne as we walked—"Wyatt's been smiling a lot more lately. Does that have anything to do with when he talked to you the other night?"

"Did he tell you?" she asked timidly, fiddling with her fingers. "I wanted to keep it a secret for a bit."

Jak smiled at her. "You kinda tell your friends when you officially start dating your crush. Why'd you wanna keep it a secret?"

"Ask Emma," she said, nudging me. "She's the one who waited a few days to mention her *first kiss*."

"She only *just* told us about the second, too," Sarah simpered.

"Are you guys kidding me?" I said, red burning my cheeks as I walked faster on the carpet runner. My friends had no trouble keeping pace.

"That's different," Jak said, brushing it off. "I *wanted* her to tell you about that."

"We need to set boundaries on what we can openly discuss," I said, just before Jak beat me to the doorway of Monsieur Goubeaux's classroom. He stepped in front of me and leaned one arm against the side, gazing down at me with that familiar playful smirk.

"Why are you in such a rush, Merlin?" he asked. "Are you embarrassed of me?"

Sarah stopped beside me, crossing her arms with a confidence I wanted to shove her for. "Emmy's just flustered because you're her first."

I wanted to crawl into the secret passageway next to us, marked by the three Callistro portraits of Caralyn and her parents. All I had to do was press on Caralyn's portrait on the far right, and a section of the wall would turn and allow me to slip away. But Jak was already entering the classroom and Monsieur Goubeaux was speaking to me in Portuguese, asking me to step inside and allow the other students in.

Portuguese was the assigned language for the day, but that didn't stop Sarah's Farsi. According to her, defying the system by speaking different languages and gathering what her opponent knew was "practicing real-life scenarios for on the field". Monsieur couldn't argue with that, being that he'd actually run into those situations before. (Momma has, too, when she was on a hunt in New York and manipulated the language barrier to win a game of Blackjack and nab the magician speaking Welsh.)

Sarah had been right about one thing: class was fairly entertaining that day.

Actually, classes had become "fun" ever since the Redway Boys had come to the Callistro Academy. It took me too long to realize how *normal* things had felt over the past month. What made me realize it in full was when Sarah, Breanne, and I left class Thursday afternoon and Prince Charming himself met us at the top of the Main Staircase.

"Hey," he said to my friends, his backpack hanging on one shoulder. "Wyatt's waiting for you in the library, and Adrien's waiting for you in the rec room."

"Ooh, thanks," Sarah chirped, pulling her bookbag strap farther up her shoulder. "And nice job of getting rid of us."

"Thanks," Jak teased back. "Have fun."

I twisted the locket hanging from my neck, watching the girls as they descended the stairs. I waited for them to reach the bottom before I turned back to Jak. "What was that about?"

"Would you like to meet me at the gazebo in half an hour?"

This sounded familiar... I was pretty sure I'd been in this same situation with him before. I was also pretty sure it'd ended really well.

"Sure," I said, slightly narrowing my eyes. "Why?"

"I'm not gonna spoil the fun," he replied, smiling and walking past me. "See you then, Merlin."

I know I don't have a lot of boy experience (or hardly any boy experience), but even I knew that this was weird behavior for Jak. Actually, not just him—all three of them. Usually we spent time together, and individual hangouts weren't planned so... specifically. Meet Jak at Capperson Park? Why? And so suddenly?

Was this a date?

Oh no, what if this is a date?

I mentally apologized to Jak as I darted up the Second Staircase. The visit to my closet was probably going to make me late.

C H A P T E R

Sixteen

Jak's eager grin was what told me that I'd made the right choice in dressing up a little (if you consider a sweater, scarf, skinny jeans, and winter boots "dressy"). I couldn't see what he'd changed into because of his winter coat, but I think my outfit gave him the confidence he needed to go all in with the romance, like I'd caught on to the right idea: he offered his hand and escorted me up the steps of the white gazebo in the middle of the snow-littered park.

"I know it's nothing big," he said, like he was anticipating a complaint, "but I thought we could just sit and—talk."

"What's that?" I asked, nodding to the paper grocery bag on top of the low-level table in front of us.

Jak followed me to the cushioned outdoor couch, taking a

spot next to me. "After-school snacks," he replied, digging into the bag and then handing me a wrapped croissant. "Do you want that, or a cheese Danish? Or do you want a gourmet biscuit with strawberry preserves?"

"What's a 'gourmet' biscuit?" I asked, unwrapping the croissant.

His grin deepened. "You wanna find out?"

I chuckled, picking off a piece of the flaky croissant and sitting up straight. "What's up, why'd you wanna come here?"

He drew in an eager breath, but his thoughts all too obviously blocked his words. His lips pressed into a thin line.

"What?" I asked.

"Nothing." He shrugged. "I just figured we deserved a break from everyday routine. It's nice to hang out for once and not chase or *be* chased by someone."

I knew that he wasn't talking about just our classmates. And I liked that he'd said it, because it made me appreciate being outside—being *here*—a lot more.

"How'd you do on Ms. Perketti's test?" I asked as he dug out a Danish from the bag.

"Pretty well." He mimicked me, tearing off pieces of the pastry. "But science has always been my best subject."

I laughed. "Funny, it's always been my worst."

"Then maybe you should've asked for help more often, Merlin," he joked. "I would've been more than willing to step up."

"My B is almost an A, I'll get there."

He looked out at the open white field in front of us. Every passerby pulled my eyes along with them as they played with their dogs and kids in the snow or simply strolled along. It was crazy to think about how Jak and I were the least normal people there—that we were the only ones attending a school training us to hunt magicians across the country and turn them in to the U.S. Government.

What *was* normal high school like?

"I'm getting you jewelry cleaner for your birthday this year."

I squinted at him. "Why?"

"You *do* fiddle with that a lot."

I looked down at the only piece of jewelry I was wearing and will probably ever wear regularly: my fingertips were around the locket. "Oh."

"It was a lot more silver when I bought it."

I shared his chuckle, shifting my weight. The talk of birthdays got the ball of thought rolling in my head, and I straightened with a question I'd never managed to ask in the five months we'd known each other: "When's your birthday?"

He scoffed. "That's the one thing we're not allowed to talk about. It's stupid."

"Shut up, no, it's not."

"It really is." His tone warned me to believe him. "I don't tell people because then they feel double the obligation to get me something. I don't like feeling guilty for accepting a present some-one bought out of moral obligation."

I sat back in realization. "It's Christmas, isn't it?"

"No."

Well, now I was all too curious—and he wouldn't get away with celebrating my birthday when I couldn't even acknowledge his. "Please?"

He leaned back, crossed his arms, and exhaled. "February

14.”

“Really?” I said curiously, as though I didn’t believe him. But honestly, what else could I expect for him?

“I told you. It’s stupid.”

“It is not.” I gently shoved him. “I think it’s pretty fitting.”

“Maybe for anyone who *likes* Valentine’s Day.”

Whoa, whoa, whoa—I mean, I guess I’d kind of expected it, but a part of me had also hoped that Jak would debunk that assumption, too.

“You don’t?”

“Well, to be fair, I don’t really know now.” His ambiguous gaze landed on me. “I’ve never had anyone to celebrate it with.”

Hang on. Was this a Valentine’s Day proposal two weeks in advance?!

Either way, I had nothing to say to that. Can you be a Valentine without being someone’s significant other? Would saying yes be a commitment that I wasn’t ready to commit to?

“What about your birthday?” I asked instead.

“Well, when you grow up with the parents I did,”—he scoffed—“sure, my dad always tries to do something, but it just... the whole thing feels like an obligation, like he’s doing it because it’s his job as my dad. It’s not what it used to be.”

Uh oh, I thought. The conversation was veering in the direction of his mother. *Get on another topic!*

“Would... would you like me to come over to Redway for your birthday?”

Jak gave a tired yet playful roll of his eyes, sitting up straighter. “That’s why I didn’t wanna tell you. Now you feel like you have to do something for me.”

"No, it's because I *want* to," I said, shifting in my seat to face him better. A defensive instinct flared in my chest. "And even if I did feel like I had to, is that wrong? After everything you've done for me just to protect me and a family you've never even met?"

"You might wanna lower your voice, Merlin," he muttered, stealing a quick glance around the people frolicking through the park. "Before someone gets curious."

I was surprised that he was the one saying it and not me to myself.

"Don't change the subject," I said with a mildly damaged pride, crossing my arms. Damp heat was gathering in my sweater thanks to my coat, my nose and fingers bitten by the cold, but I wanted to last out here with Jak for as long as I could. "What's the last nice thing I did for you?"

"You let me kiss you during the hunt. That was pretty nice."

"Doesn't count." I brought my legs up onto the cushioned seat. "Does that happen to have something to do with why you wanted to hang out today?"

He paused for a second, like he'd forgotten to rehearse whatever he was about to say. "Actually, speaking of birthdays..."

He bent down to the paper bag, took out a couple more pastries, and then—to my surprise—pulled out a purple book.

"I didn't get you anything last year," Jak began, holding it out to me, "and I never formally apologized for my parents hunting you down. And then you told me about the journal your mom got you for your birthday, so I figured... Um, did I get it right?"

I took the smooth journal from his hand, carefully placing it onto my lap like it was a bomb. In full honesty, I was more shocked than anything—surprised that he'd noted a detail like that. This journal even has the golden metal corner protectors like my red one does. Staring down at it in my lap then, though, it was like Jak really listened to everything I told him, like he really... cared.

"Okay, you're scaring me," I told him, gripping the book. "I can handle it, just give it to me straight."

That hypnotizing smile blossomed into a laugh. "Sorry, do you want me to make it official?"

"What?"

Jak maintained his smile like he had finally found the courage for the words. He turned in his spot to face me completely. "Emma, will you go out with me?"

Okay. I know almost nothing about dating, but I do know that you can't just spring *that* onto a girl without letting her suspect that you're going to ask and then mentally prepare for it!

I mean, we were already on the date in question, but the difference now was that Jak had flat out used the word and, like he'd said, made it official! Didn't that mean that, if I said yes, we were dating? And then wouldn't I be "cheating" on him by hanging out with Nolan? Or can you date multiple people at a time? Or is dating even considered being exclusive with someone?

Ugh, where's Sarah when I actually need her?

"You're already here, by the way," Jak whispered, leaning in closer as if to share his most embarrassing secret. "It wouldn't really make sense to say no."

I looked back out at Capperson Park, my chest just as quickly constricting. "No."

Jak straightened again, but my anxious stare was following the boy walking with his group of friends and nearing the gazebo area.

"Well, I guess that doesn't mean you *can't* say no."

Jak's voice reminded me that he was still there, and I turned to him. "No, not—" I said without thought. Before I knew it, he was following my eyes, and his were landing on the boy in heavy winter-ware in the middle of the group.

Why did it feel like I'd been caught red-handed?

"Do you... know him?"

Surprisingly, a part of me wanted to say no. "He's a friend," I replied, but I had to remember that Jak was a Hunter-in-training, too. Jak had grown up with professional liars as parents. Who was I to try and deceive him and imply that that was all Nolan was?

A small smile lifted one corner of mouth, and he tilted his head up. "A good friend."

"No, he's not—"

The burning in my chest was back. The snowball was running too fast down the hill.

"It's not like that, we've just talked—"

"Hey," Jak said simply, like it was really that easy. "I just wanna meet your friends."

He wasn't... upset?

"It's just him," I said, catching Nolan's green eyes at the same time. I darted my gaze back to Jak, as if looking away would make Nolan disappear. "I've only met his friends, like, twice."

"Cool. Then he gets to meet yours now. Unless he's the jealous type." Jak nudged me with his elbow. "Then we're cousins."

I blinked a couple of times, because was that even believable? All I could do was pray that it was when Nolan and his friends started walking our way.

I put the purple journal back into the bag and slapped on a smile.

"Hey, Em," Nolan said, the hesitance in his voice exposing the façade of his joy.

Is *he jealous?*

"Hey!" I was too afraid to glance at Jak and see what kind of cover he'd pulled up. "What're you doing today?"

"Just got out of school," Nolan replied, one hand deep in his coat pockets. His other gloved hand swept away his dark-brown hair, a beanie covering it as always, out of his eyes. "What're you guys doing?"

"Just catching up," Jak said, standing and extending his hand (to my complete surprise). "I'm Jak, my family's visiting for the weekend."

Well, it was Thursday, but close enough.

"Oh!" Nolan chirped, his brows furrowing. "Are you guys family?"

"Cousins," Jak replied, smiling. I knew that smile. He was relishing in how he'd predicted how this was going to go.

Nolan's happy disguise melted into truth. "Oh, nice. I'm Nolan, um... a friend." He pointed behind him at the four other kids of varying heights and winter clothes. "These are my friends."

"Yeah,"—Jak nodded kindly—"Emma's told me about you."

Okay, I had no idea where this conversation was going, but Momma always says not to wait until you do to participate: that way, you can control the direction it does end up going.

"How was school?" I asked.

"Good, good," Nolan said. "You guys wanna walk with us?"

"Oh, you should!" chirped the blonde next to him—Missy, a

real-life Barbie with freckles. She didn't look at me once as she spoke. No, her blue puppy eyes were nailed on Jak. "Maybe we can show you around town for a bit."

Jak is plenty familiar with Capperson, thanks.

"We should actually be getting back soon," Jak told her kindly. "But thanks anyway."

"Oh, sure." Missy nodded, tucking a curl behind her red ear.

"We might be in town this weekend," I said, grabbing the paper bag of snacks (and my new journal) Jak had brought. "It was nice seeing you guys, though."

This was to Nolan, whose smile seemed to deepen. He stepped down and out of the gazebo, allowing me and Jak to follow. "You, too, let me know. See you later."

I waved at Nolan's friends as Jak and I started our walk back to the school across the field. We knew to keep quiet until they were out of earshot, but just as Jak opened his mouth to speak, crunchy footsteps approached from behind us.

"Hey, uh, Jak," a sweet voice called, turning us around. Missy was jogging forward, her breath fogging every time she exhaled. A smile came to her pink lips as she finally acknowledged me but just as quickly looked back at Jak. "Hi, sorry," she said breathily, "I was just... I was wondering if I could get your number and we can just—talk."

"Thanks, I'm flattered, seriously," he said warmly, placing a hand on his chest, "but I have a girlfriend."

Why did my chest tighten at that?

"Oh!" Missy said, glancing at me as if I were the imaginary girlfriend in question. "I'm so sorry, I didn't mean—"

"No, no, you're fine. Thanks, though."

"Sure. Um, nice to meet you!" she said, taking on a professional tone. "Nice to see you again, Emma."

I nodded, forcing a smile. The first time she'd *really* acknowledged me, and it was to say goodbye. "You, too."

She turned away and walked back to her friends in front of the gazebo.

"Huh," I began as Jak turned the other way with me. "So do I tell your girlfriend that you're cheating on her?"

"Go ahead. I'm interested in someone else, anyway."

I laughed, smacking his arm. "That's horrible!"

On went his infamous smirk. "Why are you jealous? I never said it was you."

"Keep it up and it never will be," I joked back, almost freezing dead in my tracks. There was no way I'd just said that.

Jak bent his head back in laughter as he slowed his pace, slinging his arm around my shoulders. "You're cute."

His arm was around my shoulders. He'd just called me "cute"!

"Wait," I whispered, stepping away and almost tripping in the fresh snow. "They'll see."

"It's not your waist," he said in a tone all too Jakson-Bleu casual—with words that blew the butterflies to life again in my stomach. "It's fine. We're cousins."

SEVENTEEN

"Don't forget, ladies, we have our unit test the week after break!" Mr. Hartman called over the Callistro Girls and Redway Boys filing out of his classroom the next day. "Have a good winter break, everyone."

As my friends and I walked out of the math wing and reached the top of the Main Staircase, I looked down at the bustling Grand Foyer. The last time it had been this full, it had been last August's orientation. A buried reminder tried to resurface in my mind after almost two hours of advanced algebra.

I started my descent with my friends. "Why is everyone crowded in the—?"

"Hey, Merlin," a familiar voice called over the sea of Callistro Girls flooding down the stairs. In less than a second, I located Jak swimming upstream. "Can we talk for a sec?"

I glanced at Sarah and Breanne, whose giddy smiles were practically pushing me toward him.

"Sure," I said, letting him take my hand.

He guided me through the crowd and down the rest of the stairs. We instantly sneaked away from the crowd, skulking into the English wing and to Mrs. Durrett's door at the end. With a cautionary glance behind us, Jak slid open the secret passageway behind the daisy painting and pulled me inside.

It's like that morning we walked around the school. Where I'd seen the black figure. Right here in this very—

No. Jak's here. We'll be fine. He won't let something happen.

I rubbed my arms, adjusting to the suddenly damp, cold air. "Is this another impulse date?"

"First of all, I'm offended you think I'd ever take you *here* for a date." Meandering to me, he cupped my face and caressed my cheeks with his thumbs. My mind was lost in how soft his skin was. "Second... I just wanted to get in my last few moments with you alone."

Last few moments? But we had all of—

It dawned on me. Winter break was after this weekend, the first full week of *February*. Today was the first—the day the Redway Boys were leaving the Callistro Academy.

"Oh," I muttered.

"I was wondering why you were confused about yesterday," Jak mused. "Why wouldn't I do something for our last afternoon here?"

I sighed tiredly. "I'm sorry, it... Today somehow *completely* slipped my mind the last couple of weeks, I got used to it, I don't know how it..."

He wrapped his arms around me, his cologne strong as he rested his chin on top of my head.

No, don't do this. You can't do this to me.

Because today wasn't the only thing that had slipped my mind the last couple of weeks. And now I didn't know when I'd see Jak next, which meant this could be my last chance to undo what I was terrified was making our connection so strong at all.

I have to do it now. I don't have a choice.

Unless I released him from the trust spell now, I'd never know how far my boundaries with him truly went. I wasn't ready to let go of it yet—the comfort and familiarity I had with him—but I was putting it all on the line. I had to. For the sake of my family's safety, I had to. *They* were my priority, and they would always mean more to me.

I squeezed Jak tighter. I would miss this.

Converte.

Jak held me for a few seconds longer before pulling away, giving himself just enough space to kiss my forehead. His hands fell to my waist.

I bit the inside of my lip and locked eyes with him. The trust spell's weight fell straight off my back like water. Now there was no denying the brand-new resistance rearing its head around the corner. No matter how much I still wanted to trust the boy in front of me, my rationality had been set free. And it was telling me everything I already knew but couldn't face head on: it would never be okay to fully trust Jak. He had his own secrets that I didn't know, and that fact alone threatened me and my family.

"It was a pretty fun month," he said softly. "We should do it again sometime."

"You're gonna give Redway ideas." I hugged him again. "Do me a favor and don't."

"Trust me. I'd never subject you to that place."

With a twinge, my heart betrayed me. Maybe it was because of the sadness overwhelming me; the anxiety that he had to leave in a few seconds to catch up with the rest of his class before they left; or my desire to confide in him because he hadn't done a thing to break the trust we *had* already built, artificial or not—but I needed Jak to know that he still meant a lot to me. In a way, I needed him to know that I *wanted* to trust him.

I wish I could tell him about Adara. Like she's Tristan's descendant, or something to—

Wait a minute. Could I? I'd already planned to set Alexa off the scent with it, and if I planted that seed with Jak first, it just might buy all of us more time: he wouldn't be lying in case he was ever debriefed about it, so he wouldn't be punished. And Alexa would start her next hunt for someone who "wasn't me".

Maybe I *could* reward Jak for the trust he'd given me already.

"Tristan's daughter," I whispered. "Her name is 'Adara'."

His hands rose to cup my face one last time. Our noses grazed each other, and I let him meet our lips in a soft kiss. He held it for even longer than our first two and then released, his round eyes glancing back and forth between my top and bottom lip, as if taking a mental picture.

"I've told you I have feelings for you, right?"

A butterfly-infused laugh escaped me, and I pushed down his hands, self-conscious. "You have the worst timing on the planet."

He simply flashed me his million-dollar grin. "You can write about it in your new journal."

Without letting me reply, and with my mind half blurry, he turned around and opened the passageway entrance. We strolled back into the crowded foyer, where over half the Redway Boys had already left through the propped-open double doors. Daylight pouring inside onto the red rug, inviting Jak outside next.

"One more thing," he said, taking my hand and walking backwards toward the doors. "If Beanie Boy ends up seducing you and then breaking your heart while I'm gone, I know where he goes to school. And how to find out where he lives."

This wasn't happening. This wasn't happening. This wasn't—

"Hey," Adrien said, jogging up to us as we reached the middle of the foyer. "Your dad's looking for you, we're leaving right now."

This was happening.

Jak turned to me. Most of the sophomore class was standing all around us, along with younger and older Callistro Girls who wanted to catch one last glimpse of teenage boys at the Callistro Academy.

But Jak gazed into my eyes like I was the only girl there right now. And he didn't care who saw as he cupped my neck, bent down, and met our lips again.

He was actually doing this in front of everyone.

Breaking away, I tried to bite the inside of my lip as discreetly as I could to cope. Jak let me know that he totally saw it by gently brushing my bottom lip with his thumb.

"See you later, Merlin."

I couldn't cage my smile in time before I replied, "See you."

The eyes of every Callistro Girl in the room pressed heavily against me. Jak walked to the front doors with a grinning Adrien, who turned his head of blond hair to look—and wink—at me.

"*Who* could've seen that coming?" Sarah said, hands on her hips as she appeared beside me. The last two Redway Boys strolled through the exit of our school. "I did!"

"Emma!" Breanne squealed, running up to me on my other side. "He kissed you! In front of *everyone!*"

"Wow, and we were doing so well at keeping it a secret." I tightly crossed my arms, muttering, "I noticed. Everyone noticed."

With a child-like grin, Breanne squeezed me tight enough for me to know that Defensive Calisthenics really was making a difference in her.

"*Wow,*" chirped a sweet voice from the side of the crowd. When the three of us turned, Opal Dubois was skipping up to us, purple contacts glittering as she told me, "You kept *him* a pretty little secret! I'm impressed!"

"It's not like that—" I began, but she playfully rolled her eyes, her fair hands taking mine.

"He and I talked a couple times," she said with a higher, airy register. It just as quickly dropped back to normal, like she was emphasizing it when she said, "He's a *keeper,* Em, go for it. If you don't, I will. That was amazing."

Sarah glanced around, noting the dozens of eyes still on us like the four of us were the most interesting soap opera in the world. "Yes, they kissed," she announced. "You did not imagine that. Please hold all questions for the rest of your lives, thank you."

The outskirts started to disband with excited whispers and giggles, but Opal stayed where she was. She let go of my hands, smiling generously at the three of us as she pushed her straight black hair behind her ear. "Told you last year that joining schools would be a great idea. A *lot* more than I thought."

A smirk trailed the words as her amethyst eyes switched between Sarah and Breanne. Sarah beamed proudly while Breanne crossed her arms, rolling her eyes.

"He's a *study partner* first," she argued.

Opal hummed her sarcastic agreement. "Don't worry," she said with that higher pitch, "I nabbed a secret date, too, while they were here. It just didn't work out. But..."

Amelia Baker approached from behind her, calling her name. Briefly turning to acknowledge her, Opal then turned back to us with a ginger smile.

"I'm happy for you guys," she said. Something about the sincerity in her tone sounded impossible to fake. "We need to hang out sometime soon."

As she and Amelia disappeared into the dispersing crowd, all around us and across the school, there was giggling, there were enthusiastic whispers and gossip, and then there were the three of us: me, Sarah, and Breanne. There we stood in the Grand Foyer together, something familiar renewing itself over us: excitement. Excitement for whatever was next in the school year, because we'd never felt so ready for it.

That was how I knew that I'd made the right decision to tell Jak Adara's name, after all: *security* was what blanketed my chest at the thought of going the rest of the year without him, because trust spell or not, I knew he would keep that secret out there.

To my surprise, it *did* take a slight adjustment period to not having the boys around despite how they'd only been here for a month. That was especially because of all the eager questions my classmates asked about Jak. Also because Sarah refused to let us *peacefully* acknowledge that they were gone.

"You *miss* him," she teased that night from the bathroom, pouting at Breanne as she braided her long hair for bed.

Breanne sat at the desk, organizing the extra credit work that she'd managed to snag for break the coming week. "You realize that I was a devoted academic *before* him, right?"

"But you're not as happy doing homework now." Sarah grabbed a hair tie and tied off the end of her braid. "There isn't even a *hint* of a smile on your face like there was before."

"Is that all you plan to do over break with your family?" I asked from my bed, noting the deftness of Breanne's delicate hands as she rearranged her papers in her folder.

"No. It's just that the plans came up so last minute that I'm trying to get as much of it done as possible before Monday."

"And you're going to Connecticut?" I asked Sarah as she shut off the bathroom light.

"Yep, family visits," she replied, walking across our room and into the closet. "You?"

"Probably visiting my aunt and uncle."

Translation: I seriously couldn't wait to spend an entire week uninterrupted with Dad and Aunt Becca.

"Well, go crazy," Sarah said, walking out of the closet with our candy box. "I'm bringing back more next weekend."

Breanne stepped away without hesitance, but my phone dinged on the bedside table before I could stand.

Friday night. Right. It was always Friday or Saturday.

I remembered to put on my best poker face, like Momma had been the one to have just texted.

#: Your patience is thinning, I understand.
Only you, though, must see the strand.

So they *knew* how frustrated I was getting about this, and they were still withholding hints about who they were?!

Do they even know we're trying to trace them?

I tried a dozen different beginnings to a text message: I wanted to ask them for a hint as to who they were, but I didn't want to be polite. I wanted to demand for answers, but I didn't have a threat. I wanted to tell them that I'd block them if they didn't tell me what they wanted, but this was no doubt someone who knew me—who knew that I couldn't block them until I did know who they were.

I hate this, I thought as I screenshot the text, sent it to Jak and Momma, and then tossed my phone onto my bed. Taking a cozy spot on the carpet between my best friends, I grabbed a KitKat without another thought.

CHAPTER

EIGHTEEN

"Welcome home, kiddo." Aunt Becca sighed contently as she plopped down into the recliner the next afternoon. She ran a hand through her shoulder-length hair, whose roots she'd finally touched up with more platinum blond. "You ready to have the best week ever?"

I sat up from my spot on the sofa. "You have something planned?"

She scoffed. "No. I'm all the fun you need."

Right.

I slid my arms around Dad beside me and clung to him, smiling at Auntie. "I know."

"Whatever," she said, rolling her icy-blue eyes and picking at her nails.

"Hey," Momma called from the kitchen. "Is anyone gonna help me make these?"

"Sorry, kiddo," Dad said, patting my knee before slipping out of my grasp like a fish.

I didn't mind—Dad baking, I had to see.

I followed him, taking a seat at the bar while he planted himself at Momma's side and scrutinized her workstation. He grabbed the brownie box, turned it around, and quietly read the instructions to himself.

"You're actually gonna bake this?"

He only said it because of the reaction he knew he'd get out of Momma: a backhand to his chest and a glare. My dad's a romantic, though, so the reason he tries to get those reactions is so he can wrap an arm around Momma and kiss her cheek. Which always works, because she kisses him on the lips after.

"Wanna help us, kiddo?" he asked, turning to the refrigerator and grabbing the eggs.

"Sure." I leaned forward on the island. "I'll lick the spatula and bowl clean when you're done."

Momma's soft chuckle was a second delayed.

"What?" I asked.

She shrugged as she pulled open the bag of brownie mix. "Nothing. I'm just realizing that I waited your entire life to have moments like this. I really underestimated how much they'd be worth the wait."

Her words took root before I could respond: family moments. Momma had waited my entire life to have these family moments with Dad, something we'd never gotten to experience while I was growing up. Not completely, at least.

The fact must have whispered a new role into Dad's heart, because after he set the carton of eggs onto the counter, he wrapped Momma in a hug from behind.

"Well, now you can forget about the waiting," he whispered. Her hands comfortably rested on top of his, which sat on her stomach.

She rested the side of her face against Dad's and closed her eyes. As his shut next, I noticed my parents lightly swaying to imaginary music, a song only they could hear. I wondered if they were both humming it to themselves in their heads, maybe even to each other somehow.

My mom and dad. This was my mom *and* dad.

I turned around to look at Aunt Becca, whose grin spread so far that I was scared it'd permanently stretch out her lips. When she caught me staring, she pressed a finger to her lips and just as quickly darted her eyes back to Mom and Dad.

My parents. I had a whole week of this to enjoy.

My stomach uncomfortably bubbled at the thought. If something is too good to be true, it is. As tempting as it was to believe that I *did* have a straight week of this to enjoy, I was scared—no, terrified—of what Hunter danger lurked beyond the walls of my childhood home. That invisible kidnapper still had my hair, which is a sentence I *never* thought I'd have to write; I didn't know how many more Fridays and Saturdays I had until the anonymous messages would stop; and I didn't know how many days I had before the texter *or* kidnapper would expose me. And, of course, Alexa was *still* at large without any hint or clue as to what kind of game she was playing with us. Until we had an idea as to what she was doing behind the scenes, we couldn't do anything.

Three enemies at once... The thought was almost sickening enough to stop me from licking the brownie bowl clean.

Paranoia curdled in my brain all throughout the week. During the movie nights, game nights, and even midnight strolls in the park (only possible thanks to my and Aunt Becca's invisibility cloaks), the daily challenge was not letting reality impede on what was supposed to be my break from it. Jak still had no guesses as to who the texter was, and Momma had hit dead end after dead end trying to figure it out in the Hunter's Room. Which meant that Jak was probably right about them using multiple layers of concealment, and that made things even worse for my anxiety.

So I made a decision: depending on the message I'd probably get on Saturday at the end of break, I'd come clean. A sixth message *had* to be enough to put some kind of theory together, and with that, I'd tell my family about the invisible kidnapper so we could possibly put two and two together—if they were related.

For the first time since the texts had begun, I waited every minute of every hour on Friday and Saturday for my phone to chime with message number six. Go figure, Saturday night, it was kind enough to wait until I'd had a relaxing bath and was ready for bed.

I took my phone off my dresser. No matter what it said, I was going to fight back, prepared or not:

#: Unless my message still isn't clear,
A glance to the side will bring you here.

What?

Then my first theory had been right, after all: whoever this person was, they'd been trying to tell me something through every mysterious text.

I glanced all around me, but nothing was out of place. I was right on top of it, I had to be! They were *telling* me how to uncover their real message!

A glance to the side... Speaking in couplets that ultimately crafted a main message, alluding to the side... It was like Caralyn's riddles to find the secret passageway entrances, even to find her second letter that had been hiding behind the first—

Identical to Caralyn's riddles.

Goosebumps pricked my skin. I looked at the beginning of each line of every text I'd gotten over the past few weeks. Eyes widening, my heart shoved itself into my throat, cutting off my breath. The side had been their real message all along.

Another appeared, completing it:

#: Ready to know the truth,
Emmalynn "Marie"?

I.K.N.O.W.W.H.O.Y.O.U.A.R.E.

C H A P T E R

Nineteen

It wasn't the fact that my life as I knew it was about to be flung upside down yet again—no, it was how my brain was twisting itself into a knot, trying to figure out if this person was an enemy or ally. They knew who I was, yet they'd sent their messages as... a *warning*.

Jak was right: Alexa wasn't nice enough to do this. Who else was I supposed to guess?

Could it be Breanne...? She's kind enough to let me know like this. I hope.

This was crazy! I couldn't be suspecting my best friend for something like this!

I leaned against my dresser for support. Now I *had* to tell my family about this; if I was exposed, we all were.

We need to figure this out.

I moved toward my bedroom door when another text came.

#: – Come meet me at
Caralyn Callistro's secret at midnight.

The dash at the beginning was new... And looking at the message from the side, it became a signature:

– C.C.

As in... *Caralyn Callistro?*

No. That's not possible! Not even magic can resurrect the dead or make someone immortal! But I didn't know anyone else who knew her secrets, let alone where they were hiding—let alone who knew who I was!

I mindlessly gazed at the foot of my bed, rolling my lips in thought. So I didn't know this person. Yes, I'd made the promise to get my family involved, and I'd even had every intention of following through on that—but this changed things, didn't it? This was now my responsibility to do as much damage control as possible. Maybe it wasn't game over yet. My family still had a chance. On a much lesser scale, so did I, but it was a chance nonetheless.

If someone comes with me, we're all going down. I couldn't do that to them. This was my fight.

I'm the only teenager I know who would actually *meet* the anonymous person who's been terrorizing her for weeks—only because, just this once, I had too much to lose in *not* going. And I promised myself that I wouldn't keep my magic on a leash.

A couple of hours later, my parents were in bed and Aunt Becca was on the sofa bed, all fast asleep and snoring (even

Auntie, who swears that she doesn't snore). Still, I played sorceress just to be safe:

Dormio, times three. The sleeping spell would just make sure that they *stayed* asleep and didn't prematurely notice I was gone.

I grabbed my invisibility cloak and slipped out of the house. Few people were on the road at this time, even fewer in a town as small as Capperson, and the darkness would hide that someone invisible was driving. I had to park on the side of the main path through the Callistro Forest so I could walk the rest of the way to the tree stump passageway entrance, which was terrifying on its own—but at least I had self-defense *and* Hunter training built in now.

I quickly opened the stump entrance and practically leaped down. A cold, dark chill writhed through my body as my magic closed the entrance above me. I had to do this. I was invisible. I had my magic. I could defend myself. I'd be fine.

Each step down the stone tunnel took me twice as long; someone *was* down here, and I didn't need my echoing footsteps giving me away. Caralyn Callistro or not, *ally* or not, I needed more information before I exposed my presence.

Okay. This was it: the secret passageway behind the Atera family tree in the Hunter's Room. Someone would be standing where Caralyn's documents had once been as soon as I turned right.

One step. Then another.

The back of the figure dressed in a black cloak stood under the one lantern at the end of the passageway. My heart palpitated against my chest as I finally faced the anonymous texter.

No—I couldn't let my fear speak for me. I threw off my hood.

"Who are you?"

With a gasp, an ethereal-like woman spun around to face me. Innocence was plastered on her slim, delicate face. Refined eyes that matched the shade of rainclouds, a triangle jaw, and sleek golden-brown hair. Upon seeing me, she quelled the smile playing on her thin lips, keeping her distance.

"Emmalynn." Her warm, toned voice reminded me of the way Momma used to read to me when I was little. "Thank you so much for coming—"

"Who are you?" I snapped.

"I promise, I'll explain. If we could just wait for my—"

"Is this her?" a clear, male voice asked in wonder. I turned my head every which way, but what surprised me was when the woman in front of me did the same.

"Steven, my love," she muttered, straightening and clearing her throat, "your cloak."

"Oh," Steven replied. He faded into view in the entrance of the passageway I'd come from as he took off his own hood. His short, feathered hair was raven black, his eyes almost a perfect match. Both complemented his dark-brown skin and round, humble features. "I still somehow manage to forget when I have this thing on. Um, how are you, Miss Atera?"

"Miss Atera"? I wasn't sure if I liked the sound of it or wanted to wince. Especially because it all the more verified that these people really did know *everything* about me.

"Who ARE you?" I demanded one last time, fear churning my stomach.

The couple shared a glance with each other and then me. With a rush of my heart, I felt myself fall into the deep end.

"Well, um, I'm Steven," he said. He pressed his lips tightly together. "Steven Baelford."

I looked at the woman in front of me, expecting her answer next—then too afraid to hear it.

"I'm Cara," she replied slowly, as if trying to give me the chance to fully grasp her words. "Callistro. Callistro-Baelford. I'm his wife."

No. Way.

That was how she'd successfully kept the number untraceable; she *did* have training. For all I knew, she was standing in her old high school right now.

I lightly shook my head, trying to wrap it around the fact that a Hunter—from a famed line presumably extinct!—was in front of me and I was trapped down in the *Hunter's Room* with her right now!

Wait. A Hunter who was wearing an invisibility cloak. Whose husband was also wearing an invisibility cloak.

"I don't... I don't get it," I murmured. "The Callistros—their line ended—"

"The Hunter line of my family ended," Cara told me gently. "They 'bred out', essentially. The only ones left are the people who were trusted with the truth about our families."

"You, um, know of both of our grandparents—I think," Steven added, like this conversation wasn't completely blowing my mind. "You obviously know about Caralyn, and you also know of my grandfather Samuel."

Samuel. Samuel the mage, the one that had found Henry Callistro out and teamed up with Caralyn!

I asked the only question that had been in my mind since the very first text: "How did you find me?"

"Magic can track a lot of things," Steven answered. "We, um, spoke to a nore to get most of our information on you. Including your school and, um, your number."

A nore, of all people—they're the fastest and easiest way to get unobtainable, current information, but they're also known for being impishly cunning and untrustworthy with the information they get from their inquirers. Once you place your hand in theirs, they have complete access to the events of your life and knowledge about all present information about the world—almost like a seer's knowledge of the future. We probably would've gone to a nore to find out who the number belonged to if not for the risk of said nore selling us out to someone who mattered, whether by choice or force.

But a nore's magic puts them under a temporary "truth spell" when they answer a question. After answering their inquirer, they're owed a question back. The "truth spell" is temporarily transferred until you answer the nore...

Meaning that whoever Cara and Steven had spoken to now had information on one of them (depending on who'd asked)—information that they could remember and provide to anyone who asked for it. Including the U.S. Government if Steven was ever caught as a magician and Cara as an accomplice. They'd put themselves on the line just to have access to me.

I don't know how much I can trust them. Or if.

"We know it sounds bad," Cara began, anticipating my words a nanosecond away, "but we *needed* to contact you. We were entrusted with the truth regarding Adara's fate, and we're here to help you."

"Was that you in the forest?" I asked, her light-brown hair now eliciting the memory. "Were you the one spying on me?"

"Yes. That was me."

"And you figured the best way to contact me was by using an untraceable phone?"

"I retained a lot from my training," she replied, her slender hand resting on her chest. "We couldn't let you trace us without it ruining the timing. We wanted to ease you into finding out that we're allies. Caralyn copied the truth of her alliance with magic in a journal that was passed down to the most trusted member of each generation. It eventually landed with me, and of course Steven knows the story as well as I do. We know the truth."

"Then why are you here *now?*" I said, narrowing my eyes at them. "Why are you showing up now after stalking me for the past, what, almost month and a half?"

"Cara figured it was another way of *easing* you in," Steven answered with double the pace, like he was excited for this conversation. He kept his distance from me, too. "You needed to know you were meeting someone who, you know, already knows about you. If we'd showed up unannounced—I think your reaction would've, um, been a lot worse. You probably would've never come at all."

Granted, he had a point.

"We've done our research," Cara added, gray eyes as gentle as her tone, "we know our targets, and we're here to help. Alexa Delphine—"

I scoffed, wrapping my cloak tighter around myself against the frigid underground. "I don't even know where she is, forget what she's doing. How do you plan on helping?"

"There are a lot of ways to find out where she is," Steven said, his inflection as bouncy as his cloak was whenever he spoke. "Our ultimate goal is to just make sure she's not a threat anymore. That could mean a number of different things, even, um... recruiting her if possible."

"*Recruiting* her?" I laughed. Maybe these people were crazier than their first impression had let on. "Again, how do you plan on helping?"

"We're able to work from the outside since we don't have to stay at the school," Cara said, "meaning we'll be able to track her or any other Hunter and warn you in advance. That's the big thing. We don't have an explicit plan right now, but we *can* take steps that'll stop Alexa from getting your family's magic."

Power corrupts. There are too many examples in history that prove it but not enough for mankind to learn—or rather, enough to make us *want* to learn. And Alexa and her family had been infected since the beginning of time. I probably didn't need to tell Cara and Steven that, but I guess they didn't believe that there was an absolute zero chance of Alexa turning good. Somehow, that must've been enough for them to believe it could happen.

"Emmalynn," Cara said, daring a step forward, "we understand if you don't believe us. It's a game of life-or-death whenever you decide to trust someone. Put us under a truth spell, and we'll tell you the same thing:"—she kept her slender hand pressed against her heart, leaning toward me—"we want to help you."

I glimpsed her husband. Then her.

Veritatem dicere.

"Can I trust you both?" I said.

"Yes," they replied in unison.

"You have no tricks up your sleeve against me or my family? You want to help us stay safe from the government and anyone who'd want to hurt us?"

"Yes," they said in a tone twice as solid.

Cara was right: it was a game of life-or-death trusting anyone, no matter how secure my reasoning was to do so. But they couldn't lie right now. They couldn't lie, and if they were as genuine as my own mother and godfather were, I needed all the allies on the outside that I could get.

My impatience finally won. "Okay."

Cara smiled graciously at me, her raincloud eyes brightening. "We're gonna do everything we can."

At least you meant that. I figured I'd keep them under the truth spell until we said good night.

"I imagine you're, um, anxious to find Alexa first," Steven said, gesturing his words with his dark hands. "As you know, unless we have something that belongs to her, we can't use a locator spell, but we *can* visit a nore and then relay the information back to you. I can telepathically communicate any answers we find."

The thing was, I didn't want to waste time relying on them for answers—or let them sacrifice more information about themselves just for my sake. The option was easy so it was tempting, but it was the middle of the night and I was still wary of the two people in front of me. Besides, I wanted to be able to know on my own where Alexa was.

"Is there another way we can know?" I asked. "Could we track her based on the image of her, or even the thought?"

"Um... that would be a really difficult spell," Steven said, "and even more so to create."

"Let's try it," Cara said quickly, reading my impatience and almost cutting him off. "She should be able to know for her own sanity of mind."

Okay. I like her. For now, I like her.

Seconds of quiet passed where I could practically feel Steven weighing the task in his mind. "I'll do my *absolute* best," he said eventually. "We'll contact you as soon as it's finished."

At least he meant that, too.

With that, I let the first crack of a smile bend my lips that night, twisting the locket around my neck and rubbing the silver in relief. "Thanks."

"And thank you for meeting us tonight." Cara gestured to me. "We know the hour is nowhere near ideal, but we understand how tricky it is to break away from your friends and family without suspicion. So we hope tonight was at least a bit helpful."

"It was," I told her, nodding. "Trust me, it was."

Admittedly, with every spoken word, my roots in these two were able to grow a millimeter more. And I think I needed that night more than I was willing to admit.

C H A P T E R

TWENTY

At least that was one mystery down, and it hadn't ended in wildfire. I spent the next few days trying to figure out the least suspicious message to send to Jak about the anonymous number mystery being solved, but that proved a lot more difficult than letting him in on it to begin with. And it took me the same amount of time to try and figure out how to tell my family because—well, in full honesty, I was just postponing the scolding I'd get from meeting up with a pair of strangers at an ungodly hour of the night. But one of the hardest pills to swallow is the fact that one more day is all it takes to worsen the outcome. I'd have to force myself to confess sooner rather than later.

After a freakish nightmare I had Sunday night about some

kind of alleyway that Ava Baleen and I were trapped in with three teenage boys, school felt even sleepier the week after break—even worse because of the tests and review packets we had due that same Friday. The weird part? Sarah seemed to be in the same stress boat with me; Breanne and I caught her a few times reading her textbooks as often as she worked on homework, but we didn't bring it up. You do *not* bother the girl when she's trying to improve her grades. (Breanne still has the pencil scar from eighth grade on her left palm to prove it.)

Tuesday afternoon, though, I graduated from lifting the textbooks two inches off the table to four—which made Mr. Dawson think that I could perform a reversal spell on a disassembled calculator. (It's a lot harder to reverse something that you didn't watch come undone. Plus, I was trying to figure out the best way to bring up Cara and Steven.)

"Are you really channeling your power itself?" Mr. Dawson asked from across the table in the back of the gym. "Or just your knowledge?"

"Why do you feel the need to bring up the same lesson every time?" I asked, fighting the bite in my tone. "I'm channeling everything I have!"

"Okay. You're still figuring it out. Never mind."

Was that an insult? I'm actually asking.

I sighed but focused back on the broken calculator in front of me. My gaze scanned each individual piece, from the motherboard to the keys to the tiny screws. I closed my eyes and drew on my magic inside, working with it to act according to my will.

Converte.

I opened my eyes. The calculator reassembled itself like a

video in rewind, Mr. Dawson's steps exposed as they reversed and pieces levitated back into place. He smiled and pulled himself up straighter, hands in the pockets of his beige blazer.

"You're getting quicker, very nice."

"The key is coming to me more often," I said, prouder than I wanted to admit. "It's clearer, too, like I'm actually owning my abilities."

"Better now than later."

One of the gym doors clanged open behind us, turning us around. Momma strode in, posture as straight as a pencil like always. "How's it going?"

It was like the woman knew I'd planned a confession today. Why *wouldn't* she come in right now of all times?

"We're making great progress." Mr. Dawson grabbed the calculator off the table and approached her. His diamond-blue eyes rested on me over his shoulder as I followed. "Emma's taking lessons a bit more seriously now."

"Good, I'm happy." Momma nodded in the direction of the doors. "Emmy, your friends are looking for you. And you," she said to Mr. Dawson. "They want to go into town."

I guess this is it. They're both here. I might as well.

"That always ends well," Mr. Dawson mumbled, passing a hand over his face. "Let's go, Em."

"Um, actually..." I began, reaching his side. "Can we talk for a bit? I've been meaning to bring up the, um..."

"The...?" Momma asked.

I took a deep breath as if to cast my net for all the right words. I'd been preparing this story for days, and the fact was that it'd never be ready—it just had to be told.

"Okay. It's about this past Saturday night—"

Mr. Dawson gripped my shoulder, sharp gaze piercing the waxed gym floor. "Did you hear that?" he whispered.

I fought to keep my voice level as I asked, "Hear what—?"

—Emma, do you hear me? Please!—

Hang on... I knew that voice. Why was it so quiet? Far away? Why did Dad sound desperate?

—Listen to me, the pack is coming. Get to the house! Becca and I have a plan and we're getting away, but—just hurry!—

"Dad," I whispered at the same time Mr. Dawson said, "Becca."

Raw panic gripped my rationality as he and I ran to the doors. Momma's keys jingled behind me as she followed suit.

"Hang on, what's going on?" she urged. "What did you both hear?"

"Becca just said the pack is after them," Mr. Dawson said without missing a beat, pushing open the gym door. "We need to get to the house *right* now."

It made too much sense, but I couldn't add reason to it: if Alexa's pack had finally gone into their SUVs' GPS input histories, why months later? And did anyone know whose house they were really going to...?

I was all too grateful that we didn't run into Sarah and Breanne as the three of us fled the school and to the parking lot. Within a minute, Mr. Dawson was barreling down the driveway and through the forest with Momma next to him and me behind them. Momma twisted her wedding ring on her left hand, gaze burning a hole through the windshield. I knew it was all she could do to stop herself from going hysterical. That ring was the only thing of Dad she could keep with her no matter what.

I mirrored her exactly: twisting the heart around my neck, hoping against hope for the favorable outcome, and telling myself that I knew the truth. I knew that Dad and Aunt Becca were sitting on the couch at home, watching Auntie's favorite show because she refused to relinquish the remote to anyone, not even her little brother. I knew that, I knew that, I knew that I was lying to myself.

My phone buzzed in my coat pocket. I barely felt it in my fingers as I took it out and looked down.

B: Where are you? We wanted to go into town
before dinner.

> **E:** A family emergency came up, my mom and I
> just left, we'll be back as soon as we can be

Thoughts and feelings remained mixed as Mr. Dawson pulled up along the curb of the house. First red flag: as usual, there were no cars in the driveway. Whoever had come for my family had already left, yet Dad hadn't said another word to me.

No, no, no, no, no.

Momma, Mr. Dawson, and I jumped out of the car, never minding the doors, and ran up to the porch. Mom burst straight through the unlocked front door. Second red flag.

The second I stepped into the entryway, my last shard of hope shattered: the dining room table had been flipped over, the couch had been moved aside, the fireplace under the TV had been dug into, and every kitchen cabinet and the fridge door eerily hung open. Strangely enough, Aunt Becca's and my father's clothes sloppily lay all around the house. No cranny had gone uninvestigated, which only suggested two things that had equal chances of being true.

—*Dad?*— I called. —*Dad! Auntie!*—

Silence rang back at me.

All too soon, Mr. Dawson pushed me and Momma out the door. "Get back in the car, go."

She and I knew not to argue. I'd learned on my birthday to trust him no matter how bleak and dire the situation seemed. Mr. Dawson, I had to understand, always had either a plan or a reason.

As quickly as we'd pulled up, we drove away. Mr. Dawson took any turn he met along the way.

"Becca said they had an escape plan, but we don't know if they were taken or if they did escape. But we do know that Grand Hunters broke in to find them, which means they could've been sitting around waiting for their next targets to walk in."

"Thomas," Momma whispered, locking her eyes onto him. Her fingers stayed glued to her wedding ring. "My husband—my sister—"

"We don't know what happened," he stated. "Push those thoughts out of your head, they'll only do you more harm than good. Emma?"

I snapped my head up, meeting our eyes in the rearview mirror.

"I mean it. Do not jump to conclusions until we have answers."

Except, I had one answer that was already inciting its damage: something had happened to my family. Captured or on the run, they'd been stolen. And I'd broken my promise to never let another power rip us apart ever again.

Twenty-One

It was now or never. And now was as good a time as ever because I didn't want to bother Jak with mortal-versus-magic war business on his birthday tomorrow.

After what had happened to Dad and Aunt Becca, I didn't dare put off telling Momma and Mr. Dawson about Cara and Steven any longer. Yesterday's conversation had been *long*, but at least everyone was on civil grounds. Still, when I told Cara and Steven that I couldn't meet them today, they offered to drive me to Topa so that we could at least discuss things on the way there—but I wasn't going to make them wait around the area while I hung out with Jak, and I wasn't going to make the birthday boy drive an hour to pick up his present.

Plus, alone, I got to figure out my cover story on the way over.

With my first step inside, the warm aroma of fresh coffee wrapped around me. Jak was sitting in a booth against the right wall. Two drinks and a slice of marble cake sat in front of him. His eyes locked with mine, his lips curving into a smile.

I approached the table, holding out the purple gift bag to him. "Happy birthday!"

His smile dropped as he eyed it. "I told you—"

"I didn't listen," I said, bouncing the bag. "You can only deny a present once. I took the journal, and that wasn't even celebrating anything."

He sighed through his nose and took his present from me, setting it between him and the wall. "Thanks."

I took my seat across from him, resting my chin in my hand. "*I* was supposed to treat you to coffee and cake."

"I didn't listen."

His smile was contagious, and I internally scoffed at myself for being so susceptible to it. He wasn't under a trust spell anymore; why was I still so eager to let him in? Why... why did I want to be honest with him? To be real in front of him?

"Do I open it now, or...?"

I licked my lips, briefly playing out each scenario in my head. "Do you want the fun thing or the serious thing first?"

Jak nodded once, carefully. "Good."

"Then open it now."

He turned to the bag, took out the white tissue paper and rested it on the vinyl seat, and then pulled out the black fabric inside. He quickly found the shoulders and let the garment unfold in front of him.

"No way." His breath lightened, eyes traveling up and down

his gift. "You got me a hoodie?"

"Black looks good on you." I couldn't stop my smile. For a second, it felt like the trust spell was still there. "And apparently they're your favorite thing to wear."

His eyes seemed to catch on what I'd been waiting for, and he gathered the fabric on the top left side. "Genuine question." He turned the front of the hoodie to me, showing me the purple rose. "Did you pick this for a reason?"

"Purple's your favorite color, and, you know—the Callistro Academy crest is a rose with a sword. So every time you wear this and look at the rose, you can think of your friends there."

Jak subtly bit his lip before crow's feet gathered in the corners of his beaming eyes. My chest fluttered again.

He chuckled, shaking his head. "Man, I really wanna kiss you right now."

I groaned as I buried my face into my hands. "You can't say things like that!"

"Why not?"

Seriously?

I sat up, crossing my arms. "That's... couples stuff, you can't say that to a friend!"

His lips folded back into a thin line, like they were a cage for his next words. I braced myself. "That depends on how you see yourself, Merlin."

I instinctively opened my mouth to reply and realized too late that I didn't have the words. Ugh. I still wanted to tell him the truth, but now it was in the same way that there's a minuscule part of me that always wants to tell Sarah and Breanne. Lying to two good friends was hard enough and only getting harder every day.

"Hey," Jak said, breaking the quiet that my thoughts had left between us. I looked up at him. He was on the edge of his seat, leaning forward yet still far enough to give me space. "I get it."

I bit the inside of my lip. More than anything, I wanted to know if he really did.

"Ready for the serious?" I asked.

"If you are."

The brown vinyl underneath me was now warm while the heated air of the café soothed my cold skin. My fingers held my locket again, and I couldn't help but laugh in the silence. I wasn't sure if I *was* ready. I wasn't sure if I could make myself lie to Jak well enough that he'd believe me.

"That... that number. We figured it out."

He blinked a couple of times, eyes widening. "Really? Did they come clean?"

I stared at the marble cake on the table, my stomach growling. I couldn't do this. He'd see right through it. It was too outlandish, wasn't it? Then again, what part of our lives weren't?

It was too late to turn back now; I'd already told him that I knew. "Believe it or not, it was Adara."

I refused to look up at him no matter how long the trail of silence lasted. A swarm of thoughts buried my mind alive, and it didn't matter if any of them made sense—as long as they kept me busy and distracted from whatever Jak was about to say.

I hated this. The nausea, the lightheadedness, how I couldn't avoid it no matter how small the situation was... not knowing if the situation was as small as I wanted it to be.

"Emma," he said. With that, I couldn't withhold my attention from him anymore. "Are you okay?"

It was a statement. Maybe I'd missed something that he'd said before that, because Jak wasn't asking for just that moment; he wanted to know in general. By how heavily his eyes weighed on me, he had to know as badly as I did.

Start acting better before he actually does find out the truth.

I nodded. "Yeah. She was warning me. I was loose last month and she was scared. Ha, *I* was scared."

At least I couldn't find the lie in that.

Jak looked at me for only a couple of seconds before standing up with his new hoodie in hand. He walked to my side of the table and took a respectful spot beside me. His index finger brushed the bottom of my chin as he leaned in and kissed my cheek.

"Look at the rose," he whispered, showing it to me on the hoodie, "and you can think of me."

Twenty-Two

You can't say that meals are boring at the Callistro Academy for two reasons: one, they objectively aren't; and two, Opal Dubois had apparently made it her mission this school year to keep us updated and entertained with any news or magic-related gossip she could find. I don't know if the girl makes a list at the beginning of each week or what, because it's always on Friday that she has the juiciest topics. That Friday at lunch was no exception.

"Guess what," she announced too eagerly, her purple eyes shining. Instinct warned me to brace myself for what the daughter of *Magic Magazine*'s chief editor was about to say. "*Magic* found something. The latest issue about to come out involves Tristan *and* Rebecca Atera. They're on the move *together!*"

My grip tightened around my fork, stopping it from clashing onto my spaghetti-filled plate. The Callistro Girls around me, even Sarah and Breanne on either side of me, gasped and stared. How did anyone already know about that? Dad and Aunt Becca had *just* run away, and *Magic* already had coverage on it? Did the magazine have an undercover Hunter?

Teresa Darci leaned forward for a better view of Opal three seats down. "Where are they, does *Magic* know?"

Opal drew in a deep breath, holding it for suspense. "In America. In North Carolina. In *Capperson.*"

The shock swelled for half of the girls, but the other half instantly lost faith. "They can't *know* that," Caroline Walker said skeptically, a meatball stuck on her fork. "How would they find that out?"

"Alexa and William's pack found him and Rebecca running out of a nearby neighborhood yesterday. They're the ones chasing them, it's just like when Tristan was first on the run!"

My father and aunt had almost been caught running out of a "nearby neighborhood". *My* neighborhood.

"Wait, how did he get all the way over here?" Sarah asked. Then, she gasped, eyes doubling in size. "Are they trying to find his *descendant?*"

"He *has* a descendant, right?" Amelia Baker exclaimed.

"It makes the most sense if they are!" Opal grinned, pushing a black lock of hair behind her ear as if to make room for more excitement. "If Alexa Delphine and William Bleu's pack is supposed to catch them, Tristan and Rebecca are gonna lead them straight to his kid!"

A rock pressed heavily against my throat, blocking my voice.

"So are they closer to finally getting them or not?" a timid Ava Baleen asked.

"The Ateras are some of the most powerful sorcerers in *history*," Breanne replied next to me, stirring her spaghetti around her plate. "Nobody knows that better than the Delphines. They're dead equal. Anything could happen."

She had no idea how spot on she was.

I bit the inside of my cheek, setting my gaze on the red roses sitting in the glass in front of me. One sat every few feet away from each other down the table. I couldn't keep my focus from the thorns magnified underwater. They looked huge until you took them out of the water, but would still hurt just as much if you touched them.

I'm okay. This doesn't mean anything. It's fine. I had to convince myself of my safety by placing myself in the shoes of all the journalists trying to find me, trying to find out if I even existed. Knowing where I was right now and who I was to the world, I'd have a pretty hard time finding me, too.

Because Alexa still hasn't exposed me. When she could. Now of all times she could, she could.

And Dad and Aunt Becca weren't as fortunate.

I looked at Mr. Dawson in the back of the Dining Hall just as his eyes fell onto me. It was like he'd heard my message before I even had the chance to speak it.

—*Alexa and William are after Dad and Aunt Becca. Magic is printing that in their latest issue.*—

He flinched, quickly pulling his gaze down to his plate. —*So you think telepathically discussing this in a room full of gossiping teenagers is wise?*—

—We have to contact them somehow! They'll be killed if Alexa and William get them first!—

—We can't, Emma. We just can't, not right now. You're playing a dangerous game as it is. You have to trust that they'll be able to fend for themselves for a little bit. There's a reason they're not using magic to keep us updated. We have to believe that until we can find them.—

—But... they're—no, I...!—

I couldn't do anything right now. I was powerless. I couldn't do anything right now. They had to be okay. They had to be okay, they couldn't just—

"Em," Sarah whispered, leaning in close to me. "Are you okay?"

I swallowed hard, shaking my head, but not at her words. Unfortunately, there was no way for her to know that.

"Come on, I'll take you to the nurse."

I don't want to.

I can't leave without everyone seeing me.

Maybe I only felt the stares or maybe they were really there. As Sarah stood from the table and I stayed in my seat, I despised my ability to feel. I wanted to bolt out of the room without Sarah instead of waiting for her to tell Mr. Dawson that she was about to take me to Julia, as if running away in the middle of lunch would *lessen* the embarrassment.

But I did anyway. I wanted to rip off that Band-Aid if it meant I'd be numb for just a few seconds.

"Em, wait!" Sarah's padded footsteps chased after me in the Grand Foyer, adrenaline pushing me forward.

"No!" I said, my hands hovering over my head like I could pull out the swelling panic. "Just—leave me alone, go!"

"My best friend isn't okay and I can't ignore that," she told me, reaching me.

I quickened my pace toward the Main Staircase. "Go back!"

"Emma," she said, "I'm trying to help—"

"You're not helping!" I cried. My chest tightened, my eyes burned, and my throat strained to keep my tears inside. "I can't—you can't help, nobody can...!"

My lungs begged for more air despite the oxygen suffocating me. Suffocating, yet I wanted to swallow it whole. We soon passed the elevator and began our way down the hall to Julia's office.

When did I start heading this way? Because I think she can help?

She's another person who doesn't know, she can't help!

Why did I have to keep feeling like this? Why did I feel like this? Why couldn't I breathe, I couldn't breathe.

"Hey, it's okay." Sarah tried to soothe me, ultimately deciding that it was safer not to touch me. "It's okay, take deep breaths."

I needed an escape. My thoughts and fears were rising to the brim of my head, and I was swimming against their current. I couldn't breathe.

Mom was right, it's my fault.

Everybody saw.

The pressure in my head was too much. Mounting. Mounting and mounting and mounting, I couldn't breathe. I needed a breath, I needed to calm down, I couldn't calm down.

My mind was pulled under the darkness as my body collapsed onto the floor.

The world spun even after I came to and realized that I was lying down on the vinyl mattress in the private room. Exhaustion drenched my limbs, and I remembered what had happened. But by now, I was pretty sick of it happening.

Julia came into the room with a bottle of water. "You were out for a few minutes," she said flatly, plopping onto the rolling stool in front of the sink. "Sarah told me your symptoms. Which sounded like a panic attack this time."

A panic *attack...?* There were two different kinds?

Julia stuck the water bottle beside me. "So drink this and then promise me that you'll consult your mother about this. You need help, Emmalynn. Treatment, counseling, anything. You need something to help bring you through the memory of last semester. Go to the guidance counselor or *something—*"

"It won't stop." I pressed the heels of my hands against my eyes, shutting out the fluorescent lights glaring down at me. "It won't leave me alone! You don't get it!"

Julia rested to silence next to me. I could almost hear the gears turning in her head, but she didn't find something to say until I opened and started drying my eyes.

"Here."

I turned my head and hesitantly took the room-temperature water bottle from her.

"Drink."

I opened the bottle and gulped down a third of it, debating if I really wanted to go back to the Dining Hall. I slowly sat up, bringing my feet over the side of the mattress.

"I'm scared," I said, unable to bring my voice any louder beyond a mutter. I twisted the locket around my neck. "I'm scared

I'll deal with this for the rest of my life."

Or until everyone found out. Until every last person on Earth knew the truth. But I couldn't tell Julia that, either.

She heavily exhaled. "I think I finally see the problem. You don't trust yourself."

I looked up at her. Where had she gotten that from?

"But you need to," she said, green eyes holding my gaze with a steadiness I needed. "You have to believe that you are not helpless, you're not defenseless, you're a strong and more-than-capable girl. Belief might be the only thing that'll help you. Once you believe that you can get through whatever life throws at you, even if you don't find the solution immediately, you'll stop inviting as much panic and fear and likely stop the attacks."

It had never sounded so within my reach, but at the same time... Julia didn't know. She wasn't in my shoes. Her family wasn't in danger. Her family's lives weren't on the line every single day.

Hang on, I realized. That was exactly why she was right: I had a family not just to worry about, but to protect. I *had* to be bigger whether I liked it or not. I did have a role to play in these attacks—but it also wasn't that easy to stop them.

What would she tell me if she knew what I was really going through?

I was looking for a way out, and I was desperate enough for one at this point. It was the only reason I had the courage to tell her next, "What I went through last year—gave me a glimpse into a Grand Hunter's life."

Julia's movements slowed until she ultimately froze. "You were... involved? With *Grand* Hunters?"

"There was a huge misunderstanding, and sometimes I felt

like—my life was on the line." I took another swig of water. Somehow the words were drying out my mouth. "But you're right. I got through it. I fought and I got through it."

Julia curtly exhaled. "This whole time, I figured you'd accidentally slipped the Hunter secret about Callistro to someone outside of the school. But you were involved in an actual hunt?"

"It was a pretty big case. I understood why they didn't want to take any chances."

She stood up, grabbed another water bottle from the cabinet above her, and sat back down. Crossing her legs, she opened the bottle and took a large gulp. "If I may ask," she said, swallowing, "who were the Hunters after you?"

I shrugged, lightly shaking my head. Even though it was only the two of us in that room, it felt like Alexa somehow had a microphone or camera looking in; revealing her and William's identities—or, more accurately, that I'd been *their* target—felt like moving a rook into the clear path of a queen.

"It doesn't matter." I took another sip from my bottle. "They're finally on a new hunt."

"Wow. I never would've guessed."

Time ticked by, and for once, I rested in every second. This was a rare moment in itself, where I truly felt safe, where I was convinced that nothing would happen as long as I stayed where I was. I prayed and hoped for the same for Dad and Aunt Becca. I just wanted to know their location, that was it. The journey couldn't scare me; as long as I knew where my family was, I'd walk the earth blindfolded to reach them.

"Hi, honey, what can I do for you?" Julia asked freshman Elena Aleger as she stopped in the doorway.

"I've had a headache all day and lunch just made me nauseous," she replied. "I was wondering if I could have a note to go to my room."

"Oh, sure, let's see what's going on." Julia set down her water bottle onto the counter. "Have a seat out there, I'll be with you in a sec."

Elena disappeared back into the main room, giving me the courage to stand from the mattress. "I think I'm okay now," I told Julia. "Thanks for the water. And the advice. I'll be thinking about it."

"Good." She trailed behind me as I moved to the door. "I'm glad you're feeling better."

Well enough, at least.

I walked into the main room of the nurse's office, finishing the last of the water and throwing the bottle into the recycling bin next to the door. Julia's words echoed as I took a deep breath in. Maybe it was just to relieve myself, but I felt my lips bend into a small smile. I had a direction to move in now. A stronger one, at least. Another attack wasn't impossible, but it felt further away— and I'd protect my family with every new weapon in my arsenal.

I was riding a growing wave of confidence until Mr. Dawson stopped me in the middle of the corridor. A frown pulled down his sharp features, setting me back on alert. What had happened in the few minutes I was out?

"Emma." He nodded once as we approached each other. "Are you okay?"

"Better, yeah. Thanks."

"Good." He exhaled, nodding toward the other end of the hall. "Come on. I need you and your mom in my office."

C H A P T E R

Twenty-Three

Momma came in seconds after me and Mr. Dawson and closed the door behind her, which didn't ease my concern. I knew this wasn't an academic or behavioral issue, but it was definitely a magic one. And our meetings regarding magic issues didn't exactly have the best track record.

"I told you," Mr. Dawson began, glimpsing me, "we just needed to wait until we *could* locate them."

He walked across the room and over to his desk, opening a drawer and then pulling out a maroon glove. I immediately recognized it: Aunt Becca's gloves during our girls' weekend to a resort in the mountains when I was seven. We'd only been able to take her because it promoted "private stays and activities" and she used her invisibility cloak any time she wasn't locked in the suite.

"This'll help us find Tristan and Becca," Mr. Dawson said. "One of them, at least."

A locator spell.

"When did you take that?" I asked, my heart soaring on grateful wings.

"When we went to the house," he said, coming back to us in the middle of the room. "They left those clothes lying around for a reason. They were trying to remind us to take something before we left."

Momma sighed of relief, a heavy hand on her chest. "I love you, Thomas, you're literally a life-saver."

"Go ahead, Emma," he said, handing me the glove. "You do the honor. Just like we taught you."

I pressed the glove between my hands and closed my eyes, feeling my magic accumulate. I pictured Aunt Becca in my head, used the glove to remember her, and took a deep breath in with my focus on my magic.

"*Invenio.*"

A burst of blue and gold flashed in my vision, fading to the image of my father sitting next to me—no, not me, Aunt Becca. This was her point of view. They both sat on a couch in a small, dimly lit house with brown walls and a darker floor. Dad nodded and rubbed Auntie's hand. She looked to her right, her vision passing a fireplace in front of her. A dark man sat on her other side, waiting for her to speak.

The internal compass of the locator spell whispered to me: south. Still in the state, in the county—in the Capperson Forest!

My eyes shot open. "They're not caught, they're in a house with someone, in the Capperson Forest!"

"What exactly did you see?" Mr. Dawson urged. "Was there any furniture or windows?"

"There was a window in the left corner of her eye. A fireplace was in front of them, and a man was sitting in a chair next to her. It looked like they'd just agreed on something."

Mr. Dawson's posture sagged as he sighed, passing a hand over his face. "I know where they are. They're desperate, they must not be able to use magic. That's why we haven't been able to communicate with them."

"Where are they?" Momma asked.

His deep-set gaze fell onto me. "They can't use magic to respond, but they can still hear us. Tell your dad that we'll be following them. We'll just be a couple hours behind."

"What?"

"Just do it," he told me, sounding like a... well, like a headmaster.

—Dad,— I said, —*we know where you are, we took Auntie's glove. We'll be following you, just a couple hours behind. Please, please stay safe. We'll do our best to stay in touch.*—

"Amy," Mr. Dawson said, turning to her, "I'll send you the address, and then I want you two to follow me there after school."

"After school?" I repeated disappointedly.

"As long as your dad knows that we'll be in the loop with them, we have to wait until then. We can't easily justify the three of us simultaneously disappearing in the middle of the day."

I couldn't help but sigh of relief, because for once, for *once* I was getting an answer when I asked for one—even if I had to wait a couple more hours.

I write that so easily now, but every minute of it dragged like a car stuck in mud. The second Momma pulled out of the school's parking lot, I realized that the day had moved at the exact same pace for her: she broke more traffic laws than I could count on my fingers to get to wherever we were headed, but I couldn't complain or worry. She once drove through the Sierra Nevada in a SWAT truck for a hunt she went on when she was only twenty. And right now, the safety of her husband and sister-in-law was riding on wherever we were going.

Deep down one of the roads in the Capperson Forest, Momma parked in front of a cottage. Talk about something straight out of *Snow White*: vines and leaves hung from the roof and roots grew from the ground, wrapping around the structure like a shawl. When Mr. Dawson told us that he knew where Dad and Aunt Becca were, he'd said they were "desperate"—and he'd clearly been disappointed. He didn't want to be here. Why? How bad could a person living *here* be?

"Well, this is it," Momma said, sharing my confusion with furrowed brows. She put the car in park just as Mr. Dawson climbed out of his car next to us.

"Let me handle introductions," he said after we closed our doors. "Trust me, it's better if you get a feel for his personality first."

Well, this is sounding more and more interesting...

With our steps crunching on the wet ground and chunks of dense snow, we walked up to the front door. Mr. Dawson took off one glove to knock curtly. When the door opened, his warning instantly made sense.

"Well, now," the man that had sat next to my aunt chirped playfully, "*this* is an even better surprise!"

Interesting light accent... What is that? English mixed with Scottish?

"Hello, Moren," Mr. Dawson replied, fully embodying his most professional headmaster demeanor. "May we come in?"

"Oh, please!" Moren grinned, his nearly black eyes twinkling as Mr. Dawson stepped over the threshold. "You're letting in the cold."

Momma gripped my shoulders as we entered the house. The furniture was at least three decades old, and the room's only light sources were two small windows against the front wall and a lit fireplace in front of the sofa. Vegetable stew and, strangely enough, wet clothes saturated the warm, damp air.

Interesting...

"So," Moren drawled, his index fingers dancing as he sang, "what can I do for *you?*"

For lack of better words, he was an eccentric man. But at least the accent, with his inflection, relieved some of the tension.

"You know why we're here," Mr. Dawson said, taking off his gloves and stuffing them into his coat pocket.

Moren kept his grin like the house would collapse if he let it fall. His curly hair that stopped just before his shoulders nearly matched his umber skin, just a shade lighter. What stuck out to me most, though, were his rather-sharp features—something that, I could just tell, resembled his wit.

His eyes fell onto me, sending a defensive chill down my back as his arms reached out. "Is this her?" he asked lightly, looking back at Mr. Dawson. "Is this the savior who's come to unite our worlds once and for all so that the folks of magic no longer have to live like *this?*"

How many people has Mr. Dawson told that to?

Momma squeezed my shoulders through my thick coat. "Yes," she said tightly, "this is my daughter, Emmalynn."

Moren giggled spiritedly, pulling his eyes up to her. "And you're the ravishing Hunter Tristan fell in love with the moment he laid his eyes on you! I know all about you, dearie. I remember everything he and Tommy told me. That's how they knew that they could trust you."

"Thomas, remind me why we're here," Momma said, impatience raising her voice.

"This is Moren," Mr. Dawson replied, putting his hands in the pockets of his blazer. That relaxed me somewhat; he didn't feel the need to be too defensive around this guy. "He's a nore. He can answer any question we have—at a price."

Oh. Wonderful.

"That's right," Moren sang in a higher-pitched whisper. He looked back at me, the chill boomeranging. "You know about nores, don't you, hero?"

"Thomas," Momma began warily, but Mr. Dawson held up a hand and nodded once in reply.

"Nores are completely neutral in any and all affairs," he said. "They don't care who comes to them asking for answers. They only care about the information they gain so they can transfer or sell it to the next person who's interested. That's the cycle. Nores stay out of personal things otherwise. And Moren's... a friend."

"All true, I concur." Moren smiled, striding to stand tall beside Mr. Dawson (even though he was a couple of inches shorter).

"Then why did Dad and Aunt Becca come here a *day* after almost getting caught?" I asked.

Mr. Dawson faced his "friend". "I'm guessing they didn't

want to lead anyone here."

"Unless that's your first question…"—Moren's eyes took turns with each of us—"who's first?"

"We only need to know one thing." Mr. Dawson walked to the small wooden table against the left wall and sat down. "I think you can guess."

"Of course." Moren took the seat across from him. "Let me see."

Mr. Dawson placed his hand into Moren's, who placed his other hand on top. Just as with Ingrid when she prophesied, amber flooded into his irises when he activated his power. He started with a smile. Then a grin. Then, he giggled all too helplessly.

"You've been on quite a few adventures since I last saw you," he said. "You've been naughty, too. Lying to an entire school seems risky, don't you think?"

"Please, we're pressed for time right now," Mr. Dawson said. "Where are Tristan and Rebecca on their way to right now?"

"To a mage," Moren replied flatly. "They're on their way to find a mage in Capperson named 'Steven', who can give them a powerful weapon to help them evade their enemies!"

I suppressed a breath of relief; my family was with Cara and Steven. They were safe.

I wonder if Moren's the nore they talked to, to get my info.

"Thank you." Mr. Dawson looked at me and Momma. "Amy, go take Emma—"

"No, no, no," Moren chimed. "You *all* owe me an answered question. You wanted to know where your loved ones ran off to, so you all pay the price. I'll answer one question of yours and your daughter's, Mrs. Atera—that means you get two for the price of one. Isn't that fair?"

Momma lightly exhaled, her grip on me loosening. "Yes, that's fair."

Moren giggled again. "Well, then, Tommy, this is my question to you: have your feelings for Alexa Delphine *completely* withered away?"

Wait. What?

Nores know present *external* circumstances; they have no idea what goes on in our heads. But what could Moren gain out of knowing the answer to *that?*

Disgust carved Mr. Dawson's face, almost like he was offended that Moren would waste his question on that. "Of course! My feelings for her died as soon as she became a Grand Hunter."

"No need to be so defensive." Moren smiled. "It was just a question. I was curious."

Mr. Dawson was the only one who knew what he really meant by that, because he paused before he stood up. As he walked back to me and Momma and swapped places with her, he blocked himself from being readable to me.

"I'm *very* excited about this one," Moren said. Momma pulled off her gloves, put them on the table, and then let Moren take her hands.

"Why would he ask you that?" I whispered to Mr. Dawson.

"He's a friend." His gaze stayed glued to Momma sitting in the chair. "Trust me, he was giving me an easy one."

I couldn't accept that so easily. Moren *definitely* knew something that Momma and I didn't.

"What would you like to know, dearie?"

Momma was quiet for longer than I'd expected her to be. I

imagined her temporarily tearing down the walls she'd built since August to let herself find the question she was always begging for the answer to. She couldn't get that answer anywhere else.

She looked up. "Who can we trust? Who can we *really* trust?"

"You?" Moren asked. His voice settled into a lower register that was almost his natural tone. "Only you know where your trust lies, dearie. And it's with the right people."

Momma nodded ever so slightly as if to tacitly thank him. In a blink, his impish, spirited grin returned. He shifted his weight, his next question ready to knock down the front door.

"Amy Atera," he announced like a game show host, "this is my question to you: are you willing to do absolutely, positively anything for your daughter?"

Momma's head jerked back. "Anything, I don't care what it is."

Moren's head danced as he sang, "That's what I like to hear."

She seemed a little too eager to take her hand out of his as she stood. Taking her gloves on the table and coming back to us, she touched my shoulder with consolidation and comfort in her fingers. Two things I couldn't get enough of right now, because it was time for my gloves to come off.

Moren's laugh intensified. "The grand finale!" he announced. "I'm *most* excited about you, dearie, come sit, come sit! I simply can't wait."

I took my time to obey, like the seat had spikes attached to it that would impale me once I sat down. That was definitely what the whole thing felt like, because as soon as I placed my hand into his, my entire life would be transferred into his mind. He'd know every lie I'd told; every sin I'd committed; and, most terrifying, every one of my weaknesses. There were things I hadn't even told my own family, but now a stranger specializing in the exchange of information would have it all.

"I don't think I've ever had a customer more nervous than you, savior." As if to persuade me to relax, his tone settled into its natural register, his accent lightening the words again. "All you have to do is ask me a question. Easy as magic."

I ripped off the Band-Aid and then my gloves, and then gave him my hand. Amber flowed like streams through his irises as he placed his other hand on top of mine. His jaw opened slightly, just enough to show his pleasant surprise.

"How interesting... My, dearie, haven't you been through a loop? Well, then, what would you like to know?" He went back to his quiet, higher-pitched whisper. "If I have to ask."

The question had been burning alive in my brain for years, and this was my shot at finally knowing the truth once and for all.

"I wanna know who knows the truth about me that I don't already know about. Do my friends secretly know? Does Alexa's pack know?"

"I can only answer one question, dearie."

I licked my lips. One of those could eliminate the most possibilities if I formed my question right.

One question would eliminate over two hundred possibilities.

"Who in the Callistro Academy knows the truth about me that I don't already know about?"

Moren's eyes narrowed in satisfaction, his thin lips stretching into a smile. "There's only one, savior, and don't blame yourself for never realizing it sooner: Julia plays her part very well."

Twenty-Four

I sprang up from the chair like a jack-in-the-box, adrenaline searing my veins. Julia? Julia couldn't know—Julia didn't know! How?

In my peripheral, the same fear had settled into my mother and godfather. Since October, we'd been living with someone who knew the truth, the whole truth, and hadn't said a single thing about it! Why had she been so friendly? Why had she insisted on taking care of me—*helping* me?

"How does she know about me?" I exclaimed.

"Ah, ah, ah!" Moren shook his index finger with another grin. "That's two questions!"

"I'll answer another question, just tell me, please!"

He smiled down at the table and then looked back up at me

with twinkling eyes. "Somebody told her," he chimed slowly. "And that somebody... is you."

She couldn't... It wasn't possible... How could *I* have told her? And when?!

"You told her?" Momma hissed with eyes bulging out of her head. "You *told* her the truth?"

"No!" I cried, glancing back and forth between her and Mr. Dawson. It was getting too hot to keep my coat on. "I never—I didn't! I never told her anything!"

"Well, now I need to find a new nurse." Mr. Dawson sighed as he turned away, rubbing his face with both hands.

I dared to look at Momma. She furiously twisted her wedding band on her left ring ringer, taking deep breath after deep breath. Someone was lying. Someone had to be lying, but it couldn't be Moren, and it wasn't any of us as far as we knew.

"My turn!" Moren said like a child, unfazed. If I'm being honest, it angered me to a fault. "Are you ready, savior?"

I looked back at him. In a way, I actually was; nothing could be worse than finding out that one of my friends was potentially an undercover agent. I couldn't have cared less about the next question Moren wanted to ask.

I rested my hand back in his, my focus gone with the rest of my thoughts.

"A simple yes-or-no, dearie: have you ever wondered why sorcerers are the only class of magic without a distinct ability?"

In my peripheral vision, Momma straightened, but Mr. Dawson held up his hand in front of her. My mind spun with confusion, because what? Why that question from Moren, and why that reaction from Mom and Mr. Dawson?

"Um..." I said, like the word would break the table in front of me, "yeah. But—"

"Then that's all I'd like to know," Moren said, pulling his hands away and his eyes fading to black.

Why would he ask that? What did he gain from knowing what I wondered about magic, how was that an answer for him?

Unless... it wasn't the answer to the *question* that he was looking for. It was the answer he would get from someone's *reaction* to it. Someone in that room would answer the most dangerous type of question of all: unspoken.

Mom. Why *had* she reacted that way, like she was defensive about it?

Moren tapped my hand, and I looked back at him. "Next one," he said.

As I gave him my hands again, my phone buzzed in my coat pocket. I knew better than to reach for it—and yet that split-second-long glance at my pocket seemed to alter Moren's demeanor as he straightened in his seat, his hold on me loosening.

"Mrs. Atera and Mr. Dawson," he said, turning to them, "would you mind temporarily turning to your own conversation?"

"Where was this confidentiality when you asked Thomas about his feelings for his ex-girlfriend?" Momma arched a brow, her narrow features challenging him.

"Some answers are reserved only for the ears of fate."

Mr. Dawson put a hand on Momma's shoulders, silencing her. Maybe him being a druid guiding me with my own dance with destiny was the only validation she needed, because he understood. She turned with him and walked to the other side of the room.

Moren returned to me. "Go ahead," he whispered, glimpsing my coat pocket.

I tentatively drew out my phone and then tapped the screen. A new message sat in a notification—a message that belonged to a number and not a name.

No, not again. Not again, not again.

#: Hello. I know you don't know me, this is
probably really...

Moren leaned in, bright amber streaming through his irises. "Are you afraid of the message you see?"

Why he wanted to know that, I didn't know, but I knew the answer even without the "truth spell".

"Yes," I whispered, eyes trained on the number as if it'd switch to a name.

"Don't be."

I met Moren's stare just as the amber faded. His hands changed their purpose as they rested on the bottom and top of mine.

"I know that your road has narrowed and declined in safety," he said. "But despite Julia's secret, she provided you the tools you need to walk the next part of it. I'm only here now to assure you: you can be open to this ally."

"*Ally*"?

"When do I read it?"

"When you're alone," he told me gravely, like he needed me to hear the weight in his words. "Give this conversation the time it deserves."

I looked at Momma and Mr. Dawson at the wrong time, because they both met my glimpse then. I turned back to Moren. "How do I know you're telling the truth?" I asked, realizing that he'd spoken outside of the amber.

"For the same reason you could trust Caralyn's and Samuel's grandchildren."

I felt a smile surface out of relief and accomplishment. "So I *can* trust them."

Moren briefly opened his mouth before realizing his carelessness—how I'd gotten an answer without needing to ask for it.

A satisfied smile rested on his lips. "Well played, savior."

As much as Momma wanted to demand the conversation out of me after we left, she had to go after Dad and Aunt Becca while Mr. Dawson drove me home. Meanwhile, my roommates were blowing up my phone with texts and calls asking where I'd "run off to this time". Excuses were running thin, so I prayed that Momma would be back by that night for "My mom went to check on my family" to seem true.

But there was one thing I needed to address before I could make it back to Sarah and Breanne, and I had to do it where nobody could interrupt. Otherwise known as underground.

I closed the tree stump above me and leaned against the freezing cobblestone wall of the underground passageway, bracing myself with my breath in. The freedom of solitude surrounded me with a sense of safety. Taking off one glove, I tapped my phone screen and clicked the notification.

#: Hello. I know you don't know me, this is
probably really creepy and I'm sorry for con-
tacting you like this, but I really think we need
to meet. It's about Adara.

Panic was ready to pounce until Moren's words revived in my memory: an ally. I prayed that he'd been telling the truth, after all.

E: I need to know a LOT more about you before
we meet, someone else's name won't get you
anywhere

#: You're right. My name is Morgana. I'm from
Canada but I'm in Charlotte right now visiting
family. Everything else is not safe to text about.
I *believe* you're in Capperson? I'll meet you
there, anywhere you're comfortable with so I
can explain. It won't make sense here and it's
safer to tell you in person.

Talking about Adara was dangerous enough, but I ques-tioned if Morgana was a magician, too, for confidentiality over the phone to be that important. After all, not even Cara had risked revealing my identity over text.

As much as caution warned me otherwise... I had to throw my trust in Moren's promise. Meaning I had to believe that meet-ing this person was my best option.

E: Joe's House in the back of Publisher's Ink,
Sunday at 1:00?

#: I can do that. I will see you then.

Finally, a new message *with* a name showed up before I could shut off the screen:

C: Hi, honey. Did you know that your family
just came to visit us?

E: Yeah, I'm just happy that they're safe for
now

Was Moren the nore you guys went to?

C: When we first found you, yep. He's charming.

Ironically, when you managed to grab his *serious* side, he was.

C: Steven almost has everything figured out on
our end, but he's not quite there yet. Would
you like to meet tomorrow anyway and discuss
a plan?

I sighed in exhaustion, briefly resting my head on the cobble-stone behind me for a break.

E: There's a lot going on right now, I hate to
keep pushing it back, but... it's too much

C: I know, honey. No problem. We'll talk when

Steven's done and you're ready.

Well, that was some semblance of relief, at least.

That, and the fact that Momma did come back that night with the news that Dad and Auntie were safe—but Alexa and William's pack were using a prototype of a new magic sensor that detected whenever and wherever magic was used (which actually made me worry for Moren that night). And that included telepathy, which was a deadly breakthrough in the Hunter technology industry. Telepathy is such a subtle form of magic that it's usually undetectable. At least, it always had been until now. Dad and Aunt Becca had been stripped of their magic privileges.

But the reason they'd gone to Steven was so that he could create an appearance-altering spell for them, so they were at least safe from public eye. Everywhere in Capperson was compromised for them for now, so one of Auntie's friends in Marion was kind enough to take them in until things died down.

Sunday morning after breakfast, on my way to lessons with Momma and Mr. Dawson, I went over how I'd stay safe when meeting with Morgana later and which choke I should use if things came down to it. It was a good thing I had self-defense and magic lessons first—a warmup. And I had the perfect motivation to start lessons with as I walked down the large hall that led to the gym: Dad and Aunt Becca. They'd sacrificed themselves as a reminder that Alexa could pop up at *any* moment without warning, and I wouldn't let that be in vain.

That's the ironic thing about mentally preparing yourself for self-defense and offensive lessons: when you get so caught up in your head that you end up switching off your awareness to your surroundings. Two ex-Master Hunters were just down the hall while a gloved hand clamped over my mouth and dragged me into the secret passageway. Momma and Mr. Dawson were so close, but not even my instincts were close enough to help me fight back as I slipped into sleep.

C H A P T E R

Twenty-Five

I woke up in the corner of a small, dimly lit room, my ankles tied together and wrists bound behind me. It was nothing new, I'm practically a professional hostage at this point, so I forced myself to focus on strategizing an escape—

Wait. I'd been here before. Concrete walls, white-painted brick walls that scraped my cold fingers... I'd *been* here before—

An all-black figure faded into view as they threw off their hood. I gasped, barely suppressing a scream in time. Dressed in a black bodysuit with matching gloves, boots, and what had to be an invisibility cloak, my kidnapper stood in the middle of the cold room. The hanging light hung like a noose above their head, as still as a picture. The person—Hunter, I decided to call them— stepped up to me.

The black bodysuit. So they are the one who followed me and Jak in the passageways that day.

Suffocating panic flared in my chest. But for the first time since last month, my thoughts didn't build the fire; they were trying to extinguish it.

Julia's right. I'm no one to act helpless, I can't let them make me feel anything less than what I am!

Finally, my fear no longer overrode my anger.

"Okay, you have magic," I began. If they'd knocked me out in the hall without even touching me, I knew that for a fact. "And you clearly know who I am, so please, just tell me who you are! Or why you're doing this, or how you even know me!"

Hunter laughed in a whisper, kneeling down to me. Grabbing my chin, they viewed both sides of my face. I was still just afraid enough to not dare shake away. They brushed a brown piece of hair out of my face, slightly lifted my head up, and then stood. Like they were appraising me.

"Who are you?" I demanded again. "Where are we?!"

I was still trying to convince myself otherwise that I wasn't afraid or as vulnerable as I really was. Unfortunately, if Hunter was this good, they knew that even more than I did. I tried turning that fear, that frustration, into anger, and I had to keep failing until I got it right.

Hunter reached into their side pocket and pulled out a folded-up paper. One by one, they unfolded each square before showing me: a photo of a man I'd never seen before. With blunt, rugged features and dark-oak stubble across his oval chin, his sad eyes were as green as pears.

Two red letters sat in the bottom-right corner: "M.G."

"Who's that?" I asked.

Hunter held the picture by its sides, kneeling down to me again.

"Remember," they whispered.

I stared as hard as I could through their fabric mask, almost trying to burn a hole through it. Wait. This person had magic. Which meant I had an advantage that I didn't have with every other enemy.

I glanced down at the ropes that bound my ankles together, imagined the ties around my wrists, and then ignited the word in my head: *Exsolvo.*

With Hunter trying to figure out what I'd just cast, I threw my right fist at their cheek and then push-kicked their chest. Telekinesis threw them across the room. They rolled backwards on their shoulder and ended in a runner's starting position, one hand on the ground.

They're good. They know what to do. But so did I.

"We're equal," I said, standing in the basic position Momma had taught us last semester. "Tell me who you are."

Hunter snickered, standing. My heart started beating a hole into my chest. I told myself again that fear would not overcome rage this time. I couldn't be afraid, I wouldn't let my feelings dictate my victory.

Amber peeked through Hunter's mask as their arm shot forward. Before I could blink, my feet were no longer on the ground.

No, we were *far* from equal—not only was my telekinesis not strong enough to lift a person yet, but the conflict of my emotions was too transparent: they already had the mental victory. I'd given them the—

Hunter's other arm extended. Their hand slowly began to close into a fist—closing my throat with it.

Two spells at the same time. At the *same time!*

Literally speechless, the thought blew open the front doors of my head: *I'm gonna die.*

I was going to die. Before I could save my family. Before I could say goodbye to my friends or Jak, before I could help the millions—maybe even billions!—of magicians live a life absent of fear and premature death, I couldn't die!

"P—pl—*please!*" I choked out.

Hunter walked toward me, moving me to the wall until my back was against it. They slowly placed me back down, releasing my throat and letting me breathe. Kneeling in front of me again, they pressed their index finger against the center of my chest, branding the image of their covered head into my mind.

With another flash of amber, I fell back asleep.

I found myself on my bed when I woke up. My memory flooded into my mind, and I shot up, instinctively asking myself where Sarah and Breanne were: Breanne was studying in the rec room and Sarah was out in the garden with some classmates. I was safe to panic alone.

Did Hunter want to *kill* me? They definitely knew who I was, but they'd nearly choked me to death! Who were they? Someone I didn't know?

Or were they someone I just didn't know was my enemy?

Like Julia.

I swung my legs over my bed, swallowing hard. The trip to Moren's a couple of days ago felt like a dream now. It didn't make sense: why would an enemy try so hard to help me overcome my greatest obstacle?

Mr. Dawson is in range for telekinesis. If anything goes wrong when I confront her, I can tell him—

Mr. Dawson. Lessons!

I darted out of my dorm and ran to the elevator for the fastest way down. —*Mr. Dawson?—*

—*Emma, thank God! We've been looking all over for you, we were ready to use a locator spell! I've been telepathically calling you for ten minutes, where are you?—*

—*I'm visiting Julia to see if I can get anything out of her. If I stop responding again, it'll probably be because she actually is an enemy and kidnapped me.—* The steel doors slid open, and I scurried down the corridor on my left. —*Give me a few minutes.—*

—*No.—*

I stopped in my tracks on the carpet runner. No?

—*Despite what Moren said, we don't want to confirm anything for her. We need to let loose ends fly until we have more information.—*

I tightened my jaw with reluctant agreement. In other words, let sleeping dogs lie. I couldn't rock the boat, which meant I was straight on my way to magic lessons with the memory of Hunter throbbing in my mind.

All they'd done was show me a photo... If anything, it had almost served as a warning, hadn't it? Why would Hunter show me a photo of someone and tell me to remember them unless it was to let me know to watch out for them?

What if Julia was Hunter but she couldn't reveal herself to

me because she'd expose herself as a magician?

If Cara and Steven turned out to be allies, and possibly even Morgana... I wasn't dumb enough to assume, but I did know that there was just a small possibility that Hunter wasn't an enemy. They were anonymous, but they had magic, and they were warning me about something. I needed to know more, at least wait until I knew what they wanted—what their goal was—but at least I had more confidence to stay in this fight. I didn't have to drag my family into it yet.

I repeated that to myself the entire way to the gym.

C H A P T E R

Twenty-Six

One girl sat alone at a small, round table in the middle of Joe's House, facing the ordering counter. A jacket covered her hunched-over body, her white floral skirt narrowly avoiding the ground.

Just as she had told me. This was her.

"So what family," I began, walking by her and sitting myself down across from her, "are you visiting in Charlotte?"

Her maroon-brown eyes looked up at me in fearful surprise at first, but then relaxed. Two wavy bangs from her bun framed her oval face. A long, flat nose elongated her jaw, and her full lips stayed slightly parted as she stared back at me.

"Emmalynn," her soft voice said, almost too quietly for me to hear, as she pushed back one of her black bangs.

She has an accent—but not Canadian. Where was she originally from?

"Morgana."

She glimpsed the table as if the name ashamed her. Every time she spoke, her eyes took quick turns between me and the surface. "Um, I'm visiting my *tante* and *paman*—aunt and uncle, I mean."

"What language is that?"

"Indonesian," she replied, trying to raise her voice from its natural whisper-like quality. "My family is originally from there... but we moved to Ontario a few years ago. My family's... *gifts* are illegal in Indonesia."

Just like here.

"How did you survive that move?" I asked, temporarily forgetting why we were here. Magicians are killed trying to make the move to a legal country just as often as they are in a hunt, at least in the United States. How had Morgana's family done it, let alone a move *that* big?

If it was possible, the girl in front of me shrank a little more, her voice falling again. "We gave it up."

What? Gave up their magic?

"In Indonesia, you can do that—in exchange for your life. But we didn't... want to stay there after that. We had a 'family friend' in Ontario. So we moved."

I swallowed hard. Something about the softness in her eyes made it impossible to not believe her, and I wasn't sure how to feel about that.

"But that is..." she said next, keeping her hands in her lap, "partly why I'm here."

Right. That.

Despite the girl's transparent timidity, I didn't know if I wanted to restrain my caution; she knew that I was associated with Adara. Depending on how she'd gotten that information, she was either a valuable ally or a formidable enemy. And first impressions are usually more deceptive than a Venus fly trap to an insect.

Morgana swallowed, laying both of her palms on the table. "I should start from the beginning."

—*I'm a druid,*— she said. I almost jumped at the voice, which was even softer in my head.

My lips parted in confusion and caution. —*I thought you said you gave up your magic.*—

She leaned in, never keeping her eyes with me for longer than two seconds. "I did. But I need to start from the beginning. A couple of months ago, you started... showing up in my visions. Every time I dreamed about you, we were always—meeting up and talking. Sometimes you came in your uniform—*dari Akademi Callistro*. That's how I knew what town you lived in. But out of all my visions, two of them recently told me... that you weren't just any new friend."

—*They were of the same thing: us fighting in the war of mortal and magic. Doing our part in it. Where you were referred to as 'Adara', and me as 'Morgana'.*—

I cleared my throat to fill the silence. I wouldn't speak unless I had everything I needed.

"Then I..." Morgana said, "I knew that our paths were meant to cross. It was my last vision that made me finally reach out to you—I'll get to that in a bit."

"Hold on," I told her, licking my lips as I gathered my next

words. I leaned in to keep them between us, eyeing a tall gentle-
man as he walked by our table and into the bookstore. "How do
you know my real name, then? Who told you about Adara?"

"Because 'Morgana' isn't my real name, either," she whispered. "It's 'Annisa'."

—*My parents always told me,*— she began in my head, —*how 'Morgana' is just the name I'm*—

—*known by in the magic world,*— I said, in a daze so deep that
I was sure I was hallucinating. I had to be hallucinating. Or I was
having the most *insane* case of déjà vu ever!

"Our destinies," Annisa added, seeming to find comfort in
my knowledge, "are intertwined. I know that."

It wasn't... Could she really be telling me that...?

I was almost too scared to ask. —*So you're destined to become...*—

—*According to my parents, the most powerful druid to ever live.*—

"*But in the very end, you will be recorded as the most powerful sorcerer to ever live.*"

The words felt ancient in my memory as I recalled the day
Mr. Dawson told me that he was a druid. Only then did I realize
a crucial detail: he'd never said "magician". He'd said "sorcerer".

Commotion in Joe's House seemed to swell as my head ran
just as busily. A barista called out two ready orders; a group of kids
under the supervision of two teenage girls darted to the ordering
counter, laughing; and conversation grew louder because of it.

"Are you the next hundredth?" I finally asked. "Of your family's generation?"

Annisa's full lips parted as though I'd literally pulled the
words straight out of her mouth. "Yes. Have... have you been told
something similar?"

I discreetly bit my lip, crossing my arms. I didn't want to admit my side of the story yet; I didn't want to be transparent with a total stranger, not like I'd been with Jak.

"I've been told that I'll be feared, hunted, and betrayed," I said. "With all due respect, you haven't given me a reason to believe you. I don't even know how you got my number or my real name, and you still haven't told me how you have—*that thing* after giving it up."

Her lips tightened in what her worried narrowed eyes exposed as fear. "You have to hear me out completely. I can even show you after, just... not here."

I doubted that I'd be leaving Publisher's Ink by her side, but there was no harm in letting her think otherwise.

"I love history," she began. "I've always had a passion for reading the stories of the past and unburying what makes us who we are, what—" She shook her head, shooing away the words. "Sorry. Last year, before my sixteenth birthday... I found an old sketchbook from a cousin in the 1940s. I opened it, and his first sketch was of—this beautiful rose tree in his backyard, with the original photo attached."

What does this have to do with anything?

"I found the date behind the photo: April 3, 1942. I stared at the picture and started wondering about what it must have been like to live in those days... I started imagining myself in that timeline. I imagined that date and just let it... sweep my imagination."

Hang on. She couldn't be going where I thought she was. This was starting to sound frighteningly familiar to what I'd explained to my family when Dad and Mr. Dawson had come home last year, about using my will to cast my magic instead of a spell. Except, what Annisa was implying was literally impossible.

"Suddenly," she said, "I was—there. In the garden where my cousin had sketched the rose tree. In 1942."

Time travel: one of the few things that not even magic can do. And yet here Annisa was, trying to convince me that she'd managed to go back DECADES in time by, what, staring at a photo?

"I know," she quickly said, "but please, I promise, you're not wasting your time."

I managed to catch myself before I could start fiddling with my locket. I didn't want her to know anything about me yet, not even my habits.

"To make a long story short, once I realized that I was really in 1942, I figured that, if a date and imagining a location was what brought me back to the past, maybe… that's what I needed to go to the future.

"I always wear my watch,"—she held up her wrist for me to see the white digital watch around it—"but that day, I was extra grateful that I did. All I had to do was concentrate on the date on my watch and picture myself in our attic, and after a few tries—I landed back there, with the sketchbook in my lap."

This girl was claiming that her will alone had cast her magic to *time travel*. She couldn't have been telling the truth—and yet she was telling me a story that I'd already told to my own family.

"That day," Annisa said next, "I got my magic back. But it was only me. I don't know why and I feel… guilty about it. Because of my family. But since then, I've found out that I can use any picture to time travel. I can also travel with just a date, but I will… stay in place, I won't go anywhere." She tilted her head. "Does that make sense?"

That last part did, at least. "I don't know how, but yeah."

"Okay. And I can only travel to the past, not the future."

"So then going off of your visions," I said, leaning forward in my seat, "how did you get my real name and number?"

"I time traveled to your school using a photo I found online so I could—go through the student records. The realities I travel to exist... like a layer. My 'layer' never intersects with the real one, so I can explore without changing anything. So after I got your full name—I asked for your number from a friend. Who's a nore."

It made sense. I kind of hated to admit it, but it all made sense.

"That's all I have for now," Annisa said timidly, shrinking again. "Unless you want me to show you... my ability."

I did. Her ability could offer me every answer I'd been wanting since Alexa Delphine had walked into my life! But I didn't want Annisa thinking that that was the only reason I was offering my friendship. Actually, I had better questions.

—*Time travel is supposed to be impossible. So can other druids do it, too?*—

—*My parents can't. Not unless I take them with me. I don't know if I'm the only one who has an impossible ability... Maybe you have one, too, but you haven't tried it.*—

I mean, I hadn't. This was supposed to be impossible!

I shook my head. —*You said one of your dreams involved us... fulfilling our destiny.*—

She nodded. "Playing our part, I mean. I can't recall any explicit detail. Everything else is... more of a feeling. I can't describe it, I'm sorry."

I bit my lip as if to hold on to the last bit of sanity I had. I didn't trust her enough to let her in, but I trusted her to the point where I didn't want to tell my parents about her in case they prohibited us from meeting again—and me from finding out more.

Unless...

—*Can I put you under a truth spell?*— I asked.

—*If you can do it with your eyes closed.*—

Suddenly, I was that much more grateful for my lessons with Mr. Dawson as I closed my eyes. *Veritatem dicere.*

"You're telling the truth?" I asked. "Everything you just said is true, and you're not my enemy?"

"Yes, every word is true, I mean it. I promise."

Good. Then I could tell my family about her as soon as we were all together again; this would take a lot more explaining than the typical "I met a new friend" conversation, and I wanted us to think it through collectively. Everyone's minds mattered for this.

Whenever we will *be together again,* I couldn't help but think. From that perspective, this somehow seemed... *low* on the priorities list.

"Do you have—any other questions?" Annisa asked.

They all clouded in my head. There was too much to discuss and not enough time to discuss it.

"You won't be mad if I tell you that it's gonna take a bit of time before I can completely trust you, right? Truth spell or not?"

"*Tidak,*" Annisa said, shaking her head. "No. I understand."

I stood from my seat, but I didn't feel ready to leave. If I was already here with her, she was telling the truth, and we were going to become friends, why not... well, try to befriend her?

"Do you wanna—shop around?"

She took the long-strapped handbag in her lap and stood with me, a soft smile reaching her eyes. "Sure. Do you like books, too?"

I chuckled. "If I had more time to read, I'd have a lot more books."

"They're why I have hope for the world." She slung her bag over her shoulder. "If we can create better worlds on paper, we can do the same for the real one."

Twenty-Seven

Unfortunately, Opal Dubois's big news story on Monday at lunch was that the school was banning phones next year because they were a "security threat". For now, we had our own signal blockers and VPNs to hold us over until June, but my phone was literally a survival tool by that point—not to sound like every other teenager in America.

I was finally able to visit Cara and Steven that afternoon to discuss an Alexa plan after telling Momma that they'd invited me over for cinnamon rolls—which was true (and she only trusted them enough to have me over because they'd helped Dad and Auntie). I left out the whole "plan" part because I knew Momma would have one or a dozen rebuttals about my involvement; she'd want to take care of it with Mr. Dawson. Depending on what Cara and Steven wanted to do, though, I'd just be scoping out our options today.

Bigger than my childhood home, Cara and Steven's house was built next to its own small lake in the Capperson Forest. I was pretty jealous of that, considering that, with the arrival of March, the ice had melted and left behind a private swimming pool glittering in the sun. Then Cara told me that I was welcome over anytime to swim once it got hot enough.

I followed her onto the porch, and she opened the front door for me. Past the sleek, white entry foyer and passing a lounge room on the left, we walked straight down to the dining area and the large kitchen (where Steven was happily over-icing cinnamon rolls). The living room sat on the other side, and two doors straight ahead opened into the backyard. Full-length windows showcased a well-trimmed flower garden and the forest scenery beyond it.

Wow. I was all the more jealous that I hadn't grown up here.

"I told you not too much icing!" Cara scolded Steven in her traditionally gentle voice, setting the car keys down onto the granite-top island. "I can never taste the cinnamon when I let you ice them."

"Um, please tell her she's wrong, Emmalynn," Steven said, plopping another dollop onto the dripping cinnamon roll in his hand, "and that icing is the best part."

I shrugged at Cara, smiling. "It is."

She rolled her eyes and draped her coat over the shoulders of one of the barstools. "Come on, time to get to work."

Steven placed six cinnamon rolls onto a china plate and followed us into the living room, setting the plate down onto the coffee table. As he sat across from me and Cara on the white couch and leaned forward, he reminded me of Mr. Dawson a bit—especially with the black Elton John T-shirt that was almost too small for his upper body.

"So the spell," he began, resting his elbows on his knees. "I think I was, um, able to create what you wanted. But like I warned you, it's a *really* difficult spell. Even I had trouble successfully casting it."

"That's okay." I exhaled with relief. "Thanks, it's gonna be really helpful."

"Yep, and not just to you," he warned, his dark eyes growing heavier on me. "Too many bad people—and, you know, government authority figures—could do a lot with this. So once you're done with it, tell me ASAP so I can destroy it."

"I will."

"You'll use the words '*ratione locate*'. You can either look at a picture of someone or visualize them in your head, cast it with that clear image, and the rest works just like a regular locator spell."

I weighed the words in my head a few times before visualizing Alexa: her emerald eyes, her defined jaw, and her shoulder-length red hair.

Ratione locate.

I wasn't that disappointed when it didn't work—especially because I was being watched.

"Okay," I said, sitting up a little straighter. "I'll practice it as much as I can."

"Yeah, just, um, don't let it fall into the wrong hands."

He tossed a glance to Cara, who'd just polished off the last bite of her cinnamon roll.

"We think we have the start of a good plan," she said, taking a napkin from the pile neatly stacked next to the plate. After wiping her hands clean, she dabbed the corners of her mouth. "Do you know how to temporarily suspend someone's magic?"

"That's possible?"

"Yep. With an entrapment cloak." A mischievous grin stretched her thin lips, reaching her refined gray eyes. "They completely nullify someone's magic and freeze them in place. They're a lot harder to enchant, but Steven's an expert in that area. So he could enchant one—and then we could use it on Alexa."

"How?"

"We need to somehow lure her to the Callistro Forest," Steven answered, pressing the tips of his dark fingers together, "or have her follow you to a remote location. I'll jump her, Cara will put the cloak on her, and she won't be able to move or use her magic. Then we'll, um, try to reason with her, and if that doesn't work... um..."

Exactly. There was no end to that sentence, no *moral* end, at least. No end that I could ever carry out with my own hands.

"We'll get there when we get there," Cara told me gently, placing a comforting, slender hand on my back. "This is just what we think our best option is right now."

"Okay." I nodded, staring at the dripping cinnamon rolls on the plate in front of me. My next words turned my stomach. "Let's... try that."

Steven was quick to break the cautious silence that followed. "We have a plan, then."

A wave of relief flooded my chest; I couldn't remember the

last time I'd heard those words with such solid truth behind them. After all, I couldn't carry out my plan of baiting Alexa with Adara if Alexa wasn't around. But I had a couple of ways of luring her out.

"So," Steven said, drawing to a close, "kick back, relax, and have a cinnamon roll."

I happily obeyed and picked up a napkin from the pile. Placing a roll on top of it and taking a bite, I blinked with surprise. I'd agreed with Steven in the kitchen, but Cara was right: there *is* such thing as too much icing on a cinnamon roll.

A flash burst through the darkness. Bright lights were installed above me. Round tables and booths were scattered across the large space, a tile floor under me. The mall food court.

A hand grabbed my arm, stopping me from marching to the group of teenage boys approaching Ava Baleen in the mall's main aisle. "No, wait," a familiar voice told me.

I turned to face who'd grabbed me: Jak.

Another flash burst in my vision.

Dim yellow lights lit the alleyway against the night sky. Ava trembled behind me. A boy kept his arms around her, trapping her. Two more stood in front of me. We'd been cornered.

I glared at the brunet in front of me. "—made it my—"

A faster flash. Ava stood behind me. The boy who'd kept her captive was slumped against the wall.

My elbow burned. I didn't know why. Ava faced the wall behind us. I glanced between the two boys standing in front of me.

Forget it.

Flash.

I dragged Ava down the alleyway. She writhed in my grip like her life was on the line. *"You're one of them—!"*

Flash.

Ava was no longer with me as I sprinted around the corner. I slammed into a towering figure, knocking me to the ground.

My body jolted awake. I shot up in bed, heat radiating off me. My hand darted to my right elbow, where it had burned in the dream: smooth, uninjured. Deep, ragged breaths racked my chest as I dropped my hands into my lap.

This wasn't déjà vu I was feeling—I recognized that dream. That was the dream I'd *been* having lately. It finally had somewhat of a plot. I could remember it clearly. And that meant facing the fact I was all too afraid and in denial of: I recognized how that dream had *felt*, too. Just like the vision Mr. Dawson had shared with me last year about William interrogating me.

But Mr. Dawson hadn't gotten his druid visions back yet—at least, not that I knew of. He would've told me if he had, wouldn't he? To share important things with me? To warn me of the horrors of the future like the one I'd just witnessed?

Was... Annisa sharing her dreams with me? Did sharing visions have a range limit like telepathy did?

I had to be brave: I called out to Mr. Dawson until his groggy response finally filled my head.

—What're you doing up at this hour?—

—Did you get your visions back yet?—

The longer he stayed silent, the louder my heart thrummed. I could almost hear his sigh before he said, *—Seriously? That's what* *you woke me up for?—*

I guess my shame was loud in my silence, because he eventually added, —*No. They're still gone. Since last year.*—

Okay. So this had been a *really* bad idea.

—*I'm sorry.*— It was the only thing I felt safe to say. —*Good night.*—

Despite the fact that she was an hour away in Charlotte, out of range for telepathy, I tried my next option: —*Annisa?*—

Silence.

—*Annisa. Are you awake?*—

After one more attempt, I took my phone off the nightstand: no new messages. She would've woken up with the same dream and texted me about it if that had been her vision, wouldn't she?

But if that dream had really been a vision, and that vision wasn't either Mr. Dawson's or Annisa's—and if it had been *repeating* for the past few weeks...

No. It's literally impossible. It couldn't have been *my* vision. I wasn't a druid! Magicians only inherit one class from their parents, and a sorceress had been my only option to inherit!

Who was I supposed to ask about this? What if nobody believed me and it actually came to pass? What if everyone believed me but it never came to pass? How would my mom or Mr. Dawson be able to stop it from happening, let alone without arousing suspicion as to how they knew it would happen? I couldn't tell Jak because—well, *duh*, and I couldn't tell Ava for the same reason! And I couldn't ask Ingrid if it would happen because I'd lose my magic again—but how else was I supposed to know if this was a dream or a vision?!

Wait. Hadn't this happened before?

I'd somewhat dreamed of the moment Dad, Mr. Dawson, and I confronted Alexa in the basement of the beach house—the same moment I'd gotten my magic back—but I wasn't sure if that counted. Ingrid had said so herself, I couldn't dream of the future. It wasn't even *magically* possible.

The question continued to press heavily against my mind: did I have the ability to dream of the possible future or not?

C H A P T E R

Twenty-Eight

When Momma got a call from the governor of Vermont two years after graduating high school, at first it was a thank-you for saving his daughter from an undercover warlock seeking vengeance for her family. But the governor's offer for Momma to join the Vermont State Hunter Agency was a complete surprise.

In the same way, when I got a text from Nolan asking me to meet him in the square Friday night, I thought it was going to be like any other time we'd hung out—and it was. At first.

The walk there, I called Annisa and got to practice my oral history report about the American secrets of World War Two. (After six and a half hours of research in the library, I was finally able to prove that a senior Callistro Girl *was* partly behind developing the enigma that the British used to decode German secret messages. She tested it out using her own code that spelled out the name of the runaway magician she was hunting.) After that, I started thinking about what Nolan could want to do in town tonight. Usually we walked around, got something to eat, or saw a movie, but this time I started wondering about the new book café that had opened down the street as I approached the fountain.

"Hey!" I said, glancing between Nolan and his friend Ryan in their baseball uniforms as they met me. A duffel bag hung over Nolan's shoulder. "How was practice?"

"Good!" he said. "Except for how they're making us practice when it's still fifty degrees outside."

"Yeah, sucks that the season started earlier this year." Ryan ran a hand through his messy black hair, smirking at me. "Have fun."

What was that supposed to mean?

He walked past us, but Nolan waited until he climbed into his sedan parked across the street before facing me again.

"How've you been?" he asked, taking off his baseball cap. (His helmet—or, I guess, hat—hair is pretty hot, if I'm being honest.)

"Good, you?"

"Great." He sheepishly smiled, casting his green eyes down. Weird—he never struggled with eye contact. That was one of the things I admired about him. "Actually, um..."

This was officially the most awkward conversation we'd ever had.

I couldn't believe it when red flooded his pale cheeks. This was the shyest I'd ever seen him! What if Sarah was right? She'd predicted that the next time he saw me, he was going to ask—

"Um, Em, there's something I've been thinking about for a while. You're, um, really cool, and you're *so* much fun to hang out with, so... I was wondering—I've *been* wondering, sorry—if you wanted to go out with—"

An SUV with the passenger window down pulled up next to us along the curb. "Look who it is!" the driver's rough voice called, leaning in our direction. "Are you the young lady Nolan's been talking about?"

Oxygen evaporated in my lungs. The blood in my veins turned to ice.

Oval jaw. Green eyes. Dark hair and stubble.

That photo Hunter had shown me *had* been a warning. That hadn't been a photo of just anyone, that had been a photo of Nolan's—

"Dad!" Nolan snapped, his duffel bag stiff beside him as he turned to me. "I'm sorry, I didn't know he was gonna pick me up today."

That makes two of us!

"What're you doing here?" he asked his father.

"I'm on my way home from work, why? Were you about to take her out to dinner?"

I couldn't laugh. I couldn't smile. I stood there, petrified. I stood there, completely blowing my cover.

"You okay, miss?" Mr. Greenwell asked. Oh no. He was talking to me.

"Sorry," I finally sputtered. "It's nice to meet you, I'm—Emmalynn."

"I know." He grinned. The two words chilled my bones.

Nolan sighed, almost scowling. "Please stop."

"I'm sorry!" Mr. Greenwell laughed, shaking his head. "Oh, but let me say, miss, Nolan was right, you *do* have the most striking blue eyes. Never seen anything like them."

Joke with him now before you really do *give everything away!*

"He talks about me?" I asked with the biggest smile I could muster. Another Hunter. Another Hunter after my family.

"Oh yeah. A lot."

Nolan took one look at me, gave up on his original plan, and marched over to the SUV. He swung open the passenger door and threw his duffel bag into the backseat, his cheeks on fire. "Drive away right now."

"Okay, okay, fine..." Mr. Greenwell put his hand on the gearshift. Then, like he'd missed something, he looked back up at me. "It was great to finally meet you, Miss Emmalynn. I can't believe it took this long, do you not have any classes with Nolan?"

"No, I told you," he said, "she goes to the Callistro Academy."

He did not just say that.

Mr. Greenwell's eyes locked with mine, but for a second, something new flashed over them. Not long enough for me to name it, but enough for my anxiety to have a field day with the what-ifs. "Oh, right. I hear it's a great school."

"It is," I said.

I'm bombing. He's gonna know. I'm giving it away. Hunter schools weren't anonymous to agents, not even ones in other federal agencies. Nolan's father already had a handful of pieces he could connect if he wanted to.

That something new flashed again in his eyes, returning long enough for me to name it: suspicion. My anxiety *hadn't* been lying to me.

"You actually look familiar!" he chimed. "Are you sure we've never met before—?"

"No, I don't think so," I said.

Too quick. I was too defensive. I prayed that I wouldn't have to lie again, because my mistakes were mounting up high against me and only priming me to slip up.

"Dad, just go," Nolan said.

"Hmm. Okay. Have a good night, Emmalynn."

Mr. Greenwell and his son finally drove down the street, leaving me standing with a thousand nerves popping like sparks in my chest and my stomach folding in on itself. I had to have imagined what had just happened. Things like that only ever happened in my worst nightmares, and that's not including the nightmare that had actually come true last year!

So my worst nightmares always can come true.

Tears blurred the world in front of me. I had to tell Momma. Tell Mr. Dawson. Tell anyone who could tell me what to do about this. This wasn't about me, this was *all* about my family. I had to warn Momma before the events of last semester decided that it was her turn.

Calm down. Calm down, please calm down.

Deep breath in. Same breath out.

It's gonna be okay. It's okay. It's gonna be okay.

I sat on one of the benches against the fountain in an attempt to liberate myself from my head. I didn't have the answers, but I couldn't escape the lie that there was something I could do to get them. The only thing I knew was that I didn't have them. I didn't have them and I needed them. I *needed* them, I needed them—

Get up, get up, and move!

I jumped to my feet and started running back to the school.

"Mom?" I squeaked as I entered her classroom in the Hunter's Room. I almost hated myself for going down there just to tell her practically the same thing I'd told her at the end of August last year: that our enemies were one step closer to finding us.

It'd been at least ten minutes since I'd stopped crying, but my mother has had enough training (Hunter and parental) to read me like her favorite book. She instantly closed her laptop on her desk and stood, stepping off the platform to meet me. "Honey, what's wrong? What happened?"

"Agent—Agent Greenwell..." I stammered with shaky breaths, taking minimal steps toward the front desks.

"You met him." Her shoulders dropped, her honey-colored eyes sharpening. "How?"

"He picked up Nolan tonight," I whispered.

It felt like every ounce of bravery and courage I'd built over last semester had dissipated into thin air, like it had never existed at all. I'd told myself that I couldn't be anything weaker than what I'd taught myself to be, what I had to be. Now I was telling myself that I had no right to pretend my bravery, to pretend what I wasn't.

I used my hand to lean on the table. My head was too light, too dizzy.

"Nolan told him what school I go to." I barely managed the words, squeezing my eyes shut. I gripped the heart around my neck for dear life.

"You have to go," I cried, refusing to face my mother, knowing I wouldn't be able to let her go if I saw her again. "Y—you'll be found here, you have to follow Dad!"

Which didn't make the situation any easier. Thanks to Auntie's glove, we knew that she and Dad were still safe in Marion almost an hour away, but they were still out of telepathic range. Telepathy wasn't even an option with Momma. If I let my mother go, I didn't know when I'd be getting her back.

"Em," she said gently, placing a steady hand on my back. "I'm safe here. Security's *significantly* improved since they reopened the Hunter's Room—"

"He's a *Master* Hunter!" I exclaimed, whirling on her. "H—he could break in—!"

"Emma." Her voice melted into honey as she took my shoulders and then cupped my face. "I'm safe here. I promise."

My mother had never broken a single promise she'd made me in her life. That was why she almost never made me promises. She *had* lied to me, but whenever she promised something, I never wanted to live to see the day it was broken.

Twenty-Nine

"Miss Gardner and Miss Burnell," Mr. Lambert shouted to the freshman table a few days later, leaning away from his seat in the back of the Dining Hall, "we do not create secret codes with food at the table!"

"That totally would've been us if we went here freshman year," Sarah whispered to me and Breanne, pointing at Miranda and Aurora with her fork. "Ooh, let's do that tonight."

"With linguini and chicken wing bones?" Breanne asked with wide blue-hazel eyes, grinning like a child. It kind of scared me, because she sounded dead serious.

Sarah cocked a perfectly arched brow, smirking. "Duh."

I wish that Miranda Gardner and Aurora Burnell making codes with gourmet tuna salad and bread crusts *had* been the weirdest sight at lunch that afternoon. But the weirdest and, well, scariest was when I turned my attention to my mother's seat and an empty chair still stared back at me. We were halfway through lunch. She *definitely* wasn't using the bathroom.

No. Don't freak out. I'm not gonna freak out, don't freak out.

I refused to do this to myself again, I couldn't.

I called Momma just before leaving the Dining Hall and then again on my elevator ride down into the Hunter's Room: no answer. She's one of the busiest instructors we have, so I did my best to excuse it—but under present circumstances, paranoia was easier to run with. Momma was safe here. I knew that she was safe because she had the proper training to get herself out of situations like this. And that was if we were in worst-case scenario.

The elevator doors slid open. Muffled quiet followed my cushioned steps to Momma's classroom, heightening my nerves. Nothing could comfort me then except the sight of my mother sitting at her desk, grading papers and planning her next lesson.

I drew closer and closer to Momma's door. I was ready to calmly turn the knob and push it open. My mind repeated that everything was fine, that she was catching up on work or even getting ready to leave because—

The knob resisted my twist. The door was locked. She was already gone?

I didn't think—I acted on what I knew and ran back into the elevator for Mr. Dawson's office. He'd know where she was: the copy room, the teachers' lounge, maybe her bedroom, even outside to enjoy a walk!

My knock was a little too loud and I swung the door open too quickly, prompting Mr. Dawson to jump up from his desk.

"This doesn't look good."

"Where's Mom?" I asked, calling upon every ounce of strength in me to push down my panic.

Mr. Dawson glimpsed at the clock hanging on the wall behind him. "She's usually in her classroom preparing for next period."

"Could she be doing something else?"

He shrugged. "Copying lesson plans? Why?"

"Okay, did—?" The words fell off with my breath. I was terrified of the answer to my next question, but time was passing, and every second mattered. "Did you see her at all before lunch?"

As quickly as he'd opened his mouth, he closed it. He pressed his lips together, looking away in thought. "Well... no. I didn't see her at all before or during lunch."

"Because she wasn't there!"

"Okay," he said, holding up his hands, "calm down. What's going on?"

"I think—I think Agent Greenwell took her."

With his abrupt pause, the way his eyes shifted over me, there were probably a hundred thoughts already competing in his head. "Why?"

I told him what had happened on Friday night. And to my dismay, afterward, Mr. Dawson didn't immediately shut down my theory of what could've happened to my mother, which meant he was beginning to consider the probability of it. That was the scariest part: if Mr. Dawson thinks my crazy theories could actually be true, I know that they're not so crazy.

"Okay," he finally said, resting his hands on his desk and leaning forward on them. "First things first, you need to calm down. I need your mind to be clear so that you can think rationally before you act."

He'd already dealt with my spontaneity on more than one occasion the past few months, so I couldn't be mad at him for saying that.

"Second of all, the chance she was taken against her will is slim. So if she *is* with him, she went on her own accord, and if that's the case, she went because she knew she could. She had a plan. She acts based on whether or not she knows that she'll have an escape route—"

"She would've been back by now if that's the case," I said, pacing the front of the office. "It wouldn't've taken her this long to escape—"

"Being skilled and trained doesn't always mean being quick, Emma," he told me. "Some of the greatest plans take the longest to execute. If she's with him right now, she's in Hunter territory. Hunters don't let their targets escape easily. You know that."

From firsthand experience, in fact. But I also knew that my father was in hiding with my aunt, and my mother was now most likely with a *non*-retired Master Hunter, probably being debriefed and doing everything she could to keep her family safe. My family was crumbling apart before my eyes.

"I have to do something," I finally said, "I'm not gonna sit here and wait for her to come back."

"There's not much you *can* do without exposing yourself." Mr. Dawson exhaled, plopping down into his chair. "You have to trust your mom. Look at everything she's accomplished in the past seventeen years. Do you really think she'd fail you now?"

I wasn't worried about my mother failing me; I was worried

about the Hunter who'd kidnapped her failing to let her live.

I shook my head, fiddling with the charm hanging from my neck. "A locator spell."

I'd never heard him sigh so deeply. "Okay. Go find something that belongs to her, bring it back here, and we'll do it."

My breath stabilized as I released it, hope flickering in my chest. "Thanks."

"Just be careful. And if she *is* with Greenwell, don't freak out. We'll get her back, but we'll do it together."

I forced a nod before leaving his office and then ducking into the elevator again. For obvious reasons, students aren't allowed at the teacher dorms and vice versa, but being an instructor's daughter has its perks. In other words, I had a lot more viable excuses for walking into my mother's room than anyone else did.

Reaching the top of the staircase, I turned left. Everyone was enjoying the latter half of lunch downstairs and prepping for next period, so I had privacy. I'd be down the hallway where Momma's room sat, grabbing a cardigan or something, and then on my way to her within... well, hopefully the next ten minutes.

My feet raced past the doors faster the farther down the hall I traveled. *There it is, there it is, there it is—*

I never saw my next step. Only felt my knees fall to the carpet beneath me as the world around me blacked out.

THIRTY

The second my eyes opened to the same small, dimly lit gray room, my awareness snapped awake. Hunter stood in front of me in the middle, my wrists and ankles bound again, igniting my desperation.

Are you kidding me? Now, now of all times?!

"Please!" I cried, my fingers carelessly scraping against the brick behind me. "*Please*, just tell me what you want! I won't fight you, I'll give it to you, just tell me! Please!"

That desperation is the only reason I can think of for why I begged; hearing any answer, even if it was a simple no, would've surprised me more than getting the silence Hunter kept.

Wait. Why was it so cold in here?

I caught sight of my sleeves: the white dress shirt under my blazer. Hunter had taken off my blazer.

I didn't bother asking that question, especially when Hunter shook their head at me. They turned around and faced the door dead ahead of me. For a second, they seemed to debate leaving, but I knew better.

"W—what do you want?" I asked, forcing bravery into my voice. I had to deal with this whether I was scared or not. "Are you gonna kill me?"

Hunter looked at me over their shoulder, shaking their head. For some reason, the relief was minimal.

"Then what do you want?"

They turned around to face me, placing one hand on their chest and then pointing at me.

I scrunched my brow in confusion. "My—heart?"

They shook their head again.

"Just ANSWER me!"

Despite almost strangling me last time, the scariest thing Hunter had done yet was stand perfectly still under that hanging bulb in the silent, damp air. My chest tightened, bracing me.

Hunter kneeled down in front of me. They were close. Way too close.

In one swift motion, they pulled a syringe out of their jacket pocket. It was... empty.

"No, get away from me!" I tried kicking Hunter away, numb to the scraping of my fingers as I thrashed, but I had too little leverage and control to even keep my balance.

Amber briefly glowed through the black fabric of Hunter's covering. An invisible force gripped my body, freezing me in place like a victim of Medusa.

No, no, no, no!

Hunter gripped my arm, rolled up my sleeve, and pressed against my forearm until they found my largest vein. As if I were made of silicone, they stuck the needle in without another thought.

I sat frozen against the wall. My blood slowly filled the barrel of the needle, redder than the carpet runners all throughout the Callistro Academy—as dark as the wallpaper in the Hunter's Room.

I wondered if Hunter could feel the heat radiating off of my face as they withdrew the syringe and held it up to the light. Looking back at me, they chuckled, telling me that there was a satisfied grin behind that mask.

I cursed the tears brimming in my eyes, how they exposed me so blatantly. "What're you gonna do with that?"

With a gloved hand, Hunter brushed a piece of my hair away from my eye, releasing me from the freezing spell. Their fingers took my chin, tilting my head up as if appraising me again.

Bright amber peeked through the mask again, and I fell back asleep.

Maybe it shouldn't have been a surprise, I'm not sure, but the *last* place I'd expected to wake up in was the private room in the nurse's office.

I sat up with my crimson blazer back on—and a sore spot in my right forearm. Oddly enough, something sticky slightly tugged on my skin when I moved my arm: my fingers grazed over where

Hunter had stuck the syringe into, the subtlest lump buried under my sleeve. At least they'd been "kind" enough to bandage it...

Julia walked in seconds later. I couldn't tell if the sight of her brought me more relief or fear. This was the first time I was seeing her since finding out that she knew the truth about me.

I wasn't ready to let go of my theory of her being Hunter, especially not now. Why would I end up in her office right after someone—who knew how to draw blood, like a medical professional—had taken me from somewhere she also lived at—?

"An attack?"

I snapped my head up. All words sat blocked in my head as I recalled the moments before passing out in the hall: that wasn't it at all.

"No." I moaned, holding my tired head. "What am I doing here?"

"Nora found you passed out cold while she was cleaning the staff dorms." Julia pulled a water bottle out of the refrigerator and handed it to me, her auburn ponytail swishing like a cruel familiarity. She placed the back of her fair hand on my forehead. "You still don't have a fever. What were you doing before you passed out?"

I almost wish I could tell you that.

"Uh... I went to see if my mom was in her room, and then I got dizzy. I don't even remember passing out. But it wasn't a panic attack—or anxiety attack."

Julia's brows furrowed in unfiltered confusion, her head jerking back. "Huh. Okay... I guess it could be dehydration. Or stress. I did tell you to take it easy."

Easier said than done!

"But I'm glad it wasn't an attack. Has my advice helped at all?" She smiled at me, wearing compassionate green eyes that made it impossible to accuse her.

"Yeah, actually," I told her, monitoring my every word. "It's… helped a lot."

Which was pretty unfortunate, considering how this woman had lied to me and was *still* lying to me now.

The longer she kept her smile, the more violently my feelings clashed; I'd never been more conflicted about a person in my entire life, not even on the night Jak and I first met! Did I trust her? Did I not trust her? Did she have magic or not?

What was I supposed to do?

Surprisingly, and for once, my visit with her was fairly quiet. She even occupied most of the minutes she kept me by taking care of some work on her computer in the main room, and then she came back to give me a pass for class. Oh, right—*class*.

I remembered what I'd been doing before Hunter had grabbed me. Momma. I still needed to get something that belonged to Momma!

—*Mr. Dawson?*— I said after saying goodbye to Julia, starting down the corridor outside of her office.

—*There you are. Are you okay?*—

—*Yeah.*— I hoped shakiness couldn't come through in telekinesis, because that word sure felt shaky. —*Sorry, I got distracted, and then class…*—

—*We'll do it after school, okay? Try to get through the rest of the day. Trust your mom.*—

If I could do Steven's spell, I wouldn't need something of hers at all. Now I had more than one reason to master it despite the sheer amount of failure I'd experienced on a daily basis since Steven had given it to me.

After school, Mr. Dawson and I found Momma's phone stashed in her sock drawer. She'd *purposely* left behind all methods of contact. When we used a locator spell, she was in the town over.

But Agent Greenwell wasn't with her. To my surprise, I didn't know how to feel about that.

Mr. Dawson promised to keep an eye on her with her phone throughout the next couple of days, but I grabbed a scarf from her room for my own sake. Except, every time I used the locator spell, her location *changed*—from remote areas of the county to even coffee shops and bars in neighboring cities. She was never close enough for me to reach in time before she'd already be somewhere else. Still, though, Agent Greenwell never showed up in the perspective the spell gave me.

Speaking of, that Friday marked almost two weeks of practicing—and failing—Steven's spell. How was I destined to become Adara but had hopelessly spent weeks trying to cast *one* spell? This was a *must* if I was going to be able to find Alexa, and now my mom, without needing something of theirs. I practiced on anybody that popped into my head: Alexa, my classmates, Momma, my teachers, even Mr. Dawson—and nothing.

That afternoon, on our way to Mr. Hartman's, I was pretty sure I'd grown desperate enough to sneak in a few attempts during class. The spell was the only thing on my mind until Sarah took out my buzzing phone from my backpack's side pocket.

"Don't tell me you're not the cutest couple you ever did see," she simpered, showing me the screen spotlighting Jak's name.

I didn't bother arguing, Breanne giggling on my other side

just as we approached Mr. Hartman's door. Snatching my phone from Sarah, I stepped aside from the open door and picked up.

"Aren't you in class right now?" I asked.

"Teacher went to get more paper," Jak replied. He was smirking. I just knew it. "I'm good."

"Well, we're about to start class, did you need something?"

"Ouch, Merlin," he said, chuckling. "It'd hurt less if you just told me you didn't want to talk."

Sarah was on the side I held my phone (my mistake), hearing every word. She tossed back her long hair and puckered her lips into a kissy face. I jabbed her with my elbow, the last couple of Callistro Girls stepping into Mr. Hartman's classroom.

"You have ten seconds," I told Jak.

"10's a little late, but how about 7 tonight? I'll meet you at the mall."

He can never be direct, can he?

I was about to ask why he'd drive the hour over here just to hang out—until I remembered that, in his mind, Jak didn't really need a *good* excuse as long as I was in the question. "Is that all?" I asked, Breanne clinging to my arm in hopes to hear the rest.

"You're sending me mixed signals," he teased. "I thought I had you melting last time—"

"7 tonight," I said, Mr. Hartman calling the three of us to come in. "I have to go."

Sarah snatched my phone before I could hear his response. "Take pictures, babe, lots of pictures! We're always left out of the loop—"

I grabbed my phone and caught a laughing Jak.

"She's my favorite."

A quick glimpse at Sarah's smirk pushed the words straight out of my mouth: "You'll change your mind tonight."

C H A P T E R

Thirty-One

Back when Mr. Dawson was a Master Hunter, he had every right to be suspicious when a regular Hunter from his agency asked him out on a date. First of all, she wasn't supposed to know what he looked like; second, back then he wore a silver band on his left ring finger so that people would think he was married; and third, he'd never seen or heard of the woman before, yet she'd managed to get his name, appearance, phone number, and date of hire within the agency.

It turned out that she was a magician undercover, planning on blowing up the Hunter agency once she was promoted to Master Hunter. She really did want to go out with Mr. Dawson and hoped to "change his mind" about being a Hunter (not knowing that he was a druid). Mr. Dawson told her that he wouldn't expose her if she quit the agency and left everyone alone, because apparently, blowing up our enemies isn't how we're supposed to go about things.

To this day, it's one of my favorite stories. That night, as I walked to the Capperson mall to meet Jak, it grew into an alternate universe in my head—if Jak were the Hunter. Except, if Jak were actually a magician, he'd never stop trying to telepathically talk to me.

On the way, I tried Steven's spell on Jak. A target on his way to me was perfect practice—at least, I assumed so, if the spell was easier the closer my target was to me.

As I stepped onto the sidewalk in front of the mall entrance, I spoke the spell in my mind again. A flash of sunset scenery burst through my vision.

I jumped and gasped, startling the people walking in and out of the double glass doors. With that fire of embarrassment, I dropped my eyes to my black flats.

Did that work...?

I closed my eyes again to hide the amber in case it did this time. *Ratione locate.*

Too quick to jump back in. Focus. Jak—his chocolate eyes, dark-mahogany hair, light-brown skin...

Accumulate your magic. Give the words their power.

Ratione locate.

A flash of the sunset returned, long enough to catch the perspective turning toward the fountain in the Capperson square. It was a second long at most, but I opened my eyes, breaking the concentration. The realization shook me awake: Jak was only a few seconds away.

A smile stretched my lips as I gazed at my flats in blinding excitement. I'd gotten it, I'd actually gotten it! The cold air tickled my skin on the top of my feet, the numbness stimulating my nerves. I turned to look behind me at the main entrance: the glass doors sat, unoccupied, ready for someone to pull them open.

I only had a few seconds. *Alexa. Alexa, Alexa, Alexa.*

Gather your power, focus.

Ratione loc–

"Look who's here first for once."

I shut down my thoughts and looked up. Jak approached with his hands in the pockets of his—wait—of his new hoodie!

I forgot all about Alexa, beaming. "You're wearing it!"

"Duh." He flashed his signature grin. "It's my favorite one."

I'd never been more tempted to hug him. And, honestly, *keep* my arms around him.

"I just wish it still smelled new," he said, examining his sleeves. "Now it just smells like... well, me."

"I prefer that."

No way I'd just said that out loud. I'd just said that *out loud.*

Even Jak was surprised, his brows rising high above his eyes. "Um—" He laughed, covering his stupid grin. "I can either pretend you were talking about the new hoodie scent... or I can keep my arm around you while we walk."

Go with the second, go with the first, go with the second–

I scoffed. "You'd love that, wouldn't you?"

He shrugged. "Well–"

"Come on," I said, turning around and walking straight to the mall doors.

He jogged to beat me to them, and opened one for me.

"You're a real tease sometimes, you know that?"

Just as quickly, I stopped in the doorway, gaping at him. "*Me*? Me—?"

"You're blocking the entrance, Merlin."

This boy knew the game all too well, and he never gave me a chance to win.

On the bright side, we were able to stroll past the stores in comfortable silence. We glanced left and right in case we'd find somewhere to browse. At least, that was how I interpreted it until Jak took a breath in—a different kind of breath, one that pricked my instincts to ready themselves.

"Can I be completely honest?"

I instinctively slowed. "Sure."

We passed Juniors' display window, which earned Jak's attention. He stopped once we reached the other side of the entrance, turning to face the mannequin kid on display.

"I don't remember a ton about her, but this reminds me of when my mom and I would go shopping on the weekends."

I looked at him and then the mannequin: denim shorts, a red T-shirt with a yellow truck painted on it, a gray baseball cap, and a stylish pair of red-and-gray sneakers. It was too easy to picture Kid Jak in that.

"Do you go to the mall that often anymore?" I asked.

Jak smiled, almost laughing at himself. "No, I don't really need to. I get new clothes for my birthday and Christmas, I prefer cafés over the food court—"

A flash boomed in my vision, brightness overcoming my world as familiar images sped too rapidly for me to absorb. Wait. A feeling. My feelings were telling a story, one composed of just scenes and… imminence. A dim image repeated itself: night, brick walls, shadows… I'd seen this before. A classmate behind me…

My nightmare.

Tonight. It's supposed to happen tonight.

"Emma!" an anxious voice echoed, swinging open the door to reality as I stumbled into Jak. He caught me, grasping both of my arms before I could crash into the display window.

"Em," he said again, quieter this time, "are you okay?"

My eyes froze on the white tile below us. That had been magic. Just now, that had been a vision. My magic had activated without my permission.

Tell me I blinked in time. Tell me my eyes were closed during that.

"I'm sorry," I breathed, the stares of shoppers heavy on me. I kept my swirling head down. "I just got this—random stabbing pain in my eyes."

"Come on, look at me."

I knew that he was only saying it for my health's sake—to make sure I was okay, that my pupils weren't dilated or my eyes weren't unnaturally bloodshot, the works—but I didn't want to risk it. I just couldn't. What if that flash happened again?

So I did the only thing I felt safe to do: I buried myself into Jak's hoodie, catching his warm scent off the fabric. Surprised and hesitant at first, he wrapped his arms around me and gently rested his chin on top of my head. He held me there for as long as I let myself stay in his arms.

"Are you okay?" he whispered.

I nodded, never minding how I was messing up my hair. Juniors' stayed busy in my peripheral vision, and everything else was the black fabric of Jak's hoodie.

"You sure you're not about to pass out?"

I had to ask. I had to ask. "Why?"

"Isn't that what almost just happened?"

I suppressed a sigh of relief. *He's not suspecting anything. My eyes didn't give me away.*

I exhaled. "I'm fine."

But what had that been? Even if I were a druid, I knew for a fact that they didn't get visions while awake!

Could this have been my "impossible gift" Annisa had talked about?

Jak took his chin off my head, resting his cheek against it instead. I couldn't help but swallow, fear passing in my throat.

"You're good at comforting someone," I caught myself saying, desperate to control the conversation.

His chuckle vibrated against his chest. "Thanks. My mom taught me."

Of course, I wanted to say. Could I say *anything* without reminding him of her?

"She hugged me like this whenever I was upset. She'd whisper things like 'It's okay, *lalu.* I'm here.' Especially whenever I got in trouble and she and my dad had to discipline me. There was this one saying she told me almost every time... '*Manas matra bhul ne patra.*'"

I slightly pulled away, curiosity furrowing my brows.

"It's Gujarati." The pride in his smile was new—something I actually wanted to see more of from him. "It means it's natural for us to make mistakes, so it's important to forgive and understand that it's okay as long as we learn from it."

Finally, my own smile. "So that's where you got it from."

"A lot of it," he replied. "She was... great."

Of all people, Jak's mother. Jak's mother had been taken by Hunters.

Like mine.

I swallowed, mad at myself for allowing the thought. My mother wasn't dead, and we didn't know for a fact that she'd been kidnapped by Agent Greenwell. (I was just 90 percent sure of it.) I couldn't call her, but Mr. Dawson and I could still locate her. She wasn't dead. She had a plan. She was taking care of herself, she knew how to, and... I couldn't ruin it. No matter how badly I wanted to slam Agent Greenwell against a wall and drag Mom into my car to drive us home, wherever she was at right now.

A new thought seemed to weigh on Jak's mind now, his eyes falling to the floor. His lips tightened into a thin line.

I almost thought that I'd imagined him say, "Her name was 'Aastha'."

I didn't know how or why, but the name warmed my chest with a comfort I bet Jak missed almost as much as he missed her.

"Jak..."

"I wanna say it," he said softly. He clenched his jaw as he nodded, warm eyes bouncing back up to me. "I don't wanna let her name be forgotten."

"'Aastha' is beautiful."

We stayed in that moment for a few seconds longer until we regained sense of touch—and realized that we were still holding each other.

We both stepped back, Jak scratching his nose and clearing his throat. He pulled down his hoodie to straighten it.

"I hope you know how to iron," he said, pulling at the sleeves.

Jakson Bleu was back. "Because I don't."

"Then now's a great time to learn."

I walked straight past him with a proud smirk.

"Have we switched roles or something?" He laughed as he rushed up to my side again. "When did you get so bold?"

"I've been spending *way* too much time around you."

"I completely disagree, but okay."

Dinner had been over half an hour ago, and when Jak suggested dessert... I didn't know what was wrong with me, but I wasn't thinking about the kind at the food court. It was easier to say no after that.

So we silently walked throughout the first floor, Jak's hands stuck in his hoodie pockets and mine in my jacket's. He didn't stop us again until we got to Forever 21's windows.

"What's up?" I asked, trying to pin where his eyes were focused. They seemed to be jumping from every clothing rack scattered across the store's glossy black-and-white floor.

"Wanna go in here?"

"I'm sixteen."

"I'm aware."

I scanned the inside from left to right. There was a row of clear plastic boxes with different-colored and -sized bras sitting against the right wall. There was *no* way I was going inside with this boy.

"Yeah, no," I said, "let's just—"

Jak pulled out his leather wallet and handed me a twenty. Looking back up at him, I realized that his eyes weren't looking *through* the window—they were looking at it. "Buy yourself something pretty, I'll be back."

"What? But—"

I didn't have time to hand him back the bill. He was already turning around and walking toward the center of the mall, where the fountain and a kids' play area sat.

Snickering voices grabbed my attention before I could follow Jak's route. I turned my head in the original direction we'd been heading in: the Kohl's that occupied the back of the mall. A group of teenage boys surrounded a girl, laughing and walking her out of the store and to the hallway next to them. I remembered only four doors in that specific hallway: two bathrooms, a janitor's closet, and an emergency exit.

A suppressing dizziness swirled in my head, a new flame kindling in my chest. I'd never felt this before. It almost resembled… instinct.

I've seen them before, I realized. *The teenage boys and the—*

Ava. The vision I'd just gotten in front of Juniors', my nightmare, this *was* magic. My magic was telling me to go.

I can't believe this, I thought, stuffing the twenty into my jean pocket and then running down to the hallway once the group disappeared into it. At the corner, I waited until the emergency door clanged shut.

No alarm. I was too worried and alert to think about the safety hazards of that.

I dashed down the hall, passing the bathrooms and closet before bursting through the emergency exit. Three boys turned in my direction, my eyes quickly trying to adjust to the sudden dimness of outside. A bitter cold nipped at my face, the sulfurous odor of a dumpster farther down the alley carried on the low breeze. The heavy metal door slowly closed behind me, silence trailing it as the five of us stared back at each other. The tallest boy gripped the girl's arm, standing closest to the back wall of the alley.

My shoulders dropped. It *was* Ava.

Part of me had been hoping against hope that maybe I'd mistaken her for someone else or that she wouldn't actually get caught up in all of this. Anything but be here tonight.

She found out about me in one of my dreams, I reminded myself. I couldn't let that happen, I couldn't use magic. We had to get out of here on our own.

"Emma?" she squeaked. The boys sneered, hooting.

"You guys know each other?" the only blond said, his shaggy hair sweeping over his eyes. "Awesome!"

Idiot.

Focus on Ava. Only her. "Do you know them?"

"Um..."

That's a no.

"Yeah, she knows us." The second tallest—a couple of inches higher than me—smirked. The dim alley lights revealed the fawn shade of his curly hair. He stood in front of us all like the leader. "We go a little ways back."

Waves of anxiety, a familiar angry fear, seared their path in my chest. I fought the tremors and heat as I focused on Ava again.

"What're you doing with them?"

"I..."

The leader of the group swayed a step toward me, gesturing in her direction. "We were just chilling—"

"I didn't ask you," I stated, meeting his fierce hazel eyes.

My anger had spoken, and not even Annisa could take me back in time.

The boy's smirk dropped. I almost took a step back—but the fight raging in my chest pushed against the instinct. I'd vowed to myself to never believe that I couldn't do it, especially not when I had the training for this. And the experience! I'd faced Alexa Delphine and William Bleu, these guys were teddy bears!

"Okay, and I didn't ask you to butt into our business," the brunet leader said, slithering toward me as if every stride were meant to intimidate me.

"She's my friend and she clearly doesn't wanna be here. You made it my business when you took her back here anyway."

He scoffed. "That involves you, how?"

I narrowed my eyes. "I'm not gonna waste time explaining it to you." I turned to Ava and reached for her. A bony hand clamped down onto my wrist.

"Listen, brat," the brunet hissed, yanking me to face him, "shut that pretty mouth before you ask for too much."

I wondered if he felt the trembling in my arm. And I hated that he probably did.

No—I'm the one who's trained. I could throw him down the alley at the drop of a hat, I'm the only threat here!

"I'm not asking, I'm *telling* you, back off!"

His eyes and grip hardened as his blond friend stepped forward. "Somebody needs to be humbled—"

"Stop!" Ava cried, grabbing our attention. Every time she jerked in the tall boy's grip, he held her firmer. "Stop, let her go!"

The brunet slightly loosened his hold on me as he glared at the tall boy. "Hey, shut her up, Justin!"

"Ava, elbow and roundhouse!"

I didn't turn to watch as I twisted my wrist out of the brunet's grip. Grabbing his wrist and the back of his neck, I slammed my foot into his chest. The blond darted toward me, too slow with his approach. I took his wrist and squeezed with every muscle in my hand, bending it backwards. He cried out, leaving his arching back open. I brought my knee up and turned my body, thrusting a kick at the center of his spine.

"Ava!" I spun around. Justin had her in a chokehold from behind, his leg wrapped around hers.

Someone's arm wrapped around my neck. Just as I was ready to actually throw the boy down the alley, my dream's ending—Ava's words—rang across my head. No magic. I couldn't use magic right now.

"Believe me, this isn't all I can do, princess," the brunet sneered in my ear. "You *definitely* don't wanna hear what I'm sending to your head right now."

—I can't wait to have those pretty lips all to myself. Just wait until I get my legs around you.—

Horror constricted my chest. A bolt of disgusted rage racked my body, blinding my rationality.

Momma's right: sometimes, the basics are all you need.

I bit down on his arm with unrestricted force. His yelp burst in my ear as I turned and elbowed him in his cheek. Just as quickly, his opposite hand hooked my lip.

The sting ignited a fire of blood and adrenaline. All I knew, all I could see, was my training—Hunter and magic—controlling me now. My hand flew to his wrist that had struck me and twisted his arm. I shoved my palm against his elbow, snapping his arm. His scream ripped through the air, placating an ounce of my fury.

"You asked for it!" I snarled.

You know what? Forget it.

I closed my eyes, called upon the strengthening spell that I now knew existed, and threw a roundhouse kick to his chest again. The boy fell backwards and clung to his blond friend, taking him down with him.

With those two the last thing in my vision, I briefly closed my eyes. *Dormio-obliviscor.* Now they'd eventually wake up here with no memory of us or the fight.

I let a foggy breath out before turning back to Ava. Her eyes stayed on an unconscious Justin slouched against the wall. Both of her hands sat on her chest, her shoulders jumping with every pant.

I repeated the forgetting spell on Justin before turning to Ava, breathlessly crying out her name.

She whirled to me, remembering that I was there, and ran into my arms. "Emma!"

The sweet scent of her blond hair immediately combatted the odor of the dumpster. Her cardigan was cold but quickly warmed in my embrace, the heat from her adrenaline-exhausted body radiating.

"Are you okay?" I asked, breaking away.

"Yeah." She sniffed, trying to catch her breath. "Yeah, but—"

Glossy blue eyes fell to my mouth. "Your lip, you're bleeding!"

"It's fine," I said, wiping away the wet trail on my chin. In truth, my bottom lip throbbed with a stinging soreness, but I pushed it away to reassure Ava. "I'm okay, come on."

Her fragile breaths, exposed by the cold, finally began to steady, but they weren't shaking with just exhaustion anymore. I'd breathed those same pants in the Hunter's Room with Jak, the Grand Foyer at lunch with Sarah, even with Hunter. I'd become more than accustomed to those breaths that were stuck in Ava's throat right now.

"Are you okay?" I asked again.

"I don't know," she squeaked, hugging herself and rubbing her arms. "I was really—scared. I—I still am, I don't know why."

I only knew to wrap her in another hug—because for a second, before Julia's words and past experience had come back to me, I'd been scared, too.

"I wish I knew what to say. I'm so sorry."

Because the only weapon built in me was magic. I'd so intuitively used it as a weapon against other human beings, yet for the sake of someone else. My magic was all I had to show Ava how much I cared about her, enough to play risk for reward. The only work I *could* do was invisible. But she was safe and unharmed, and that was what mattered.

She waited until her body calmed before releasing a final sigh. Now her breaths were gentle, and when I stood still enough, I could feel her heart hard at work to calm the rest of her down.

She pulled away from me, looking behind her at the three unconscious boys. "They came up to me and—I couldn't get them to leave. I just stood there and let them talk to me. I was so stupid, I let them—"

"Stop," I told her, a sting zapping my lip with every other word. "You're not stupid. This wasn't your fault."

"But I threw him, I shoved him against the wall," she cried, briefly turning to Justin.

I took her shoulders. "Hey. The second someone invades

your personal space, they're in *your* territory. And you have *every* right to push them back out of it if they won't leave."

"I hurt him."

Blood warmed a single stream on my chin as another drop fell down my skin. "He wasn't planning on letting you go."

Ava sniffed without another argument. She starkly resembled the terrified girl I'd seen in my vision, the one who'd found out I was a magician. "Stupid" left a longer stay in my head than I wanted it to: if I really had known about this beforehand, wasn't I to blame for it coming true?

I weighed the effects of the situation, the effects of my magic and what had happened because of it—what *hadn't* happened because of it. My magic had warned me. My magic had used me as an intercessor.

For the first time in my life, I felt bad for a mortal because they didn't have what I did.

Ava... I'm sorry you can't trust me.

"I'm here for you," I finally said. "I have your back."

Her small arms squeezed me one more time, tighter than I thought they could. But what warmed me from the inside out in the winter cold was the fact that Ava Baleen felt safe and comfortable enough with me to sob in my arms.

Thirty-Two

"Yeah, I think it's stopped. And you scratched most of it off your chin."

Ava sniffed again as we stopped near the perfume department of Kohl's, facing the mall from the store's exit. My lip was more sore than stinging, and I wondered how much fun Breanne was going to have analyzing the wound and treating it when I got home. (She'd probably get to me before Momma could.)

"Thanks," I said, to Ava, gently dabbing the middle of my lip, the area that wasn't cut. "I guess I'll grab a drink from the food court and ask for a bag of ice."

"What if everyone at home asks what happened?"

"I... have really chapped lips during the winter."

Ava smiled gratefully and rubbed the tip of her nose. "Thanks, Emma. I'm here right now because of you."

Jak flashed in my mind for only a second when I asked, "Do you want me to walk you home?"

"Actually, I'm only here because I have to get my dad a birthday present. Teresa was supposed to meet me, but then... *that* happened, so I have to go find her. I'm gonna call her."

I nodded. "Got it. Stay safe. Remember what I said."

"You stay safe, too. Thanks again."

My body reset into a comforting familiarity as my fingertips met the silver locket around my neck. I watched Ava walk deeper into Kohl's before I turned around and stepped back into the mall. My nails went over the "Emma" engraving on the charm, then the sapphire set in the top. The adrenaline had left minutes ago, but my stomach was still bubbling with disturbance. That brunet boy had been a magician. His friends... Had they been magicians, too? How could they prey upon an innocent girl? Take advantage of someone who had less power than they did?

I cursed the tears pricking my eyes. Not even the new-clothes scent of the mall could distract me then.

"Emma!"

My body stiffened. *Oh no. I'm in trouble.*

Forever 21 sat a few spaces down from Kohl's. I strode toward the entrance, but Jak was jogging to me.

"I came back and searched the whole store—"

His eyes fell to my lip. I was *definitely* in trouble.

"You're bleeding."

Guess the cut is deeper than I thought.

Jak stepped closer to me, carefully cupping my face in his

hands. "You're bleeding, what happened?"

"It's fine," I said, shaking my head away from his hands. "My lips have been really chapped—"

He scoffed, narrowing his eyes. "Trust me. No, they haven't."

Ha. He *would* know, wouldn't he?

I went to lick my lips and then remembered. I went to bite my bottom lip and then remembered. I bit the inside of my lip, but that seemed to pump more blood through the cut.

"What happened?" Jak asked lowly. His eyes bore the wrath of a lion's, fear stretching its claw into my chest. I'd only ever seen those eyes once in the time we'd known each other: the day I'd formally met Alexa.

"I don't wanna talk about it tonight."

"Who did this to you?"

I leveled our eyes. "Jak. I'm not telling you right now."

"Fine, but are you okay—?"

"I'm fine!" I exclaimed, starting down the main aisle—starting my way home.

"Merlin," he said from behind me. "Emma—I had to know if it was Alexa, that's all!"

"Why would it be Alexa?" I snapped, spinning back around to face him. "She's not even in Capperson!"

"My dad's here."

Everything in me but my heart froze. Now he had my attention. "What do you mean?"

He closed the gaping distance between us. "I saw him in the window reflection. That's what I went to check out. That's why I wanted you to stay in the store."

Why was William here? Why was William here but Alexa

wasn't? Why was anyone in the pack here?!

Jak drew closer. One person away. "I didn't know if she took you while I was talking to him."

His breath warmed the cold cherry of my nose. Conversation buzzed amidst shoppers, their shoes clicking on the tile and bags swaying against each other—but the silence between me and Jak seemed to only amplify the throbbing pain in my lip. That was the only thing I had to focus on when we weren't talking.

"She didn't," I whispered. I crossed my arms, eye contact impossible to pair with my words. "Why is your dad here?"

"He doesn't completely trust that we're not holding out on the pack. He was watching us."

Watch–?

The memory dawned: William had never explicitly answered no when I'd asked him in the passageway if I was still a target.

"We're no longer hunting you..."

We're *monitoring* you.

How long had this been going on? What had they gathered since then?

"He can't just stalk me like that," I said, holding myself tighter. "Not after they already ruled me innocent. Then it's just regular harassment, that's illegal!"

"He can get by under the excuse that he's looking out for his son's safety."

"So they've only been watching when I'm with you?"

"Yep."

"Every time?"

He rubbed his lips together. Mine cringed watching them. "I'd like to *think* they haven't been watching us every time."

The day before his birthday. Surely his dad would've given his son at least some privacy, dropping the hunt for a day, as a "present", wouldn't he?

That'd be the least *he could do for him.*

Jak's hands slipped into the pockets of his hoodie. "You're okay? Actually?"

"Well, I mean,"—I sighed, nearing laughter—"you just practically told me that I was almost kidnapped in the mall."

"You've got a niche for that, Merlin."

If *only* he knew.

His stare fell onto my lip again, a new thought weighing on him. "Man. I can't kiss you for a few days now, huh?"

I quickly closed the cage to the butterflies. "Normal people would argue that that's just for *couples*, anyway."

"Last I checked, we weren't normal."

I was ready to scold him for using a technicality, but shook my head instead.

A familiar tune began playing over the mall speakers. Ever since that night Momma and I had come home from the New Year's party, and then in the Grand Foyer weeks later, I was never able to hear the song the same way ever again:

"'When I fall in love...'"

Jak and I gazed up at the brightly lit ceiling, searching for the speakers.

"Your dad hums this song."

It was the first thought that had slipped into my mind, which I was comfortable enough to do with Jak even without the trust spell. I was a bit grateful for that, but I couldn't tell if I regretted the words or not; I could've just opened a door that Jak didn't want to open.

That seemed to be the case when he looked down at the floor and said, "I know."

He knew—he knew why his father kept this song in mind. But if my silent curiosity wasn't going to get anything out of him tonight, it would just have to wait.

Jak took his eyes up but kept them low. He was stuck so deep in a daze held by thought—maybe even memory—that he was forgetting to hide it.

"Can I hold you?"

Okay, I hadn't been expecting *that*. Jakson Bleu is bold, but I couldn't pin a time when he'd ever been *that* bold.

Which had to mean that... this song meant something. To *both* of them.

"My hand?" I asked, ready to oblige and avoid assumptions.

"You." His hands respectfully stayed in the pockets of his hoodie. "Just you."

I had to admit it to myself: I trusted him. Besides keeping his parents a secret, he had never purposely broken my trust. He'd risked his home life, the opportunity to amend his relationship with his dad, and practically everything he knew for the sake of my and Tristan's daughter's safety.

So the word was easy, even on my cut lip: "Sure."

He wrapped his arms around me, locking his hands together and resting them on my lower back. I leaned my head on his shoulder and he leaned his against mine. A mild sway moved through us. I didn't know if he had his eyes closed or not, but paranoia warned me to keep mine open and scan the mall in front of me. For my sake, and for his.

We were safe.

Jak pulled away a minute later, but he kept his arm around my waist. Together, we walked through and then eventually out of the Capperson mall.

C H A P T E R

Thirty-Three

My head fell onto my pillow so heavily that night that I was scared I'd break my bedframe. Tens of thousands of thoughts weighed down my mind: my mother, the safety of my family, the need to meet with Cara and Steven to solidify our plan about luring out and taking down Alexa... oh, and taking down Alexa.

The ceiling stared back at me as I exhaled and tried to set myself down into the proper mindset. Now was the best time to practice. I'd succeeded with Jak tonight for two seconds, so at least I could actually do it.

Ratione locate.

I sighed carefully, mindful of my two sleeping roommates. *You're* not *getting away from me this time, Alexa.*

I pictured every detail of her and let myself feel the magic buried in me, the magic that had already done impossible things—what I'd used so easily to do those things. I allowed my will to grow, bending it how I needed it to, and I revived the words on my sore lips:

"*Ratione locate.*"

White bled into my vision before flickering into a cobblestone hallway. It flashed three times in front of me, and I jolted upward.

There it was—the last bit of confidence I needed.

"*Ratione locate.*"

My vision was thrust into Alexa's perspective as she walked through familiar tunnels. Vintage lanterns glowed above her head, her steps softly echoing on the concrete. The spell whispered her location to me.

My blood ran cold. *No.*

She was in the secret passageways—the *underground* ones. She was in the school.

A staircase appeared in front of her. When she approached, a circle opened in the ceiling. Alexa walked up the stairs and stepped onto... the Callistro Forest.

Away from me? Why?

I guess she doesn't plan on kidnapping me tonight. What was she doing here at all? She was supposed to be in another city on a hunt! How had she snuck all the way over here without her pack noticing?

My head lay all the heavier against my pillow. The dozen more questions eventually ran my subconscious into the ground, pushing it into sleep. At this point, first semester had been a lot lighter compared to second. I'd already spent the last two months gaining two enemies and then two allies, losing my entire family, figuring out why my greatest enemy seemed to be avoiding me, and training to become an agent eventually meant to slaughter my people. My world was turning upside down right before me, jostling me and making me bump my head against the wall behind me.

Wait. That was *me*.

A running engine hummed under me, road noises just beyond. Those weren't in a dream. My subconscious was fading back to reality. Upon the soreness in my arms from being behind my back for so long, I shot my eyes open.

This floor was black. These walls were metal and white. I was sitting. And the person in front of me was—*Momma*!

"Mom!" I cried, nearly falling forward as I jumped out of my seat. Thin ropes bound my ankles and my wrists, cutting into my skin if I tried to break past them.

"Did he do that to your lip?"

I opened my mouth to speak, but the memory closed it. I had no idea if she'd appreciate the fact that I'd used magic (albeit discreetly) to defend myself and Ava against three rotten boys, and a lecture was the *last* thing either of us needed right now.

"No," I said. "My lips have just been really chapped—"

"I told you, blink more often when you lie," she said. "You have a daze-like stare when you lie. Anyone who's trained and spoken to you twice will know. Second of all, I've been in more fistfights than the number of years you've been alive, so I know what a busted lip looks like. What happened?"

Well... all right, then.

"Ava and I were at the mall tonight and these guys wouldn't leave us alone. They attacked first. We just defended ourselves."

"So it was a fistfight? How many boys?"

"Three." Even though I was telling the truth, I still counted each word and blinked on every other one. "I had two, Ava had one."

"Stop counting. Did you use your magic?"

Is now really the time for a Hunter lesson?!

"To make them sleep and forget us and the fight. I had my eyes closed."

Hearing it out loud, I almost expected praise of some kind, but I knew better. This was my mother; I had to brace myself for discipline, for something along the lines of how I should've been more careful.

Or... maybe, for the first time ever, that was what I *wanted.* Any sign to tell me that my mother, not just the scared and trained part of her, was still there. But we were riding in the back of a van against our will—if anything, my story just reminded us of our current situation.

Instead of discipline, instead of praise, Momma pressed her head against the wall of the van. Her voice was too dreary to be hers. "I'm so sorry," she whispered. "You—you handled that well but now you're here, and... I told him not to come after you. I told him to leave you alone."

Agent Greenwell.

Wait... Was he the reason Alexa had been *leaving* the school? Had the two of them met before grabbing me?

"You were kidnapped, weren't you?" I said.

Momma's gaze moved up slightly, but it was still too low to

meet mine. She wouldn't look at me, almost like she *couldn't* look at me. She'd never done that before.

"Mom, were you kidnapped—?"

"No."

Wait. What?

"You *came* to him?"

Her sigh was much heavier now, drawing my attention to how low her shoulders had sunk. "I know you disagree with what I did the day I found out about you. But the circumstances are the exact same right now. I had to go with him."

"When did he even come by?"

"He called my office and asked me to meet him at the front gates of the school."

"Weren't the guards there?"

"Yes, but for all they knew, I'd be back by the time lunch was over. I just—I hadn't expected him to..."

I did what I knew she wanted me to and looked away. There are excruciatingly few moments in my mother's life when she wasn't prepared, when she was fatally careless. Even after last semester, even after the past two decades, she'd made another critical mistake. For someone like Amy Dalbert, that was unacceptable, at least in her eyes. Part of me regretted that I couldn't fix that for her.

"How did he break in tonight?" I asked. "How did he get past security and defenses and...?"

Please don't say it was Alexa. Please don't say—

"I helped him in. Trust me, Em, it was either that or... something a lot worse."

I didn't know if that answer was any better.

"What've you been doing all this time? What has he done to you?"

"Some things are better left unsaid." At least her frown softened a little for me. "For the sake of the person who wants to hear them."

A forceful urge to pull a rear naked choke on Agent Greenwell surged in my chest, but that was probably why Momma didn't answer my question. Mr. Dawson was right: I had to trust her.

Being with her didn't make the kidnapping experience even the slightest bit less terrifying. Actually, it made it all the worse; I wasn't the only guilty party in that car. Momma was an accomplice and had been since the day she started dating Dad. According to Caldwell's law, Agent Greenwell had every right to arrest us—and kill me.

"Momma," I whispered, readying myself for the words I never thought I'd let myself say to her as a Hunter-in-training, "I'm scared."

"I know," she whispered back. "We'll find a way out, honey. I promise, we will."

She didn't dare tell me that she was afraid, too, but I knew.

The van jerked to a stop. I heard the engine turn off and the driver door open, my heart leaping into my throat.

He's coming.

"Emma," Momma said, caution lacing her words. I looked up into her now dull eyes warning me to trust her. "No magic unless necessary."

The back doors of the van swung open, frigid air sweeping inside. I shivered as Agent Greenwell grinned. The van light was the only thing illuminating him as he stood in the night. "We're quiet," he remarked. "I figured you wanted to see your daughter again, Mrs. Atera."

"How could you do this?" I spat. The scab on my bottom lip threatened to split open with every passionate word, but I couldn't bring myself to care. "You're a parent, you wouldn't want this for your son! Why are you doing this?"

"My son doesn't have magic," he hissed, his stubbled oval jaw clenching. "My son isn't an *Atera.*"

I'm sorry—was that supposed to be an insult?

I wanted to bring up Friday night two weeks ago, how Nolan had been about to ask me out right before his dad pulled up. In fact, I almost wanted to brag that Nolan could have, one day, become part of the family his father despised if things ever went that far.

But then again, Nolan didn't know that I had magic. Nolan didn't know that I was an Atera.

"What're you expecting to gain out of this?" Momma's amber eyes sliced straight through him. "I don't know how kidnapping my daughter—"

He snickered. "Patience is a powerful virtue."

Despite the fear folding my stomach in on itself, I forced myself to match Agent Greenwell's eyes. I needed to bring my anger closer to the surface, because I had a gut feeling that I was going to need it.

He pulled us out of the van before cutting off the ropes around our ankles. Gaining my footing on the sidewalk, I looked up at the small, cozy house that sat in front of us. We were standing in the middle of an unfamiliar neighborhood. I wanted to ask if we were still in Capperson, but sometimes there's more comfort in what you don't know.

I looked at Momma, wary of her silence: her lips were parted, her eyes stuck on the house like Dad was standing on the roof.

"Mom?" I whispered. "Where are we?"

Agent Greenwell closed the van doors and then came to stand behind us. He seemed all too eager to let her answer, staring her down with his arms crossed.

"This is where your dad and I lived when we got married," she whispered. Her eyes fell onto me, strangely... nostalgic. "Where I found out I was pregnant with you."

C H A P T E R

Thirty-Four

As if binding our hands and feet again weren't enough—no, Agent Greenwell had to tie us to the chairs in the dining room on top of it. Turns out that the house had been bought and preserved by an agency as "evidence" not too long after Momma moved out. And now Agent Greenwell was using it against us.

We knew better than to fight back: sure, I could put him under a sleeping spell and make him forget about us—but it was too temporary. He'd come barreling down our door again, and he'd know more than ever. We needed more intel so we could form something as we went along.

The house was definitely homey, smaller than the one I'd grown up in. I almost started wondering how my childhood would've gone if I *had* grown up here. I wanted anything to distract myself from why I was there now, anything to take myself away, but it didn't matter. No matter how much I wanted to forget for even one second, I couldn't. No matter how desperate I was for ignorance, nothing could erase or make me forget the Hunter in the room. I'd known my whole life that they'd always be there, but in that moment, they'd never seemed bigger.

"Happy?" Momma said across from me as Agent Greenwell circled us. "You have me. Now what, what do you wanna do with me?"

He came to stand behind me, placing his hands on the back of my chair. My breath hollowed like I couldn't let him hear me breathe. "I still want answers, but I want them from you. So it's not a matter of what I'm gonna do with *you*." He slid his meaty hands onto my shoulders, pressing down on them. "It's what I'm gonna do with her."

Momma jerked in her chair, held down by the ropes. "Don't you dare touch my daughter, Marcus!"

"Be honest with me and I won't." I heard his smile and then saw it as he rounded my chair. He paced around the dining room. "How's married life treated you, Amy? How's your husband?"

We still had that advantage: he didn't know that Dad was no longer in custody. But as of the locator spell yesterday, he and Aunt Becca had moved out of Marion. We hadn't gotten to find out where they were going before Mr. Broadhurst knocked on Mr. Dawson's door.

Right now, we had no idea where they were.

"I don't know," Momma stated, out of patience. "He's on the run with Rebecca again."

"Really?" he deadpanned. His hands rested on his hips, and he leaned down next to her. "Nothing's changed?"

His gaze darted to me, and I had to look at Momma's denim jeans for comfort. "Neither of you know where Tristan Atera is?"

"He's running," Momma said again. "Even if we did know, he'd be somewhere else by the time you got to him. Isn't that why you ran all over the place with me?"

To make sure nobody could track her and get to her in time. So that was why Momma had been constantly on the move whenever I'd used a locator spell with her. Had Agent Greenwell just known to "stay out of shot"?

He ambled toward me again. Never in my life had I been so incapable of moving my own body because of fear.

"Have you ever met your dad, Emmalynn? Does he even know he has a kid?"

I'd known for two weeks that I'd slip up on my next lie to Agent Greenwell. But silence would give him all the answers he needed anyway. I was trapped.

"Well?" he said, next to me. "Go ahead, tell me where your dad's hiding and I'll let you both go."

"I don't know," I said, steadier than I'd anticipated. The wound on my lip itched with each word. "I really don't."

He hummed in thought, looking at me as if I were an artifact on display in the Hunter's Room. Then, his hand rose, brushing a strand of my hair away from my face. He took my chin into his fingers.

"*Marcus—*" Momma growled.

"You do look like him." A hungry smile split his lips apart. "And you gotta be pretty special for Nolan to be so fond of you.

He's picky. Doesn't go with just any girl. Well, you're an Atera. Ateras are supposed to be gifted, right?"

"Marcus!" Momma barked again, but I shushed her with a glance. He wasn't going to give us anything we wanted, and he was willing to torture us for information we didn't have. Or he'd force me to use my magic to figure it out—and I refused that. I refused to be a pawn in any Hunter's agenda.

My anger had reached its boiling point. It was Momma's turn to trust me.

I defiantly stared back at the man holding my face, imagining the tight ropes that bound my body to the chair. *Exsolvo.*

Concern lined Marcus's rough features; he knew that I'd used magic, just not what I'd cast. The ropes fell limp onto my hands.

I stood up, shaking them off. "You forgot Ateras can do *that.*"

Marcus bit his lip, clenching his fists. My muscles tensed, anticipating his next move—anticipating what spell to use next.

"Your mom picked the right school for you," he said. "Tell you what."

"Emmalynn," Momma whispered, disappointment dragging my name. "I told you no—"

Marcus flung himself behind her. A switchblade flicked open in his hand. His other grabbed the back of Momma's head as he pressed the blade to her throat.

"Mom—!"

"Stay *right* there!" he growled when I tried to step forward. "You and I both know magic can't bring back the dead. Untie her ropes and she's gone."

"Hurt her and you're next!" I snarled, but only to hide the

sobs in my throat. My mind was split between the terror locking my chest and the enraged thrum pulsing in my veins.

"I have what you want, you have what I want." A smirk I wanted to slap right off his face slithered to his lips. "How about this: stay with me, and I'll let her go."

Momma opened her mouth, but Marcus silenced her with a wide-eyed scowl.

I wasn't about to make a deal with the devil, though, not after Mom's experience. More importantly, it was more than safe to assume that he'd learned his lesson from that—he wouldn't be so naïve this time as to actually uphold his end of the bargain.

"Who's it gonna be, kid?" Marcus's impatient glare could cut through obsidian. "Your mom or your dad, pick one!"

Ite procul!

The heat of my anger screamed for release, and I was ready to indulge: my telekinesis ripped the switchblade out of Marcus's hand. It flew through the archway and into the living room wall while I untied Momma's ropes.

With one glower at Greenwell, he was off the ground.

Momma jumped from the chair. "Good girl," she breathed, putting one hand on my shoulder as she looked up at our captive dangling in thin air. His head was almost touching the ceiling.

"Is this supposed to scare me?" Marcus laughed, trying to find his balance even though he didn't need to. "You think this is enough—?"

My fury wanted to go further, and I was going to let it. I brought my other hand up—just as Hunter had—and slowly closed it into a fist. My will alone cast my desire, curdling Marcus's words in his throat. He gasped for air, eyes wide and blaring their terror.

"Emma," Momma said, realizing what I was doing. I didn't stop. "Emmalynn!"

"Please—" the man above us choked out, holding his neck. "Please, I—I'll—!"

"*Emmalynn!*"

I closed my fist all the way and then just as quickly let go, dropping Greenwell onto the floor. Incessant coughs cut off his gulps of air, but I felt no pity for the man who'd just threatened to slit my mother's throat. I walked to him, kneeled down, and used telekinesis to force his head up.

"You will *never* come after me or my family again," I hissed, staring with fire. "Leave us alone, drop your position as a Master Hunter, and let me and my mom go. You won't tell *anyone*"—I leaned in closer—"about us or tonight unless you want this fate for your family. And if you think I'm bluffing,"—he gasped as my magic closed his throat—"their blood will be on *your* hands."

I released him. Marcus bowed his head, too afraid now to look me in the eye.

Veritatem dicere.

"That's the deal. Will you keep your end of it?"

"Yes!" he whispered frailly, keeping his head bowed. "Yes, I will, I swear!"

I released him from the truth spell, stood up, and walked to the front door. In that moment, the adrenaline and satisfaction were so addicting that I didn't even wait for Mom to follow me out of the house.

Something brand new settled over Momma during our drive to the outskirts of the Callistro Forest. I'd sat in her angry and tired silences before, but this—I'd never experienced this one. She was... scared.

It wasn't until we parked the van in a nearby parking lot and entered the forest that she finally took in a breath to speak. "What was that?" she asked flatly. Not even out of reprimanding me, but—out of that fear. "You were about to kill him."

Pine needles and dirt crunched under my feet as I stopped. The night replayed in my head, but all I could remember clearly was when I'd begun to strangle a man. And then threatened his family—his son, a boy I cared about.

I couldn't look at Momma when I told her the truth, when I had nothing to justify it with. "I don't know."

She stopped in her tracks and faced me. But she didn't walk to me. "When did Mr. Dawson teach you how to cast two spells at the same time? W—when did he teach you... *that?* Why would he ever teach you something like that?"

Tears pressed behind my eyes as I felt myself, my real self, return to me. Shame engulfed my body in flames. "He didn't."

Momma exhaled, a puff of fog betraying it.

"Come on," she eventually said, gesturing for me to follow her. She continued walking deeper into the forest and toward the school.

That was the most painful part of the night: Mom not coming over to hug me and tell me that things were okay now, that we could go home safely. Mom not coming over to me and comforting me, because she couldn't. Because, for the first time in my life, she was scared of my magic.

Thirty-Five

The silver doors slid open in front of me, Sarah, and Breanne, welcoming us back into the Hunter's Room (as much as a room filled with weapons *can* welcome you). On my screen, Annisa was still typing as the three of us walked out of the elevator and Breanne rambled about her analysis of the pharmacological chemistry in *Romeo and Juliet*.

A bubble of text finally appeared.

A: I was thinking, imagine how much you
would improve in your classes if you travelled
back to 1778 and became a spy for the Conti-
nental Army? Or, you can't actually join the
army, but you could pretend to

I grinned, finally without punishment from my lip after a few days. Annisa's power offered so many possibilities that, thanks to her, I *literally* had all the time in the world to explore. Or, rather, I would've been able to explore them if she hadn't gone back to Canada.

Also, I was pretty sure that that suggestion was more for her than for me.

E: Maybe sometime lol, just to try

"Emma, dear," Sarah sang next to me, catching up. I immediately slid out of the conversation. "You know we're not supposed to text during class."

Breanne chortled from my other side. "You're really suffering, aren't you?"

Mrs. Durrett had finally caught Sarah on her phone in AP Lang yesterday. I thought that she'd been texting Adrien, but Mrs. Durrett ended up asking her to "study for physics *outside* of class next time". Breanne and I had shared a hopelessly confused glance at each other, and then four minutes later, Sarah was caught texting Adrien about how frustrated she was that her phone had almost been confiscated.

"They're stealing the last few months I get to HAVE a phone!" Sarah snapped, stopping next to the cerebral polygraph display pillar. Her words ran as fast as a rabbit. "We can't have them next year or even while we're on the junior class trip."

"What?" Breanne and I asked.

"Oh, yeah." Sarah smirked, tossing her hair behind her shoulders. "You didn't hear it from me, but the trip next year for the junior class is gonna be *huge*. I highly doubt they'll let us take our phones."

No, no, no, if I didn't have my phone, how could I make sure that Dad and Aunt Becca were safe while I was gone? How long would the trip be? Would we be even remotely close by?

"Do we have to go?" I asked as our classmates began streaming into Momma's class on the left side of the room.

"Yep," Sarah said. "It's a *huge* part of training. The class is even sworn to *strict* confidentiality about the whole thing."

"That's so weird," I said. I quickly noticed that we were the last few Callistro Girls in the Hunter's Room, along with a late Teresa Darci and Hannah Lowe now coming out of the elevator. "Is that not ominously threatening to anyone else?"

"This entire career is threatening," Breanne said. "It's probably just for the same reasons of confidentiality."

Teresa and Hannah were now scurrying into the classroom. Sarah, Breanne, and I followed after them.

"Still, it just feels..."

"Ladies, please finish your conversation after class," Momma called from the front of the room, eyeing the three of us as we took our seats.

Two face-down photos sat in front of us on our table—one for me and one for Breanne next to me. We just as quickly returned our attention to Momma. Her posture was picture perfect as usual, her hands resting behind her back. She made eye contact with every girl in the room, commanding their silence, before taking a steady breath in.

"Photo analysis," she began, stepping down from the platform and starting her walk around the classroom, "is one of the most vital skills in a Hunter's arsenal. Photos will tell you much more than setting and the people there at the time if you let them. Every picture tells you an entire timeline of an event. They can contain the past, present, and future all in one."

She strolled along the back of the room now. "Today, I'm going to teach you a method that, if executed *thoroughly*, will never fail to tell you the story behind a picture."

She returned to the front of the room, black heels clicking on the dark oak. Picking up a purple dry erase marker from the lip of the whiteboard, she wrote "OFTEN" on the board.

"This," she said, writing each word as she spoke it, "is 'observations'… 'facts'… 'theories'… 'edits'… and 'names'."

"First, list your observations. No detail is too small or insignificant, and every one has the potential of playing a vital role in a picture.

"But that's why you'll run into a common and sometimes fatal enemy: overlooking. Your eyes will catch something they typically see throughout day-to-day life, or something that seems normal for its setting. You could be examining the senior portrait of a Callistro Girl in her uniform, for example."

A handful of us instinctually looked down at the gray plaid skirts and crimson blazers we wore, like we were noting every detail now.

"Same crest embroidered on the blazer and everything," Momma said. "But before you allow assumptions to overlook a critical detail, you notice that *her* blazer is open because it doesn't have any buttons. You notice that the crest is sewed on the *right* side, and you notice that her dress shirt buttons from the left."

Her defined eyes swept across the room, waiting for one of

us to respond, but we knew better.

"Meaning she's not a Callistro Girl. She's an enemy who's already infiltrated your walls. Observation"—Momma rested her hands on the back of her desk chair—"is critical."

I wondered how much that night with Agent Greenwell was fueling her lesson—her passion in making sure that we understood this. If any of it even *was* running through her head, or if this was how she was distracting herself from it.

"Second," she said next, "list the facts of the case. Write this down: do not let your inferences interfere with this step. The facts not only bring you to the next step of thorough analysis, but they let you execute it *accurately*: your theories. You never form them based on a gut feeling, past experiences, or inferences. Facts are the *only* thing that will tell you what was really happening at the time a photo was taken.

"Then, you're going to *edit* your theories. Eliminate your discrepancies and any objective impossibility—in this industry, though, you'll find how few of those exist, so be careful. Narrow down every last detail and curve toward one. Then you'll be brought to your last step: names. Names of the people, the cars, the places, whatever it may be. Utilize the facts, apply your perfected theory, and determine what is really happening in your photo to answer a question about your mission."

Breanne was writing at a hundred miles per hour as usual, but when I looked down at my paper, I'd only written "O.F.T.E.N." and what each word stood for. Maybe it was because Momma had just returned home from being kidnapped a couple of days ago, but her words had carried me into the wind. It was a lot more hypnotizing and easier for my attention to fade than it should've been.

Momma snapped her fingers and then pointed up. We turned over our photographs. Mine featured a side view of an opera singer, taken from the wing of the stage. A slip of paper had been lying underneath the photo.

"Each picture in front of you has captured a seemingly normal day or a regular event. The piece of paper in front of you has the context of your case. You have one hour to figure out what's wrong."

Looking back down at the opera singer, I made sure to start paying extra close attention. I had a feeling that today's lesson would eventually extend far beyond a class assignment.

"I just want an iced coffee!" Sarah whined as we walked into the Grand Foyer after school. "They're working us to death."

"Oh, oh, wait," Breanne said, taking my arm and stopping us in the center of the foyer. She looked at Sarah. "Can you grab us a snack from the Dining Hall? I wanna get some extra study time in and eat in our room."

"Yeah, sure." Sarah sighed, her usual bounce absent from her steps as she walked toward the Hall.

Something felt... off.

"I think something's wrong," Breanne whispered to me only after Sarah passed through the entryway. Her doe-like eyes slightly looked up at me with worry. "She hasn't been herself since, like, mid-January. Maybe even a little before that, since November."

I shrugged. "This semester's definitely harder than last."

"Yeah, but I went to school with her for the last eight years." She gripped her left backpack strap with tight, pale fingers. "And you've known her for just as long. You realize that she's going without her phone right now because she was caught *studying* in class, right?"

Breanne had missed a minor detail of a story that I knew she knew well: Sarah had lost her phone for texting Adrien *about* getting caught studying. That meant that Breanne was upset enough to not care about getting the details right, and the truth was, I was just as concerned—but pretending I was overthinking was easier. It wasn't reality.

Was it?

Breanne swallowed, picking at the hair on her wrist. "I just hope she's not overworking herself."

"We can make sure she isn't," I told her, then laughing. "But studying in our room isn't the way to go."

Her eyes locked on the Dining Hall entrance, jaw making subtle movements as she grinded her teeth. Her hand hadn't moved away from her wrist. I was worried, too, but Breanne had all the more reason to be: last time, *she'd* been the one to keep a secret eating her alive from the inside out. And the only reason Momma had been able to save her from her ex-boyfriend was because I'd used a locator spell...

What was going on with Sarah?

"It's fine," I assured Breanne. "She'll tell us when she's ready. And if it gets bad, we can ask her about it."

Her gaze darted over my shoulder before she could reply. I followed them, turning around. Mr. Dawson was stepping out of his office and walking to us.

"Hi, Headmaster Dawson," Breanne said as he approached.

He gave her a gentle smile of acknowledgement. "Good afternoon, Miss Shaw. Miss Marie, may I borrow you for a few minutes?"

"I'll be up in our room," Breanne said, adjusting her backpack and extending her hand for me to give her mine. "Go ahead, Headmaster Dawson. Have a good day!"

I handed her my backpack as he replied, "You, too."

I only watched Breanne scamper up the Main Staircase for a second before the magnet of Mr. Dawson's stare became too strong. He gained my attention, nodding to his door behind me.

"My office, please."

Okay. Why did it feel like I was getting called into the headmaster's office more often lately?

And why did this time feel like I'd *earned* it?

He allowed me inside first before closing the door. The first thing I noticed was Momma sitting on the white leather sofa against the right wall.

What was going on now?

Surprisingly, she stayed quiet. I looked back at Mr. Dawson to ask my first question, but he took a breath in and asked, "In your own words, what happened?"

Oh. Agent Greenwell.

I didn't know what to say. And I hoped that I'd stay dumbfounded long enough for him to propel the conversation somehow, but his and Momma's stares started burning.

I finally found the words: "He kidnapped us."

Without acknowledging me, Mr. Dawson walked by and to his desk. He leaned against it, using his arms for support. "And?"

This was it. I had to face reality head on. I glimpsed my mother as if for help, but she'd already told Mr. Dawson everything, every detail from that night.

I was in trouble.

"Emma," Mr. Dawson stated when I didn't respond. I braced myself to have the answers to whatever questions he was about to fire. "I never taught you how to choke someone in midair. I never taught you how to lift someone into the air. I never taught you how to do either of those things *in your head*, because there isn't even a spell to choke someone for *obvious* reasons! Lifting someone off the ground requires strong telekinesis, and you can barely lift a pile of textbooks!"

Was it really necessary to keep bringing that up?

He crossed his arms. "But above all else, I never taught you how to *blackmail* a Master Hunter. I thought you were friends with his son, and all of a sudden I'm hearing that you threatened to kill him!"

The navy rug under the glass coffee table was my only comfort in the mortifying midst of his scolding. Why Momma didn't say a word, I refused to think about for too long, because hearing about what I'd done was the confirmation that Friday night had actually happened. *I* had done all of those things, and knowing that was punishment enough.

And Mr. Dawson only confirmed the most terrifying part about it all when he asked, "Where did you learn how to choke someone in midair?"

I hadn't learned it from anyone; I'd just copied Hunter.

"I just did it," I admitted. "I felt my magic and what I wanted to do."

Momma's silence changed moods—from observant to curious—as Mr. Dawson stood from his desk. He rounded it to sit in his chair and rubbed his face with both hands. A heavy sigh left his lips, one that was all too loud with the words trapped in his head.

"What?" I dared to ask.

He reserved a few more seconds to himself, but Momma's breath in cut him off.

"When you started choking Marcus," she said, keeping strict eye contact, "your eyes changed from amber to amethyst."

What...? What? But that wasn't—she couldn't have seen that right! Amethyst? A magician's eyes don't turn amethyst when they cast, they've turned amber since the beginning of time!

"Did you know?" Mr. Dawson asked me.

"No!" I finally sputtered. "I've *never* heard of that before!"

"Yeah." He lightly shook his head. "Nobody has."

Not one answer crossed my thoughts. No wonder Momma had been so afraid of me. We were crossing a threshold into an unknown that no human had ever encountered.

"Look. This could be really dangerous," Mr. Dawson said. "Not to say that it is, but that's not at all to say it isn't. We have no idea if this resulted from you casting with just your will, from a malicious thing done with it... I don't know. But because of that, the only thing I'm teaching you until we figure out what's going on is control. I think you can agree that that's the most important thing right now. Okay?"

I fiddled with the silver locket around my neck, the rest of my body unsure of what to do. "Okay."

"And on the note of violence," Momma added, shifting her

position in her seat and holding up a finger, "I want the *full* story of how you ended up with that cut on your lip."

I opened my mouth, ready to argue that it really had been as simple as defending myself and Ava against a few boys—but it hadn't been that simple. That fight had *literally* only happened because of my magic.

I took a seat across from her on the other sofa. "I had a dream—actually, I had a few—where some boys took Ava to this alley behind the mall. We fought them off and I used magic, but she saw me. Then I ran into someone and woke up. They were *really* small fragments, less than two seconds, if even a second long, and there was a flash between each one, but I felt myself *right* there, standing in my perspective as I fought."

Mr. Dawson's deep-set eyes widened to golf balls. "What?" he whispered.

I didn't want to repeat myself because of it, like I'd just spoken a death curse over him.

"Hang on," Momma said. She leaned against the arm of the couch, her brows crinkling together. "You had a dream that that would happen?"

"One of them started out with... Jak and I were at the food court, and the boys were approaching Ava. I wanted to interfere, but Jak stopped me. And then it flashed to just me and Ava in the alley with them. We talked, and it kept flashing to fight scenes. I couldn't catch more than a few words from anyone, the image would flash again... Some things actually happened but not everything."

"You had a vision."

The words were so steady that I had to look at Mr. Dawson

to see if he was actually that calm. Instead, I'd never felt more like a stranger under his gaze.

"*You* had a vision," he repeated, but I think he was trying to get himself to believe it more than me or Momma. "But that's not—that's not possible, you're not a druid."

What did he want me to say? That it was a coincidence? That it wasn't possible for me to dream of the future even though I had?

"I don't know how it happened," I said. "But when I got to the mall, this—weird flash of it suddenly hit me right before I found Ava. It was so strong, it knocked me over. It was like a vision, but I was awake."

Mr. Dawson's brows furrowed like I'd just called him stupid. "I've never heard—"

He cut himself off, lips pressed together as a hand passed over his face. I'd never seen tiredness pull down so heavily on his sharp features.

Not even he knows what's going on?

"Okay," he finally said, leaning forward. "I know neither of you want to hear this, but Moren is the only person we know who can and *will* tell us what's going on with Emma."

"I don't think so," Momma said reproachfully. "We'd have to pay his price, and I want him to have as little dirt on us as possible. He already got something out of Tristan and Becca."

"We've been asking questions for *weeks*, Amy," Mr. Dawson stated. "We can't get answers anywhere else! Unless Tristan and Becca know something about this, but they're not exactly an option right now!"

"I know it's dangerous!" Momma shot back, almost pushing me back—dangerous? Did... did she think I was dangerous? "But just because we *can* get answers from Moren doesn't mean we should. It doesn't mean we can *afford* them."

"What do you suggest we do, then?"

She opened her mouth but then closed it. Her fingers twisted the golden band on her left hand as she slouched in her seat. I hoped that she was thinking of a plan—that's what my mother usually does, it's how she keeps me safe.

Instead, she said, "Please, Emma," with tired eyes on me. My hope fell with her chest as she sighed. "*Promise* me: no magic unless necessary."

C H A P T E R

Thirty-Six

I'm not sure what I expected the evening to look like—maybe some progress on my diagram of a Higgs boson particle, finishing my Portuguese essay on the aliens-helping-the-Aztecs conspiracy theory, and an at-home spa night with Sarah and Breanne if we had time. A text from Nolan asking if we could talk? Not on that list.

The second surprise was how Mr. Dawson actually gave me a pass to leave, but it wasn't like we had to worry about Marcus. And he didn't know about Hunter, but I was taking Momma's car to avoid another run-in with them anyway.

The town square was practically empty, as if Nolan had rented it out for the night. The soft yellow glow of the streetlamps was at least some comfort. My nerves eased a bit as I approached the fountain and found Nolan pacing in front of it. A white shirt with his baseball team's logo printed on it hung off him under a denim jacket. And as always, the baby-blue beanie on his head was doing him favors.

"Hey," I said, walking up.

His head bounced up, his soft features holding something I'd never seen from him before: sadness. Disappointment, I'd seen, but not sadness...

"Hey."

Okay. Something was definitely wrong.

I crossed my arms, which, despite taking a sweater before I left, did close to nothing to preserve the little body heat I had. The crisp scent of the ending winter shot a bullet of cold through me. "You wanted to talk?"

To my dismay and excitement, Nolan took off his denim jacket and closed the gap between us, trying to drape it around my shoulders.

"Oh, you don't have to—"

"No," he said, pulling the sides of the jacket as close together as they'd go, "I do. That's probably the only time I'll ever get to do something like that for you."

I narrowed my eyes. "What do you mean?"

He stuck his pale hands into his pockets and shrugged, casting his eyes down. It seemed like he had to win a game of tug-of-war in his mind just to look at me. "My dad doesn't want me to see you anymore."

Wait. What?

Then again, could I really be surprised? Friday night, I'd threatened his entire family! I think that night, I'd forgotten that

Nolan was related to Marcus at all—maybe that was why it was so easy to look at Nolan now, to talk to him. Up until those words fell from his lips and I remembered my sins.

"Why not?" I asked.

"He doesn't 'trust' you." Anger brewed in Nolan's clear voice. "I offered for you and your mom to have dinner with us sometime, and he totally snapped. He doesn't... I'm not allowed to see you anymore, and I don't even know why."

"Oh."

I knew why. I knew exactly why, and I couldn't even tell him. My only option was to stand there and let his jacket start to slip off my shoulders. I took it off before it could fall and handed it back to him.

I could feel both of us staring at it for a few seconds. When enough time passed and he still didn't say anything, I looked up. His eyes had shifted to me, burning with some kind of worn desire that I couldn't name. Not until he walked past the jacket, cupped my face, and pressed his lips against mine.

And, well, I kissed him back, because he'd unearthed a buried whim. What was it like to have a crush on someone who had nothing to do with the mortal-magic war? What was it like to have romantic experiences with a boy from my hometown? What was it like kissing a normal boy?

It was... wonderful.

I held Nolan's jacket in one hand and rested the other on his arm. He broke away, looking into my eyes as if every answer he wanted lay in them.

"Sorry." He exhaled, my cheeks almost numb to his equally cold hands. "I shouldn't've just—come up like that but you have no idea how long I've wanted to do that. I just... I had to know."

"Me, too."

Even in that moment, I knew that it was wrong. I was remembering every reason I couldn't be with Nolan: for every reason I couldn't be with Jak and then some, because Nolan didn't even know that Hunter schools existed.

"Can we try this, Em?" he asked. "I really wanna see if we could work. My dad's always busy with work, it's not like he'll see us—"

"It's not gonna work," I told him, stepping back from him. Hot tears pressed behind my eyes, and I scolded myself for it. "It can't—"

"Why?" His hands slid down to my shoulders. "If you don't feel the same way—"

"No, I do, I just—!" I said, turning to the fountain. "That's the problem, I... I do wanna try—"

"Then why can't we?" He took the jacket from my hand and draped it around my shoulders again, taking note of my light shivers. The way his fingers traced down to my chin, I could practically feel his want for another kiss. "Why can't we make 'us' a thing?"

"No, I'm sorry." I turned around and let the jacket fall as I left. Nolan called after me, but all that was left in my courage was to turn around and shout again, "I'm sorry!"

Despite going to an all-girls Hunter school herself, Momma still had a handful of bachelors chasing after her in high school. Dad was far from her first relationship, just the only one she'd ever gotten serious with. It wasn't like I was serious with Jak or even with him in the first place, but... I still felt like I'd crossed a boundary I'd had no business even setting eyes on. I already knew what Sarah and Breanne would say about it—I needed to talk to someone who knew me *and* how to separate the emotions from the facts.

And someone who could factor Nolan's dad into their advice.

At least Momma told me that I'd done the right thing in severing myself from the situation. Next time, though, I had to give him an actual explanation and not leave the poor boy hanging. She also said, for a lot more reasons, I had to cut off the romantic situation with Jak—which obviously gave me two things to look forward to.

The next afternoon, when the girls and I were on our way up to our dorm, it was like Jak knew what had happened the night before and had decided to call me just to haunt me. I tried not to complain, though; it was Jak, first of all. And anything from him always potentially meant an update on Alexa and William.

"How's it going, Merlin?"

"Things are crazy," I said casually as the girls and I reached the top of the last staircase. "What about you?"

"Things are deceptively normal," he replied. I wondered if he was walking, too, where he could be on his way to. "Pretty boring... Have you been okay? Any more attacks?"

At my extended silence, Sarah and Breanne looked over their shoulders at me. I gestured for them to keep walking as we approached our door. Now that I thought about it, it had actually been some time since I'd last seen Julia for anything, not even to escort a classmate. But the problem was far from taken care of.

"Merlin?"

"They've been happening less." I waited behind Sarah as she unlocked and then opened our door. I set my backpack down next to the closet. "It's been a while since I last had one, actually."

"Julia probably appreciates the break," he teased.

I chuckled. "And you only saw me in there once."

"Yeah, good thing she's the *nice* kind of school nurse. You two seemed like friends."

"We kind of are," I said, plopping down onto my bed. Breanne was already cracking open her textbook on the desk in the corner of the room, and Sarah was faithfully side-eyeing me as she entered the bathroom. "She's actually why I've been able to get some kind of control over the anxiety."

To my surprise, he laughed. "Okay, I'm sorry, that's just—that's kind of ironic to me."

"Why?"

"You're gonna think I'm crazy, which go ahead. But the second I met her, the way she talked, her smirk, even her walk, just her air in general—I'd never met her before but I *recognized* it."

Great—Julia was the spitting image of his late mom, wasn't she? It felt like *every* time Jak talked to me, he was just reminded of his mother. What was I supposed to say? Was I supposed to comfort him? Did I need to? Or was he about to open up a happy memory instead?

"Or I'm crazy because I haven't seen her for a couple months," he said next, "but she reminds me a lot of Alexa. Even her eyes and kind of the hair color."

I froze on my bed. No. No—why was something connecting

in my head? It couldn't be. It wasn't possible, she couldn't... Alexa couldn't be—

Steven was able to make a spell that alters your appearance.

Alexa was in the passageways when I located her using his locator spell.

Julia knows my secret.

Alexa knows my secret.

"You still there?"

"I have to go," I said, hanging up the phone and leaping from my bed and to the door.

"Emma?" Sarah called from the bathroom.

"I'll be back," I called, shutting the door behind me and dashing back down the corridor.

Why does it make sense?

I ran down each flight of stairs until I got to the Grand Foyer, adrenaline moving my feet.

All this time, this whole time.

I bolted past Mr. Dawson's office, denying his protection.

Julia plays her role well. Her role. Moren had to know. Why didn't he tell me?

I reached the doorway of the nurse's office, my chest on fire.

"Hello, stranger," Julia said, taking a quick glance up in my direction. Her eyes were otherwise glued to the pages of *To Kill a Mockingbird*. "What's wrong now? Sick? Injured body part—?"

"No," I said, closing the door behind me. "I just... I just wanna talk."

The lock clicking into place pulled her attention back to me. She set the book down onto the desk. For a second—a split second—her body seemed to tense. Her arms were almost defensive.

But instinct and training were quick to settle in, and she relaxed.

"Okay..." she said. "About what?"

The question slammed into me like a truck: I'd acted on impulse, without a plan. Where was I supposed to go from here? How was I supposed to corner her without trapping myself?

Momma's words from class last year echoed in my head: the second you let your target know that you know their secret is the second you hand the game over. It's the second you give them the power to win.

"I thought about what you said a couple of months ago," I began, leaning against the door. If I seemed comfortable, Julia would be more comfortable. "About nursing instead of hunting."

Her smile was sickeningly kind. "You want to become a school nurse instead of a Hunter?"

"Not exactly. Um... can we talk in there?"

She stood from the desk, giving me permission to walk into the private room built in on the left side of the room. Following closely behind, she closed the door behind us. Did she always look at me this carefully, or was that my paranoia?

"You chose a different profession," I said, sitting on the edge of the mattress. "You had two options, and you chose the best one for you. The one that could give you the life you wanted."

"Yes..." she said carefully. She took her spot in front of the sink, the rolling stool beside her—but she didn't sit. That was a first. "So if not nursing or hunting, what do you want to do when you graduate?"

"I still wanna leave a mark." I glimpsed the delicate red roses in the vase next to the sink. The tips of their petals were withering. "But I can't do that by becoming a Hunter. I wanna change the world with magic."

Julia's head jerked back, glancing at the closed door as if someone was listening. "Emmalynn—what are you talking about?"

The light of realization flooded my mind. My name—that was it. The detail that told me everything I needed to know about the situation, the facts of the case: the people who knew me called me "Emma". My nickname proved that I was on friendly terms with someone, that we'd at least known each other beyond being acquaintances. For obvious reasons, Alexa and William didn't fall under that category.

Julia did. We'd become friends long ago, but she'd never let go of "Emmalynn".

"Julia chose to be a nurse because she didn't want the world to see her as a Hunter," I said, pushing my feet into the ground to keep myself grounded. "She had a legacy she was born into, but she picked the other side because it was the path to getting what she really wanted. That sounds familiar, that sounds really familiar to me."

"I need you to calm down, Emmalynn—"

"Why do you call me that?"

Julia tightened her stance in a way I'd only ever seen my mother and classmates do in the gym. Her eyes were hardening by the second. She was too defensive.

I slowly stood up, surrendering my naivety. "You *do* know who I am. Julia's known this entire time because—she's not real."

Green eyes I should've recognized long ago stared back at me, angry eyes that I'd seen the early morning of my birthday right before Dad and I escaped the beach house.

Then, they softened. They were the other pair I'd come to

know over the last few months.

"You know who I am, too, don't you?"

My mind reeled with every memory I had of Julia and our friendship—every last word of advice that had seemed so genuine, so wise, and had actually worked when I followed it. Everything turned on me as I stared into her eyes one last time.

I cursed the lie of her nametag that read "Julia". "You're Alexa Delphine."

Thirty-Seven

Julia—I mean, Alexa—turned and walked into the supply closet at the end of the room. Inside, she cast something I'd never heard before and then walked out as her true self: trademark red hair, green eyes, and all.

A stormy wave of anxiety slammed over me, almost strong enough to knock me back onto the vinyl mattress. I hadn't seen this woman since the most traumatic night of my life that *she* had caused—and I'd been living with her since October.

Her shoulder-length hair bouncing with every step, her emerald eyes sharpening against the fluorescent lights, her defined lips—I had every detail of this woman memorized, and yet the sight of her struck a violent chord in me every time. A fear reserved just for her.

"You did a great job keeping what happened last year to your-self. No matter how many times I tried to get it out of you." A sinister smile slithered to her lips. "I'm glad to know that I can trust you to keep your mouth shut."

I hated how deeply her eyes dug into me as she said it. Like this was the most fun game she'd ever played in her life.

"Why are you here?" I spat—because now I was realizing that all those times I'd managed to push back fear and seemingly jump over it, I'd only stuffed it all into storage. And the container wasn't big enough anymore. "You're supposed to be hunting us, doesn't anyone notice you've been gone this whole time?"

"Where do you think I got the name and disguise from?" She sat on the black stool, as cool as a Hunter who had her prey right where she wanted it. "I switched names and looks with my sister. She's the one out on the hunt right now."

"Isn't she already in your pack?"

"Nope. The Hunter game was too outlandish for her—which is too bad, because she was pretty good. But I had a favor to cash in, and she had nothing better to do." Alexa's smile widened into a grin, twisting my stomach. "She's been leading the pack while I do my research here. I tell her what to do, and the pack follows 'my' lead."

The mall... I wondered if the real Julia had sent William to scope us out, to keep him out of the way and give him less time to suspect something was amiss with his wife.

I shook my head at the memory. "What about William's say? Doesn't he co-lead—?"

"William's wrapped so tightly around my finger, you can put a bow on him and call him a present," Alexa simpered, leaning against the counter in her seat. "Whenever he plans something that threatens our progress, I tell Julia how to persuade him and get us back on track. So while she's been busy being me"—her eyes glinted with marvel—"I've been having quite the field day."

I thought back to the night Cara first texted me, the night of Sarah's aunt and uncle's New Year's party. And I realized the question that I'd somehow managed to bury for the last two and a half months: "Does William recognize my mom?"

"As Amy Dalbert, no. He never saw what she looked like when we were about to recruit her. I was the only one trusted with her image."

"So then why? You already know I'm Tristan's daughter. You know who my mom is, you know we're guilty! Why haven't you attacked yet?"

Her hesitance struck me like a baseball bat. Her breath in arrived too late for her to hide it, but she licked her lips in recovery.

"Every Hunter had a strategy," she said lowly. She folded her hands in her lap. "Let's just say that I have to make sure the Delphines aren't exposed with you. And I also have to uphold my 'Hunter's promise' of making sure you're not a threat to anyone."

No. Something was wrong with that. Something was as off about that as it was when she'd let me go twice last semester. That, and the fact that—

"Says the *magician* who's stealing magic so she can dominate and destroy the world!"

Alexa's eyes flashed with something I was too scared to name. She wasn't Sympathetic Alexa anymore. She'd made up her mind, stripping herself of that hesitance.

"Dominate and destroy, huh?" she said, too close to a whisper. It didn't fit the Grand Hunter I'd come to know. "That's what you think I'm trying to do?"

"What would you call it?" I snapped. "I know you're not protecting us! *I'm* the one trying to save our people from you! It's the only reason I'm still fighting you!"

She breathily snickered. "Oh, sweet girl."

I didn't dare blink—not unless I'd miss what was happening behind her softening eyes. And I couldn't miss it this time because, for the first time ever, I was pretty sure Alexa was exposing who she was and not who she forced herself to be.

"You know..." she said, "you know so little."

Don't let her trick you, I commanded myself. Julia wasn't in there anymore. I couldn't let myself believe otherwise.

"I was like you."

The silence was heavy with impending information, yet no matter how hard I tried, I couldn't swallow quietly. Part of me silently begged that it wouldn't change Alexa's mind, that she'd continue even if she saw how much I had to know what she was thinking.

"My hope was abundant," she said. "I dreamed of better days, I saw the potential for understanding in people—but not from the side you'd assume. Our people—"

I think it was the unfamiliarity of the words that stopped her. She cleared her throat and made herself ignorant to my stare, looking down.

"Magicians don't stand alone in the thorns of misunderstanding. We're divided by laws, Emmalynn. But we all stand in the same chains. Always have."

Don't let her trick you. Don't fall for it.

Not after what I'd learned about history. Who was massacred by the thousands year after year? Who was being trained in elite schools to rid half the world's population? Who had to pretend to be the other to avoid being killed? Who had the rights to a free life in *every* country of the world, not just a handful of them?

"So you decided"—I dragged my eyes down to her chin, too afraid of her reaction to my words now—"that if you had full control, everything would just be... better?"

"Sure, why not?" she said, stepping back into her false sympathy. "Let's take over the world since nobody else can be trusted with it. Why do you think I've kept Caralyn's letters safe this whole time? The woman wrote a recipe for anarchy—the last thing I want is that getting into the wrong hands."

Caralyn's letters were safe—but they were safe for all the wrong reasons. I didn't know how to feel about that. I especially didn't know how to feel about her "protecting" those documents when this had been her plan the entire time: to get close to me, to gain my trust so that I'd eventually divulge *my* darkest secrets to Julia—and then arrest me for it. *Far* from protection.

My blood was boiling. I'd confided so surely in Julia, but I'd actually confided in Alexa Delphine. *She* had taken care of me when I was sick. *She* had joked and teased me with Jak. *She* had helped me stop the anxiety and panic attacks when she had been the cause of them in the first place!

She'd been my comfort when I was driving myself insane! When SHE was driving me insane! It had been her all this time!

Why would she do that to me?

"Why did you help me?" I cried. My feet felt too heavy on the tile, like I was glued to my spot against my will. "You were the one causing my attacks, you *knew* that! Why did you help me?"

"Just because I'm after your family's magic doesn't mean I live to watch you suffer," Alexa replied, almost... bitterly. Her eyes even narrowed slightly. "I was teaching you a skill you're going to need throughout the rest of your life, Emmalynn, as a magician or Hunter. You need to know how to defeat what will always be the greatest weapon against you: your mind."

I swallowed hard. It seemed to resonate as Alexa and I caught ourselves locked in the other's scowl.

I didn't know her like I'd thought I did—as Alexa or Julia. She was a master of identity, of deception and getting whatever she wanted no matter what leaps she had to make for it. No matter how she had to hide to get it.

My jaw clenched, trying to cage my words—but one last tired, frustrated exhale made everything tumble down. "Are you Hunter?"

Maybe the question had spawned from my rage—maybe I wanted her to confess *everything* she really was, the despicable person she was—because only she could match Hunter's description at this point.

"'Hunter'?" Alexa repeated, cocking a brow. She took in a breath to speak but then hesitated. "Who's Hunter?"

Great job, Emma. Fantastic *job.*

With my mouth agape, frozen by every word competing for my voice, my fear had built a strong-enough wall to trap my thoughts. I had nothing to say, and it was a death sentence.

She tilted her head down as if to ask, *Well?* And I felt an indomitable urge to spill.

"I don't... I don't know," I said. "They've been—investigating me. I guess, who I am."

Alexa took another breath, her shoulders falling. She stood from the rolling stool, and I had the all-too-familiar feeling that I'd said something I wasn't supposed to.

"You're saying," she said—no teeth, no smile, no smirk, "that I have a competitor?"

Not again. I can't do this again. Not again, please not again.

Wonder flashed in her eyes. "What's Hunter done to you so far?"

When I didn't respond—because I really didn't know how to begin that answer—she took a hard step forward, startling me.

"What've they done to you, Emmalynn?"

"They warned me about Greenwell and took DNA samples."

Amber flowed into her irises, and she forced my head up. She wasn't satisfied. The woman could read me as well as my mother could. "And?"

"They—they drew my blood the last time they took me."

She released my head, staring until she softly scoffed. "So I have a competitor."

To my cautious surprise, she walked to the door and grabbed the knob. She looked over her shoulder to say, "How about, in exchange for your memory, you don't repeat any of this conversation? Sound fair?"

My empty stare fell in defeat to the white tile below her.

"Good girl."

The door opened, and then Alexa's footsteps echoed into the main office. Eventually, the crimson carpet runner out in the hall muted them. She had left me in all my fear, anxiety, and tears.

No. No, no, no. Please stop. Stop it, stop, don't.

The room was swaying. I dropped back onto the mattress. My head was spinning, you could fry an egg on my face, and tears stole my vision as I desperately tried to hold on to the world in front of me.

Each deep, slow breath only reminded me why I was taking them in the first place, reminded me of what had just happened. I furiously twisted the locket around my neck, my world a little more fragile, a little more broken, and a few seconds closer to falling apart.

THIRTY-EIGHT

Ignorance was why I didn't use Steven's spell to find Alexa after that: ignorance *is* bliss, especially when you're a teenager and it's easier to pretend that the real world doesn't exist. I couldn't believe how easily anxiety manipulated my rationality, or, at least, overpowered it. Also because of ignorance, I didn't tell Momma and Mr. Dawson that Julia was actually Alexa—except, a majority of that reason was that Alexa had threatened me not to.

A couple of nights later, though, when I did woman up and use the locator spell, Alexa was driving through the streets of Glenwood—over half an hour out. That, I *really* wanted to believe, meant that she was hunting down Hunter. I was on borrowed comfort for the next week.

The Hunter career occupies our lives more and more the

older we get, but even as a sophomore, I was monitoring my every step and scanning every inch of my surroundings as I trudged through the week. And frankly, I had every right to when my phone buzzed with an unknown number Friday night.

I was a mile beyond paranoid by that point. I took my phone, excused myself from our dorm, and closed the door behind me to prepare. (I'd learned my lesson by then; I couldn't risk Sarah and Breanne seeing my reaction to whatever kind of horrible news was probably waiting for me.)

I forced myself to open the message and look down. , the past three months started all over again.

#: Want to know the results of your blood test?
I'd be more than happy to share.
Forests are rather peaceful,
So why don't you meet me there?
6:00, little 'Marie'. Don't be late.

Hunter had my phone number. Hunter knew who I was.
Hunter had *tested my blood.*
My lips tightened with a familiar helpless anger. No, this was it. I was done with this. I refused to give Hunter any more power with my ignorance, not when Cara, Steven, and I had developed a plan that could tell me exactly who they were. It might've been meant for Alexa, but my priorities had never been clearer.

Hunter said not to be late, but I was definitely bringing backup.

Cara and Steven agreed to meet me in the Callistro Forest, a mile south of the school, to try and use our Alexa plan on Hunter. After all, by that point, Hunter had become just as dangerous.

Dark-blue sky stretched over us by the time I arrived where we'd agreed on. Despite the little daylight that remained, we weren't about to miss the opportunity to meet Hunter.

I hugged myself in the cold, trying to convince myself that it was just to trap warmth, but my coat was growing hotter by the minute. I tried to ignore how tight my jeans were and how an acorn was poking my foot through an extra-worn part of my boot sole. Right now, I needed to be a lot stronger than mere annoyance. The aroma of tree bark and leaves was strong in my nose, my only comfort as I watched a car pull up yards away.

Cara climbed out, leaving the parking lights on. "Nobody's here yet?"

"No." I glanced around the forest, keeping my arms against my chest. "Where's Steven?"

"Hiding," she whispered, leaving her car behind as she came closer to me. "He's waiting. Are you okay?"

"I'm fine."

Alexa's warning played like a record in my head, but Cara and Steven were the ones who were supposed to help me trap her. It only took a second for me to reason that the best way to lure her out was by saying, "I found Alexa."

Cara's head jerked back, confusion scrunching her delicate face. Her gray eyes looked brown in the rapidly fading daylight. "What do you mean?"

"Our school nurse, Julia, was Alexa under an appearance-switch spell this whole time." The words rolled off my tongue with dangerous ease. "Almost the entire year, I trusted her. I could've told her everything if I hadn't..."

Delayed shame made the rest of the words fade into the cold. We were only a few days into spring, but I wished it actually *felt* like spring.

Wait a minute. Dad and Aunt Becca had gone to Steven to ask him to *create* an appearance spell... but if Alexa had been disguising herself as Julia since months before...

"Did Steven create that spell for her?"

"No!" Cara answered in a gasp. "Honey, no, Steven created an appearance-*altering* spell specifically for your dad and aunt. He never made an appearance-switching one."

My gaze rested on the dark leaves, whose colors I could barely distinguish. I tightened my jaw like it was a built-in mechanism to stop my next words from escaping. "She said that the Alexa hunting my family right now is her *sister* Julia. Alexa's been giving her instructions on how to lead the pack while she finds out more about me. I just... I'm angry I never saw it sooner."

"You've been under a *lot* lately," Cara assured me. "That's why you asked Steven for that locator spell. Have you been able to use it?"

"It's really hard, but yeah. I've found Alexa a couple of times with it."

"Good. Then I'd use it to find your Hunter." She pulled out her phone from her coat pocket. "We're nearing meeting time and they told you not to be late, which means they could show up early—"

A loud crack snapped in the distance. Too loud. We'd only heard it because we were supposed to.

Hunter was here.

I darted my stare all around me. In my peripheral, a figure too dark to blend in with the atmosphere whished by the trees. I snapped my head left. They dashed out from behind a trunk to hide behind another.

"Cara—"

She gently shushed me. Her head was as still as a statue's, moving like a cat's when she did turn it.

Rustling shook nearby, too close to my right. A curdled cry erupted into the air. Someone fell out from behind a tree mere yards from where Cara and I stood. We whirled to face them. The dark figure yanked Steven out from behind the tree by his collar.

He was slouched over, clutching his side. A knife glinted in the figure's hand, the car's dim parking lights illuminating the—

No. That was blood.

"STEVEN!" Cara screamed. His attacker jabbed the knife in her direction when she tried to step forward.

I looked them from head to toe: a black suit with matching gloves and boots, with a black cloak and a fabric mask that covered their whole head.

"Hunter," I muttered, voice shaking with anger.

"Hunter?" Cara hissed, her fists so tight that even in the near dark, her knuckles were white. "Take off that mask or I'll rip it off!"

Hunter laughed—and for the first time, she made it audible. For the first time, she gave me a clue to her identity.

For the first time ever, my blood didn't freeze, but boiled at Alexa Delphine's laugh.

"No," I stammered, as if the word could change reality,

"you're not—you said—!"

Still holding a gasping Steven by his collar, Hunter gave that hand the knife. She used the other to grab the bottom of the mask and start pulling it off.

"Honestly, Emmalynn,"—Alexa's sweet voice was muffled until the stretchy fabric came over her head, and she dropped it to the ground—"I thought you would've figured it out by now. You were *so* close, and you still let me convince you otherwise."

I'd ignored all the details that would've told me Hunter's identity, but that was just the problem: Grand Hunter Alexa Delphine was one of the best on the planet. Magic? Check. Kidnapper? Check. Out to physically, emotionally, and mentally torment me? Check. But those categories also fit too many other people for me to be sure! How was I supposed to know, to make *sure*, that there weren't people who already knew about me, who were planning my demise as I spoke?

"Steven!" Cara cried again, but Alexa tossed the knife back to her right hand and pressed it against his throat.

"Take another step and you'll be a widow," she snapped.

"No, you—" I said, "you *told* me you weren't Hunter!"

"No, I didn't," Alexa said all too casually. "I asked *you* who they were and what they'd done to you. I never told you that I wasn't them. Nice name, by the way."

"You said you had a competitor!"

"A competitor for your fear, maybe." She grinned. I was pretty sure that I had enough courage to slap it right off her face. "Still never said that I wasn't that competitor."

I hated her for it, but she was right. She'd been deceiving me from the very beginning. She had been acting the entire time.

Never let your enemy know something they don't already know.

My chest crumpled in shame. Despite the hunts we'd had this semester already, I'd failed the only one that actually mattered.

"But..." I stammered, confusion rising with the anxiety, "why would you warn me about Greenwell? How did you even know about—?"

"He finally stepped down and out of the way because of you," she replied simply. "Thanks for that. I knew you were the right person to send his way."

No way. How much did she know about me and Nolan? *Did* she know about him, or had she used me because Marcus was the agent who'd blackmailed my mother so we were already connected? What would she need him out of the way for?

"Come on, Emmalynn," Alexa said, breaking me out of my head. "I invite you out here to give you answers, and you bring other people? You *tell* these people what I told you to stay quiet about?" She clicked her tongue. "We have a problem. Like you said, I even *warned* you. I was fair, wasn't I?"

"'Fair'?" I snapped. "*Fair?* You want to steal my family's magic and then kill us so you can take over the world! How is that fair?"

"I didn't—" she began, her breath pausing before she cleared her throat. "Think of it this way: you wouldn't be hunted anymore. Caldwell wants you to suffer, but I'd help you avoid that. You know why I need your magic, you know how extraordinary it is. I need that."

I swallowed. Those words revived a memory from early this semester: Adara. This was it. Despite every fear shouting at me not to do it, that I wasn't good enough to pull it off, I had to execute my Adara plan *now*. It was my absolute last shot of getting out, getting my family out, of the twisted mess Alexa had thrown us into.

"You don't want me."

She chortled. "You're so cute! Yes, Emmalynn, I want you. Your magic is so much more powerful—"

"It's not the most powerful."

Cara and Steven gaped at me like they were praying that I knew what I was doing.

"*Veritatem dicere*," I said.

Steven's eyes, black in the dusk light, widened. Alexa stared at me with an even combination of curiosity and caution. I'd stepped onto the tightrope, and now I had to walk to the other side.

I took a deep breath, forcing myself to look Alexa in the eyes. "There's a sorceress named 'Adara' destined to help unite the mortal and magic worlds. She's meant to become the most powerful sorcerer to ever live."

Alexa's knife lowered. "I know all about Adara, darling. Most of the magic world does. That's not new."

What? No, this wasn't part of the plan! How was she not more interested in Adara when power was her main goal? If she still cared more about the Ateras, how was I supposed to lead her away from—?

Steven gasped as his body sank a little more in Alexa's grip. He was growing limper with every sentence exchanged.

Forget the plan. I couldn't expect things to go according to plan every time.

"So you know her magic is stronger than mine," I said, trying to piece together the puzzle as I went. "Why are you—?"

"I don't know why you're questioning me about a sorceress whose identity is meant to be as big of a secret as yours," Alexa said curiously. "Why would I go after a sorceress nobody knows anything about?"

This was going south. This was about to *far* south.

"Unless"—she grinned—"*you* know something about her. Ha, even better, you *are* her."

What do I say? What do I say?!

"Who else to be the most powerful sorcerer if not the daughter of one of the first family of sorcerers to exist? Let me ask you something, Emmalynn, are you carrying anyone else's magic?"

We'd transferred Dad's magic back to him last year, so... "No."

"So you're as powerful as you are on your own. Tell me something else, then." Alexa raised the knife again. "How do you know you're *not* Adara? How do you know you're not meant to become her one day?"

I fumbled for my words, and I hated myself for it. "I'm... Wh—why would I—?"

Her chuckle swelled into laughter. "Nothing except the fact that your blood tests came back with extremely interesting results. Yes, I disguised myself as Hunter to test your DNA. I had to know my enemy inside and out, like I told you. And your blood test... I couldn't believe my eyes. Nothing like it has *ever* happened in the history of magic."

I didn't want to know. I *really* didn't want to know, but Steven was (literally) hanging on for dear life and Cara was glancing back and forth between me and Alexa as if to demand the answer herself.

"Your blood wields all seven classes of magic."

I stepped back, the words slamming into my chest like a boulder. "What're you talking about?"

"Put it this way: you're not just a sorceress." Hunger gleamed in Alexa's eyes the longer she looked at me. "You have the blood of a druid, mage, seer, nore—every identity of magic you can think of. You, my dear, are a hybrid."

C H A P T E R

Thirty-Nine

"But my family...!" I stammered, questioning if I could believe the woman in front of me. There used to be no question about it, but after everything that had happened the past three months? The dream about Ava, casting without needing a spell, even Annisa! Why did it make sense? "My family is *just* sorcerers—"

"Somebody slipped up somewhere," Alexa sang. She almost reminded me of Moren then.

"Emma," Cara said, her gentle voice the only thing reminding me that this was reality, "you can't trust her, she's a pathological liar!"

But Alexa saw that I was already gone with her words, mulling them over in my head. Cara's boots became darker with the evening sky, only the edges illuminated by the parking lights of her car behind Alexa and Steven. Casting spells that didn't even exist like a mage. Dreaming of the possible future like a druid. Even that weird flash of my nightmare—a vision, after all—at the mall right before it took place, like...

Like a prophecy. A seer's prophecy.

She's right.

"The tests can't lie," Alexa said, beaming. "So? How do you know you're not Adara, Emmalynn? How do you know that that's not *your* destiny?"

Steven's eyes closed. My heart skipped a beat before his voice filled my head and I felt the weight of my truth spell lift.

—It's okay. Lie.—

—Thank you so much.—

He was in too much pain to use telepathy again; he was dying. I had to answer with that in mind and get him to the hospital ASAP.

"Because I don't *know* who she is, nobody does," I said, wanting to believe my lies. I even remembered to blink. "I know about her the same way you do."

Alexa's knife instinctively lowered again, her eyes narrowing. "All right, then," she mused. "So you're not Adara."

"I don't—think so."

"But you *do* know something about her."

"You're a Grand Hunter," I spat. "You figure it out and hunt her down! I just know her name!"

Alexa finally snapped her mouth closed, but I wasn't going to give her any more ammo. And I was definitely done playing her game.

"So put the knife down," I stated. "Let him go."

She brought Steven up farther, eliciting a gasp from him. "He's bleeding out, anyway. How much you wanna bet he won't make it past sunrise?"

"Let him go!" I shouted, acidic anger rising into my throat. "I said to put him down!"

"You're getting brave, Atera." Alexa pressed the knife against Steven's throat, pushing my anger closer to my lips with it. "You would've never *dared* to order me around last year. How *is* your father, by the way? Has the public found him yet? Has Caldwell caught him and Rebecca, and now they're both—?"

"Let him GO!" I screamed, my telekinesis ripping the knife away from her hands. I threw it into a tree beside Steven and thrust Alexa into the air.

"Steven!" Cara called, running to him.

I wanted to cut straight through Alexa's smug grin with my glare as she dangled in thin air. "Oh, this is exactly what I like to see!" she chimed. "Wow, you've grown so—"

I brought my other hand up, calling upon the mage that I now knew was in me. Alexa's throat began to close with my forming fist.

At what I had to assume was the amethyst change in my eyes, Alexa blinked. She might've known what was happening, but that didn't make it any easier to believe. "H—how—" she choked out, "did you—learn—?"

"From you. Where did you learn it?"

"M—mage!" She gasped, her fingers clawing at her throat. "Okay, you made—your *point!*"

Alexa saying so only made me believe that I hadn't. My hand

continued to close.

Thunder rolled lowly from above. The tiniest water droplets pricked my cheeks.

"Emma!" Cara called, but I kept my eyes on my target. My rage bled into my fingers and took hold, my thumb now brushing against my index finger. Harsh wind blew against my face, but I pushed against it.

"E—Emmalynn!" Alexa gripped her throat with both hands. "*Stop!*"

"Emma, the storm!" Cara cried with a shaky voice. "Stop, you're about to kill her!"

I'd heard that fear before. Momma had spoken to me that same way, she'd said those same words to me after...

After I'd almost strangled Agent Greenwell.

I jerked my hand away, the sudden emptiness in my grip as hollow as the rest of me felt. My hands lightly shook with the memory of the power they'd just wielded. Power I shouldn't have welcomed again, power responsible for the storm clouds billowing above us.

Alexa crumpled to the forest floor like a dog on the ground, her black cloak draped all around her. She gulped down the air, coughing incessantly. I didn't dare take a step toward any of the people in front of me. I didn't dare risk changing something—destroying something—by moving.

Alexa's coughing slowed, her breaths becoming soft pants. She looked up at me. Her emerald-green eyes drilled through the night air. "You're good, Atera," she rasped. "You're pretty good."

I watched, frozen, as she stood, all but hacking up a lung. She flipped the hood hanging behind her over her head, faded from sight, and literally disappeared into the night.

Someone else gasped before I could worry about her. When I looked over, Steven was lying in his wife's lap and pressing his side.

"You can't stop talking to me!" Cara cried, running her hand through his feathered black hair. "Tell me you're still here, you can't leave me! You *can't* leave me now, not now! *Not* now!"

His words had gone extinct. I immediately helped Cara get him into the car.

There was an overwhelming innocence to the hospital waiting room. With walls painted dusty rose and animal cracker crumbs locked between the dark-gray carpet threads, I almost felt like I was five again and waiting for my pediatrician. There was a corner for kids, decorated with children's magazines and toys, but the cherry on top was the people—normal people—of all ages sitting with me and Cara. All of us were waiting to hear that we could see our loved ones.

Cara went in for a check-up once the nurse pulled up her records and Cara gave her a little "context" (in other words, "Our lives were threatened and we barely made it out alive"). She came back half an hour later and took a comfortable spot next to me.

"Do I need to go in, too?" I asked.

"Only if you feel like you need to. They just needed to make sure everything was okay."

"Are you okay? Are you sick?"

"No." She smiled dreamily, softly shaking her head. "I'm

pregnant.”

“What?” I breathed, louder than intended. “Really? *Really?* You are?”

“Yes.” She chuckled, resting her slender hand on my arm—Momma’s gesture for telling me to calm down. Cara was already a pro! “With the high stress of tonight, they wanted to double-check that everything’s okay. The baby’s fine, I’m fine, you’re fine...” Her smile dissipated. I regretted that I was able to finish her thoughts so easily.

It all made sense now: the *other* reason Cara had been terrified for Steven’s life, why she had kept repeating “not now”—not now of all times. Not when their baby was on their way. Not when they were about to have a family. I didn’t know that pain from a parent’s perspective, but I knew it from a child’s: I’d almost lost my father to the mortal-magic war. That had almost happened to Steven tonight. That was why Cara had been so hesitant to do anything, why she’d obeyed Alexa so easily, in the forest; she’d been trying to protect all three lives at once.

“Does Steven know?” I whispered.

She cast her eyes down to her lap. “No.”

It struck me like a baseball bat: I was why he was even in the hospital. I was why there’d been high stress at all tonight. I’d brought this on them—I’d brought this on their whole family.

“I’m sorry,” I choked out. The tears had already made their way to the front doors, squeezing past each other in the doorway. I dried the frontmost ones with my knuckles as fast as I could. “None of this... none of this would’ve happened if I hadn’t dragged you into it, if I hadn’t told you about Hunter, I–”

“Emma.” Cara turned in her chair to face me better. Gentle

fingers lifted my head and wiped a runaway tear from my cheek. "We chose to come tonight. *I* chose to come tonight, I knew we were dealing with a dangerous enemy, and Steven did, too. In fact, he did everything he could to keep me at home, but I knew I had to come. Honey, we have so many more answers now, answers we would've never gotten had not *all* of us been there tonight. And— if I hadn't been there to help you get Steven in the car..."

She faded out. Neither of us needed to hear the end of that sentence, anyway.

"Do you understand, though?" Her voice lowered to a raspy whisper. "Have you sat back once since getting here and thought about how much we gained tonight?"

I hadn't realized any of that until now. I finally knew the answer to every question I'd had about myself since last semester, I knew why Julia knew my secret, what Hunter wanted with my DNA, and where Alexa was—thanks to Steven.

And yet, that was the one and only answer I didn't have: Steven's condition. And I wouldn't get it, not tonight, at least.

"That being said," Cara whispered when I didn't respond, leaning in close, "do you know what happened with your eyes when you cast the storm?"

"Yeah. It's a bit of a story." I sighed, leaning back in the dark-purple chair. "I'll tell you later, but I really have to go. My mom's worried, and I still haven't told her where I am."

That was an understatement of sorts; the last thing I'd texted her had been sent an hour ago, and it was "With Cara and Steven, will be back soon". Needless to say, she was blowing up my phone and asking where I was.

"I understand," Cara said. "Do you need a ride home?"

"She'll pick me up, but thanks."

I stood up to leave, but then I caught myself staring at the woman in front of me. Something struck me like lightning: she was the seventh-great granddaughter of Caralyn Callistro, the founder of the Callistro Academy for Hunters. The woman in front of me was a literal part of history—a huge representation of it, at least—yet here she was now, sitting in the hospital waiting room for news on the condition of her husband, a mage, and comforting me, a sorceress (or, I guess... wielder of all magics).

I bent down, tightly wrapped my arms around her, and said, "Thank you so much."

"No need, sweetheart."

"No," I said, letting go. Jak's words from the night he first told me about his mother, which still resonate with me today, echoed in my mind as I said, "There is. You could've picked a different path but didn't. So thank you for being mortal *and* magic."

She stood and wrapped her arms around me in one last goodbye. Heading to the waiting room exit, I pulled out my phone and braced myself for Momma's wrath.

CHAPTER

FORTY

"**D**o you have any idea how much trouble you're in?" Momma crossed her arms, standing next to Mr. Dawson as he closed the door to his office. "You give me nothing but an ambiguous text, I don't hear from you for almost two hours, and then I find out that you're at the hospital! For the millionth time, Emmalynn, what were you doing there?"

I sat myself down on the white leather sofa on the right side of the room. Right now, I didn't have the luxury of preparing the story, so I forced myself to be ready for the consequences and opened my mouth.

I confessed what the "cinnamon roll meeting" with Cara and Steven had actually been: a meeting for us to devise a plan against Alexa. Then, since I knew Hunter's identity now, I coughed up the three times they'd kidnapped me, which left me with the story of what had happened tonight. I'd met Hunter *and* Alexa, who ended up being our school nurse this whole time and that was how she knew the truth about me. I really had been the one to tell her, last year in the basement of the beach house.

I kind of anticipated "Julia" being the straw that broke the camel's back. For a second, when Mom looked up at the ceiling and placed one hand on her chest, I was scared she was having a heart attack. Thankfully, it was just a poor attempt at regulating her shallow breathing.

"The whole time." Mr. Dawson rubbed his face with both hands, sighing in exhaustion. Disappointment seemed to fight for a place in his demeanor, but he wouldn't let it in.

"Emma," Momma stated, rubbing her temples with closed eyes, "*dare* I ask how you escaped Alexa tonight?"

I stared down my lap in shame as I told her, "I did to her what I did to Agent Greenwell."

I'd expected the silence that came afterward, but cursed it nonetheless. Just as quickly, Mr. Dawson's chuckling and then *laughter* shattered it as he buried his face in his hand. The second Momma rested her hands on her hips, I knew that the man had sealed his fate.

"What, pray tell, do you find so hilarious, Thomas?"

He released his face, grinning. "Your sixteen-year-old daughter is scaring off Grand Hunters, Amy."

A diamond-like pair and a honey-like pair of eyes fell onto me. Mr. Dawson was still smiling despite the scowl marking Momma's face. Then, slowly, her scowl lifted. Eventually, she uncrossed her arms.

"I guess so."

That was the only part of the night I hadn't given away yet: *why* I was able to scare off Grand Hunters. It was arguably the easiest part of the story (because it was the only thing I hadn't done wrong), but it took me a while to bring myself to say it; I'd experienced the evidence yet still couldn't believe it in full. Honestly, I was still partially convinced that I'd hallucinated all of the evidence.

But I forced myself to recount that anyway, repeating Alexa's test results. Coming from me, though, they felt all the more false. They felt like Alexa *had* lied to me, like she'd just been trying to get into my head and make me exploit my power. In a way, I had. And by the looks of it, Momma and Mr. Dawson never wanted me to use it ever again.

"A hybrid," Mr. Dawson deadpanned, clutching his arms and turning to my mother. "She's a hybrid."

"How is that possible, Thomas?" Momma asked skeptically. "The Atera family is *just* sorcerers—"

"I'm not implying anything," he said, holding his hands up. "I'm just saying it explains that family legend Tristan and Becca mentioned last year. Emma being the next hundredth generation, why she's meant to be so powerful—why she's able to cast spells that don't exist, why she can cast spells without casting the actual spell, why she had a vision of Ava at the mall? That random thunder that happened earlier tonight—"

"How?" Momma demanded, dropping her hands to her sides. "How is that supposed to be possible, why her? Why is it just my daughter who's such a giant walking target?"

Oh no. That reminded me: I *wasn't* the only one who was a

giant walking target.

My impossible ability. Annisa had been right.

I forced myself to snag the opportunity before I lost the courage: "I'm not."

Immediately, I had Momma's and Mr. Dawson's attention again. I almost wished Annisa could be here to "enjoy" this conversation with me. You can imagine how annoyed (to say the least) Momma was at Moren for keeping Annisa a secret from her, but I got brownie points for picking a public place to meet up with her and using a truth spell on her.

It was all the parts where Annisa was just like me that was hard to swallow—also to say the least. And I got no brownie points for waiting until I found out about something like tonight to tell Momma and Mr. Dawson about her.

"What is going on?" Mr. Dawson whispered, but it sounded like he was talking to himself. "Morgana... helping Adara?"

I nodded, the only safe thing to do. Even Momma watched him carefully, the conversation having completely jumped out of territory she was familiar in.

"That... tracks," Mr. Dawson mused hesitantly, his brows scrunching together. "Remember? I told you that you'd *help* unite the mortal and magic worlds. Morgana—Annisa's probably a part of that."

"So she *is* part of my destiny?" I asked, like the answer could only be trusted if it came from him.

"And you're part of hers," he replied. "But 'how' and 'why' are two questions I can't land for the life of me."

"How could you wait so long to tell us something like that?" Momma said.

"Because I knew she wasn't an enemy." I lightly shrugged, shrinking under her scowl. "I could handle her—"

"You don't just need to update us when someone's dangerous, Emmalynn," she stated, firmly crossing her arms. "That's huge information, if there's even a chance that it ties into the Ateras somehow, we need to know everything we can about it. What terrifies me more than anything is the fact that I can't even trust you to tell me if you *do* meet someone dangerous! You asked two people who are almost strangers for backup tonight and not your *trained* mother and godfather?"

"I'm sorry," I muttered. "But we had a plan, Cara and Steven are on my side—"

"Which is practically a Christmas miracle that things turned out that way," she retorted. "But what if they weren't? What if they'd turned out to be two undercover Hunters trying to verify your identity as an Atera? Just because someone has magic doesn't mean you can trust them, Emmalynn! Take a *good* look at your greatest enemy, who's literally a magician!"

"I know—"

"No, you don't." Her glower was practically pushing me into the sofa. "I told you when you first fessed up about them—*days* after meeting them, may I remind you—you had no problem meeting a stranger at an ungodly hour of the night, sneaking past me and your dad to do it, and *illegally* driving to get there! It's them, it's Annisa, it's Hunter, it's even Julia, I mean—I can't even—was I even the one who raised you?"

"I know!" I snapped. "I knew tonight would be dangerous, but I also had a plan to defend myself. I knew what to do if things went wrong, but I *had* to find out what Hunter knew. And finding out benefitted us!"

No matter how afraid I was, no matter how painful and acidic my anger was, I forced myself to look Momma dead in the eyes with every word I was finally liberating. "The fewer people who knew about everything, the better, because I can't protect everyone, Mom. I had to do this on my own. And I got through it, I made it out, and I made three allies in the process."

Momma closed her mouth and took a deep breath. Beside her, Mr. Dawson watched her carefully. Her words came slowly, like she was trying to find a way for me to understand. "Emma. I am your mother. It is my obligation in every sense to protect you. I taught you what to do and what not to do regarding strangers. I'm supposed to be teaching you how to deal with potential enemies who know who you are. Yet you're still running into these things head on even when you're way out of your depth, you challenge them to a fault, and..."

She shook her head, fading to silence.

And? I wanted to ask.

"And you work through something on your own until you know that you can't do it alone," she said, as if she'd heard me. "I can't figure out if that's a bad thing or not."

Mr. Dawson looked at her as if he had his own two cents—but he knew better than to step in.

Unfortunately for Momma, I did have one piece of bad news—which was also possibly great news, but the former was enough to make the words frail and soft. I mean... Momma *had* asked for the secrets: I told them about Adara and Alexa, how Steven had resurrected my plan after it'd backfired.

"Does that mean you're off the hook with Alexa?" Momma

asked cautiously, twisting her wedding band.

"I don't know," I said. "Because she knows about me, but she also knows that there's someone meant to be stronger than me. But she also knows where to find me, which is a lot less than what she can say about Adara... so I have no idea what she wants to do after tonight."

"Then we're back to square one." Mr. Dawson sighed, ambling to his desk across the room. "Not knowing where Alexa is, wondering when she's gonna pop up, and needing a plan. We're exactly where we were at the beginning of the year."

Except, this time, Aunt Becca was gone *with* Dad. But now I also knew a spell that could tell me Alexa's location with just the thought of her, which meant...

"I can use Steven's spell before he destroys it." Because, in full honesty, not one part of my mind would accept even a chance that he wouldn't wake up tomorrow. I didn't know if that was naivety or optimism.

Mr. Dawson pressed his lips together, leaning against his desk and staring at me like I was a newly dug-up artifact and he was trying to figure out my origin. "Great. Okay, then, Emma—where is she right now?"

"Well—it's a really hard spell. I've only had a couple successful attempts—"

"Work on it," he stated. "Practice it until it's impossible for you to fail. We're not letting Alexa catch us off guard this time, disguise or not."

It sounded like a promise, and I wanted to treat it as such—because I was making that promise to myself, too, and I was going to do everything in my power to keep it.

"All that said,"—Momma was now wearing her mom tone, and I dreaded her direction as she paired authoritative eyes with mine—"I need you to reflect, Emma. For the past three months, you've lied to me, you've gone behind my back, you've kept secrets from me that threatened your safety and the safety of your family, and you've blatantly disobeyed me. How do you expect me to trust you after this? With anything?"

A wave of shame crashed over me, drenching me from head to toe. In full honesty, I didn't.

Momma softly shook her head. "I haven't had to ground you for a *long* time. But you've gone too far this time, honey. No phone and no going out for three weeks: one week for every month you've lied to me."

My pride was big enough to keep me silent, but a part of me still wanted to tell her that that was fair. And I thought that even as I handed her my phone that night.

CHAPTER

Forty-One

omma was merciful enough to show me the message that Cara had sent me at 5 the next morning telling me that Steven's surgery had gone well. Even the doctors couldn't believe that he'd held on for as long as he had, but apparently the wound wasn't as deep as Cara and I had thought—strangely enough. The doctors managed to conduct a blood transfusion and stitch him up in time. Cara even sent me a selfie of her and Steven in his hospital bed with the caption, "Someone's excited about becoming a father!"

By Sunday, things were finally calm. Things were normal. Things were... not terrible. And I wondered how much longer I had with that before my entire world would be set on fire and turned upside down again.

It wasn't long at all; you can imagine how tempted I was to freak out when Mr. Dawson didn't show up for dinner in the Dining Hall that night. The last three months had taught me two things: worst-case scenario is always possible, but also that my family was capable of defending themselves.

But for once, couldn't we just *stay* safe where we belonged?

Momma quickly assured me after dinner that he was fine, which sentenced me to a night of homework in my dorm with the girls. Unfortunately, I had to wait for Breanne to finish her explanation on the parametrization of Pythagorean triples for someone to knock on our door.

Sarah sprang up to open it, shouting, "I'll get it!" because the knock alone wasn't enough to cut Breanne off.

Sarah swung open the door, revealing Momma standing outside. "Hello, ladies." Her eyes glazed over the work spread out across the floor. "Having fun?"

"*Oh* yeah." Sarah smiled cheekily, resting a hand on her hip. "Tons."

"Sorry to take you away from it, Em," Momma said, gesturing for me to follow her. "I need to grab you for a bit."

Much to Sarah's dismay, it was a "mother-daughter" thing.

When she closed the door behind us, Momma wrapped her arm around my shoulder and gave me a loving squeeze. "So?" she said. "How's second semester so far?"

"Kind of weird," I told her. "I actually got used to the guys being here. They should've stayed longer."

"Oh, really?" She laughed, rubbing my shoulder as she started leading me down the corridor. "Yeah, I know why you miss them."

"Everyone is *way* too interested in my love life."

"I'm your mom, I'm supposed to be." Impish eyes fell onto me. "I bet you didn't know that I heard what Jak did in the foyer when they left."

Somehow, I'd almost completely forgotten about Jak kissing me in front of the sophomore class and then some. "What? How?"

"Gossip travels quickly around here."

Before I could open my mouth to reply, Momma stopped and moved to stand in front of me. Heavy hands rested on my shoulders.

"So do not relay a single word of this to *anyone*. Especially not Sarah and Breanne."

"About... where Mr. Dawson went tonight?"

"Yes," she said, standing a little taller. "Which was an extremely private matter that he wants to tell us about."

In other words, Momma wanted to make sure that I knew exactly what we were walking into before we got to Mr. Dawson's office. For some reason, I wanted Dad and Aunt Becca, now safely with their cousins in Spindale, to hear the news with us. Like it was wrong of me and Mom to know and leave them out. I guess we'd find a way to update them somehow.

When Momma allowed me inside the headmaster's office first and then closed the door behind us, I knew that things were *serious* when I saw Mr. Dawson pacing the width of the room behind the coffee table. He constantly switched from crossed arms to hands on his hips to one hand on a hip and the other rubbing his face, like a hundred thoughts were demanding his attention all at once. The *only* time I'd ever seen this man pace had been when Aunt Becca went missing for a month when I was ten. (She had to fly under the radar when her landlord got a little too close to figuring out the truth, and she couldn't warn us because telepathy has a range and she was already on her way to Tennessee.) It was the last day of March, but it felt like the start of something was looming over us.

"What happened tonight?" Momma asked gently, crossing her arms.

Mr. Dawson finally stilled as I took a seat on the left sofa. "Dinner with my brother didn't go… as expected," he muttered.

"Is he not going to let you see your niece?" Momma asked.

My eyes widened with the memory: a few years ago, when Mr. Dawson was visiting me and Momma at the house, I'd overheard a conversation about his niece he wasn't allowed to see because of a family disagreement. *That's* what tonight had been about?

"No, that—" Mr. Dawson exhaled, pacing again as he rubbed his neck. "That's not the problem. He's gonna let me see her. He'll be here any minute to formally introduce us."

"What?" Momma said. "That's amazing, what's the problem?"

"Wait—can I have some context please?" I asked, resting my elbow on the arm of the sofa.

Mr. Dawson released a sharp sigh, meeting my eyes. "It's a long story. *Years* ago, my brother and his wife were involved in an incident that practically exposed them, which made them pack up and leave their neighborhood. Their daughter was born soon after, but she was almost immediately taken in by their mortal friend Leah. While Leah took care of the baby, my brother and his wife tried to build a safe life for their family. But they didn't know how else to hide the fact that their daughter was a druid other than to make it look like Leah was her biological mother. So they let Leah raise her to believe that—that she was mortal. Now they visit as 'close family friends'."

He walked to the front of his desk and leaned against it, gripping the edges. "I took a job here as a self-defense instructor a few days before my niece was born, when my brother and I were on good terms. That following week, we hadn't had any time to visit or call because of how hectic our lives had become, him with his daughter and moving, and me with Tristan and your mom... The *only* thing I knew was that my niece had been born, that was it.

"So when my brother found out that I'd accepted a position here, he forbade me from ever seeing his daughter. He considered it an act of betrayal, so he didn't want her around 'someone like me'. He never even told me her name, and he's barely talked to me since."

Just because he started working here? But a title with Callistro helped alleviate suspicion. If anything, it *helped* their family.

Then again, I guess Aunt Becca is kind of the same way...

Mr. Dawson continued. "Come to find out, Ingrid recently told him about you, and the role I've played in your life. So he offered to have dinner tonight. He decided that he wants someone else of biological relation to be in his daughter's life, to help him slowly introduce her to the truth. I still knew absolutely nothing about her, but I accepted. She's... she's family."

His gaze fell to a mindless point in front of him. Mom and I waited for him to open his mouth again to finish, but it never came.

"Thomas," Momma finally said. She dared a few steps forward as if to wake him up. "What happened?"

He paused. For the first time in my life, I heard a *quiver* in

Thomas Dawson's voice. "The other reason he's letting me into her life is because she goes here. Leah enrolled her as a cover to make it seem less obvious. She's a Callistro Girl."

My head shot forward. I was almost scared my eyes would fall straight out of my head as they widened.

"The problem came up at dinner when—my brother showed me a picture of her."

Mr. Dawson's office door clicked, creaking open. A tall man walked inside, messy dark-brown hair atop his head with sharp diamond-blue eyes. Beside him stood a girl with fair skin and long, straight black hair.

My body went limp on the sofa.

Her glittering purple eyes went straight past me and Momma and landed on Mr. Dawson, hypnotized as if she were seeing him for the first time. "Um... hi, Uncle Thomas."

Mr. Dawson's gaze stayed on her and her alone. He put on a tender smile I'd seen all throughout my childhood. "How are you, Opal?"

ACKNOWLEDGEMENTS

I must immediately thank my beta readers, who showed me every change and improvement that made THITR what it is today: Lauren, McKenna, Grace, Kiera, Abigail, Azim, and Leah. You all allowed me to publish a book that I'm not ashamed of!

My friends and followers have greatly encouraged (and even demanded) the release of this book. My heart is beyond full because of all of the support Emma and I have received as we both tell our stories. Never in my wildest dreams could I have anticipated this for the EA Series, so to say that it's a privilege to have you as a reader is an understatement.

So to all of my readers, especially you on Instagram: you are appreciated more than you will *ever* know.

About the Author

Ariana Tosado is a 22-year-old author, musician, university student, book editor, and content creator for teen and young-adult audiences. She started pursuing her passion of writing novels in middle school. Today, she's homed her focus on the *Emmalynn Atera* Series, marketing *Thy Kingdom Come*, and producing music. She aims to create relatable and encouraging content through her platforms, all with her cat, Sophie, in one hand and an iced vanilla latte in the other.

You can find out more about what she's up to on her website (www.arianatosado.com) or on Instagram (@thearianatosado).